Frayed Silk

ELLA FIELDS

Dedication

For those who believed in me when I was
riddled with doubts.

It's not love you should fear but, rather, the things you might do for it.

Chapter One

"I WANT A DIVORCE."

The words ring hollowly in my ears, but they're out. I've finally said them. I never pictured myself having to, but it's done now.

I just wish I didn't have to say them.

I wish things were different.

How they used to be.

But wishing means that I have some form of hope, and hope has no place in this house or this heart of mine anymore.

"No." That's all Leo says, not taking his eyes off the TV.

My own eyes have been glued to the blank profile of his face for the last ten seconds since the words left my mouth.

I thought he'd at least ask why. Finally tell me what has gone wrong between us. Because Lord knows I've exhausted my search for answers.

Over the past seven months, he's closed himself off to me. To our children. To our once happy life together. And he's never told me why. Why he's chosen to make me feel so alone. As if I'm invisible even when I'm in the same room as him, sharing the same bed as him, and supposed to be sharing a life with him.

Ten years. We've been married for ten years this November. Ten years that I don't want to throw away. But … I'm desperate. Can't he see me? Can't he see what's happening to me? To him? To all of us?

I thought asking for a divorce would elicit a reaction from the cold, aloof mask he's so fond of wearing these days.

Apparently, I was wrong.

I don't really want a divorce. Far from it. I just want my husband back. I just want my heart to stop hurting every time I look at him, and he looks away from me.

My throat burns. I clear it and ask, "Why not?"

He doesn't answer me. Not right away. Then finally, he turns his head to look at me from where he's sprawled out on the other couch. Leo's the kind of handsome that lives inside magazines. The sculpted cheekbones, the square jaw coated in light brown stubble, a head full of messy dark blond hair, and the most piercing blue eyes I've ever seen.

"Why, what?" He blinks, looking tired and annoyed.

"Why did you say no?" My eyes beg him for things my mouth is sick of asking for.

Love me. Come back to me. Look at me like you used to. Touch me. Stop breaking me.

He ignores my question, turning back to face the TV and effectively dismissing me. But I know he saw the pleading in my eyes. He just doesn't care.

After another five minutes roll by, I sigh and get up from the couch. Placing the cardigan I was knitting into my basket under the coffee table, I leave the room.

Walking up the stairs, I can't help but pause to look at the photos adorning the walls; our family, our children, Leo and I together.

I stroke a finger along the bottom of the black frame that houses an image of Leo and me on our wedding day. I looked so happy, so full of love, and eager to move forward into the future with the man who has his arms wrapped tightly around me. While I'm smiling into the camera, he's smiling down at me. My finger moves up the glass to touch that smile, wanting to take it from that beautiful memory and force it back on the face of the man downstairs. Because he hardly ever smiles anymore. Not like he once did.

I swallow down the hurt and continue moving up the stairs. Heading toward the kids' bedrooms, I pick up Greta's school shoes and her plastic tiara along the way.

I check on Greta first, finding her blankets half tossed on the floor and a myriad of stuffed toys tucked under her arm. Typical. I manage a smile, moving into the room and picking them up, then situating them over her small seven-year-old body. Placing a kiss on her light brown hair, I move out of the room and pull the door halfway closed.

I check on Charlie next, and as usual, I find the complete opposite. His blankets are pulled up to his shoulders as he sleeps on his side. Not a toy in sight. Which concerns me a little, considering he's only nine years old. A few months ago, he claimed he was getting too old to keep playing with toys. I had frowned, feeling my heart clench at the odd statement. But Leo simply nodded, accepting his request with barely any reaction at all.

Charlie's always been a little quieter and a little more

reserved than his sister is. Whereas Greta has absolutely no issues telling the world her problems and outrage, he tends to keep his problems to himself.

I lean down to kiss his head, smoothing my finger between his brows. Leo and I used to laugh about how he'd always look so serious when he was little, even while sleeping. Tense, almost. Like he's not happy about not knowing where his dreams might take him when he closes his eyes.

I pull his door closed halfway and pad quietly down the hall to our bedroom. Stripping out of my pajama pants, I climb into bed in the same thing I always wear—my panties and a tank top. Or sometimes a t-shirt.

Leo would always comment about how crazy it made him. Except for the fact that he preferred me in nothing, of course. But with children come changes. Like not being able to sleep naked unless you padlock your door beforehand.

Yes, our Charlie picked our lock with a butter knife about eighteen months ago. Leo and I had jumped apart, and I'd hidden underneath the covers until Leo told him we'd be downstairs in a minute. Thankfully, he didn't ask any questions— like why was his mother hiding underneath the blankets like a big kid—and simply closed the door behind him on his way out.

I lay awake for what feels like hours, but a quick glance over at the clock shows it's only been about forty-five minutes. I can't get my mind to turn off. It feels like it's been tangled in knots for an eternity.

Have I tried to talk to him? I've lost count of how many times I've tried. I've bought sexy outfits, got my blond hair styled so it doesn't simply fall to my ass in its old, limp, long, typical fashion. My hairdresser went nuts, chopping it up to my shoulder blades and adding in layers everywhere, so now it has somewhat of an attractive wave to it. But when he got home that night, he looked straight through me. He didn't even notice.

I've talked it to death with Lola, my best friend since college. Has he cheated? Is he having an affair? If he is, or has, then he's been very good at hiding it. I've seen no signs of it, other than his absent demeanor, of course. Just the thought of it makes my stomach lurch over itself. Because despite how bad things are between us, I still love him.

I'm still madly, stupidly, and irrevocably in love with him.

I don't know how to just switch it off. And I don't think it works like that.

But, apparently, it works like that for him.

His footsteps travel down the hall as he climbs the stairs then pause in the hallway as he checks on the kids. Something he still does every night, even though he's happy to ignore them when they're awake most days.

I roll over and pretend to be asleep before he walks into the room. When he does, he leaves the door wide open—as expected. We haven't been intimate since earlier this year, but it's not for lack of trying. It's killing me. A part of me thinks that maybe if we were, it'd help fix this rift. We could renew this loss of connection if only he'd touch me with more than just a peck on the head each morning before he leaves for work. And that's if he's home. A lot of the time, he'll get up before us and supposedly go to the gym before he heads into the office.

I hear his clothes hit the floor before the bed dips with his weight.

Barely breathing, I wait for him to reach over and hook

an arm around my waist to drag me into his strong, warm body. Like he used to.

I open my eyes and stare at the en suite door when it doesn't happen.

We both lay there, in the dark, not talking, not touching, and not sleeping, just co-existing in the silence that screams louder than any voice ever could.

Then he speaks. "You promised me forever when I slid that ring onto your finger."

My heart starts pounding dangerously fast in my chest, but I simply retort in a sad voice, "And you promised to love and cherish me always."

He's quiet for a few minutes. "We're not getting a divorce, Dahlia."

Dahlia. He used to call me Lia, like my family and close friends.

A tear escapes, rolling down my cheek onto the pillow beneath it as I squeeze my eyes shut and wait for sleep to take me away from here.

Chapter Two

"WHAT WOULD YOU HAVE DONE IF HE'D SAID YES? Are you crazy?" Lola's eyes widen, and I shrug.

"Maybe." I lean back against my black Range Rover. "I don't know."

She stares at me for a moment. "Are you sure it's not the company? Maybe he is having trouble at work."

I shake my head. "No. I'd know if it were in trouble. Besides, I've asked him that a few times already."

I'd know if it were because he's the CEO of Vandellen Logistics. And I know a lot of his close co-workers and their wives. The gossip would run rampant if there were problems.

"Fuck me, Lia," she blurts, scrubbing a palm over her mouth before quickly glancing around to make sure that none of the stuffy moms nearby heard her. Not that she'd usually care, but Bonnets Bay Preparatory has some first-class bitches who become rabid with any sign of trash on their beloved school grounds.

Lola isn't trash at all. She's a high school teacher, and her husband, Trey, has his own carpentry business in the city. But anyone who doesn't drive a car worth over fifty thousand dollars automatically earns an entry into the 'not good enough' category in their little black books of snobbery.

"Where the hell do you go from here?" She lowers her voice. "You can't keep living like this."

I heave out a weary sigh, looking down at the pointed toes of my boots. "I have no idea."

"Oh, shhh. Here comes Fiona," she whispers.

I look up to see Fiona's smiling face approaching us. She set her pretty green eyes on us the first day our kids started kindergarten together, and we took her under our wing. She's beautiful but can also be a little snotty. She's nice, though— well, to us anyway. The three of us kind of clicked, and we've been friends with her ever since.

"Afternoon, ladies," she says brightly. "I couldn't help but overhear that Natasha's son has a girlfriend. Crazy, right?" She laughs.

"Seriously? They start that early these days?" Lola looks concerned, which is fair enough. Her daughter, Sophie, is a stunning girl with blond hair and big, bright blue eyes.

Fiona shrugs. "Apparently." She turns to me. "Hey, are you still volunteering at that homeless shelter?"

She asks me this all the time, but I nod. "Yeah, I'm heading in for my shift tomorrow."

"Oh, good, back in a sec!" She races back off to her car just as the bell rings, signaling the end of the school day.

"That guy still hitting on you there?" Lola smirks at me.

I can't help but laugh. "Oh, my God, yes."

She nudges me. "How old did you say he was again?"

"I'm not sure exactly. I think I heard one of the girls there say twenty-six or twenty-seven."

She guffaws. "You go, girl. See, you've still got it. More than got it. So don't you worry about that."

I smile thinly, watching as our kids race out of the school.

I'm not worried. Despite changing my hair and my other desperate attempts to get him to notice me, I know I'm far from ugly. But just because I take care of and feel good about myself doesn't mean I'm what Leo wants anymore.

"Mommy!" Greta yells, crashing into my legs. "Adam lost a tooth today! In class! There was blood everywhere!"

My eyes widen theatrically. "Oh, my goodness, did he keep it for the tooth fairy?"

She nods frantically. "Yes, I made sure he did."

Smiling, I lean down to kiss her head as Charlie approaches. I ruffle his blond hair. "Hey, little man. How was your day?"

"Charlie got real mad at someone," Sophie informs me from beside us.

Lola frowns down at her. "Soph …"

"No, it's okay," I tell her and look at Charlie. "What happened?"

He merely shrugs. "Aaron was annoying me. So I told him not to." He opens the door and climbs into the car, shutting it without another word.

I glance at Lola, who tries for a smile. "Bad day maybe?"

But she and I both know his outbursts are becoming more than what we can keep explaining away as a bad day.

We say goodbye, and I make sure both kids have their seat belts on. I'm about to climb in the car when I see Fiona racing back over, dragging her twin boys, Henry and Rupert, and a large garbage bag with her.

"Sorry, here." She passes over the bag. "If you could drop it in for me, that'd be fantastic. I've got so much to do tomorrow." She huffs out a breath.

I open the trunk and throw it in the back, closing it before saying, "Thank you. But seriously, you donate all the time. How the hell do you have anything left in your house?"

I swear she gives me a bag every month.

She laughs, the sound like wind chimes as it floats off into the warm early autumn air around us. "Nonsense. You know me, I have a bit of a problem with shopping. And if I don't turn out the old to make room for the new, Dylan is bound to notice how bad it's gotten." She then glares at her boys. "Not a word or no Xbox for a month." They both nod, a little wide-eyed.

I laugh, thanking her again and getting into the car.

Once home, I unpack the kids' bags as they head into the living room to eat a snack and watch TV. I know Charlie isn't going to want to talk to me about what happened at school. His father is the only one who can usually get stuff out of him, but I have to try.

I put their lunchboxes in the dishwasher and grab my coffee, heading into the living room and taking a seat beside him on the couch. I take a few sips from my mug and place it down on the coffee table, putting my arm behind his head and bringing him into my side.

"You okay?" I ask quietly. Thankfully, a music app on his sister's iPad keeps her preoccupied.

He doesn't answer. Just rests his head against the side of my chest as I smooth his hair back from his face.

"What happened? Why'd you yell at Aaron?"

And still, he stares at the TV, but I wait.

Finally, he says, "He was annoying me. I already told you that."

"Charlie," I warn. "Please, just tell me what happened. I want to help."

"What's for dinner?" He tries to deflect.

My shoulders droop with my sigh as I sit back and tilt my face to the ceiling.

I don't know whether to keep pushing or finally admit he's just like his father. Stubborn and resolved to work out whatever issues he has on his own.

Picking the clothes up from the bathroom floor, I toss them into the hamper and mop up some water with a towel. I hear the garage door leading to the kitchen open downstairs as I throw the towel in the hamper before going back down.

Worry and trepidation fill every step I take, which is ridiculous. This man is supposed to be my best friend, my lover, my husband. I shouldn't be afraid to ask him for something.

Yet I am. I'm stupidly nervous as hell.

I walk into the kitchen, pouring myself half a glass of wine and drinking it down quickly while he sorts through the mail at the other counter with his back to me.

He must have gone for a swim after work. His hair is wet, and he's in jeans and a t-shirt instead of his suit. He goes to the gym to work out, but swimming is what he's always enjoyed doing to unwind after a stressful day. I guess today was one of them.

Maybe I should wait …

No, Charlie can't wait.

"How was your day?" I ask quietly, leaning back against the counter behind me.

"Fine. Where are the kids?" He scans a letter before setting it down with what I'm guessing are other bills.

"Upstairs. They've just taken a shower, and they're waiting for you."

He grunts, tossing the unwanted junk mail and envelopes into the trash and heading out of the kitchen.

"Wait, please," I croak.

He stops but doesn't turn around to face me.

"Charlie had a fight with a boy at school today."

He turns around then, his eyes landing on me for the first time since he got home. But his features stay hard, his stance almost tense as he looks at me.

"Is he hurt?" he asks.

I shake my head. "No, at least not physically. But Sophie said that he got pretty angry with one of the boys in their class. He's acting like it's no big deal, and he won't talk to me." I run a hand through my hair. "Can you …?" I trail off.

"I'll talk to him." He leaves, and I stand here, thinking I should feel relieved that he said he would. But I just feel … drained. Like that brief conversation shouldn't have expended the emotional energy it did.

Deciding to run myself a bath, I head upstairs and hear soft murmurs come from our son's bedroom as I walk past his closed door. Stripping my clothes off, I grab a pair of panties, sleep shorts, and a t-shirt before locking myself in the bathroom and waiting as the big corner bath fills with hot, bubbly water.

Climbing in, I tie my hair up on top of my head and slide down until the water covers my shoulders. I leave the water running—better to hide the sound of the impending sobs clawing their way up my throat. I don't often do this. Wallowing in self-pity isn't usually my style. The sad thing is, I probably don't need to do this nearly as much as I used to.

But tonight, the hurt needs to be let out again.

So I let it out, holding a washcloth up to my mouth to muffle the sound of my heart breaking for the thousandth time over the past seven months.

It's moments like these, as hot tears race each other down my cheeks, I beg my heart to hate him.

But it's a damn fool because it never listens to me.

Chapter Three

"**M**orning, Blondie," Jared says, walking over to me as I pull the bags from the trunk to take inside, one of them being Fiona's.

Jared's tall, at least six-foot-one with dark, slicked back brown hair and matching stubble, plus the most mischievous grin that I've ever seen on a man. He's also got to be at least five years younger than I am. And the fact that I'm married hasn't deterred him either. Which yeah, not going to lie, kind of makes me feel good. And I need all the good I can get these days.

"Hey." I struggle to close the trunk with my hands full, trying to use my back and ass. He chuckles, grabbing some bags from me and freeing a hand for me to close it and lock the car. I'm in a pretty rough part of the city of Rayleigh, so leaving the car unlocked is not an option.

"How're you doing?" His eyes probe my face, which I'm sure is a little puffy from last night's crying jig.

"Great," I lie. "You? Have you been behaving?" I arch a brow at him.

He winks at me as we near the doors to the shelter. "Define behaving." His handsome face lights up with his grin.

I snort. "Never mind."

He hip bumps me. "Now, now, Blondie. You know you're the only one for me."

That makes me laugh. We walk inside, and I pass the bags over to Glenda, who thanks me and wishes us a good morning before she opens them up to sort through them.

Jared follows me into the kitchen after we both sign in and wash our hands. We then spend a minute pulling our hair nets and aprons on.

He's here on account of needing to complete his community service hours whereas I'm here because I want to be.

My mom raised me without my dad around. I knew him, sure, but rarely saw him, and he died when I was a teenager. Mom often went without basic things like food when times were tough with money, opting to make sure I was taken care of first. We came here to this very same women's shelter quite a few times. My mom would put in several hours volunteering so we could have food in our stomachs during those tough periods.

So even though my husband is loaded, I still find it hard to think of myself that way. Don't get me wrong; I'm more than grateful for everything he's provided for us. It's more than I ever dared to dream of. But I'd trade it all in in a heartbeat if it meant he'd come back to me.

Jared suddenly laughs, reaching over to fix my hair net.

"What?" I frown.

"Nothing," he mutters, stroking a finger down my cheek.

I blush and move away farther into the kitchen to start preparing lunch. Being that it's a half an hour's drive to Rayleigh, I can usually only stay a few hours. Then I have to head back to Bonnets Bay so I can get a few things done before I need to pick up the kids.

"Okay, so seeing as you won't let me take you out to dinner, have coffee with me."

I pause while cutting up some carrots. "Jared." I smirk down at the food. "We've been over this. You know I'm married."

I go back to chopping.

He sighs dramatically. "Yes, you've told me. Three times already."

"So why do you keep asking me?" I can't help it. I'm curious.

He moves in closer to my side. "Because I can smell a broken heart from a mile away, Blondie. And you"—he points a peeler at me—"reek of it."

Despite the accuracy of his statement, I laugh quietly. "Is that like a weird fetish of yours or something?"

He huffs. "Hardly. But it comes in handy because I usually want to steer clear of that shit." His eyes fall on me. "But you … well, you look like you need a good bit of loving or at the very least, a friend."

My heart stutters at his words. He's right. I do, but I just don't want it from him. Besides … "I have friends."

"While that may be so, it might help to hang out, you know … to take your mind off whatever is troubling you so much."

I scoop the carrot slices into a bowl and grab the cling wrap from the counter behind me, mulling over it for a few minutes.

Is it wrong to have coffee with another man? One who's made his interest in me so blatantly obvious over these past few weeks? Hell yes, it is. But I'm beginning not to give a damn about right and wrong. Not when Leo so clearly doesn't seem to give a shit anyway.

"Okay." I lean a hip against the stainless-steel counter to face him. "One coffee." I raise my brows and pointer finger in warning.

He grins, startling me when he leans in to grab my cheeks to place a quick, loud peck on my forehead. "You won't regret it, Blondie."

Let's hope not.

We finish our shift, and I wait for him outside while he fills out some paperwork needed for his probation officer. I don't know all the details of what he did, but I heard that he used to be mixed up with a bad circle of people, who were heavily involved in motor vehicle theft. He swaggers a little as he walks out to find me standing here. Beaming, as if he thought I'd renege on our coffee date.

Date? Nope, just coffee, I tell myself. And who knows, maybe caving a little will help in getting him to back off a bit.

He wraps an arm around my shoulder, and I instantly lift it off me, scowling up at him.

Chuckling, he raises his hands in the air. "Okay, got it."

We walk into an old diner at the end of the street, and Jared slides into an empty booth in the corner. I hop in on the other side, placing my purse down next to me and ordering a latte when the waitress comes by. Jared orders a flat white, and I can't help but think about Leo and his love for black coffee, no sugar. I pull my phone out to check it but find no missed calls or texts. I don't know what I was expecting really. Maybe a sign that I shouldn't be doing this? I bite my lip as anxiety assaults me and put my phone away.

Jared leans across the table between us, clasping his hands together as he stares intently at me. My teeth slowly release their hold on my lip as I realize no man has really looked at me in this way for months.

"What's eating at you, Blondie? Is that Rover of yours giving you trouble? Because I know a guy—"

A laugh escapes as I hold a hand up, halting his words. "Stop, no."

He winks. "Just let me know."

"Aren't you in enough trouble with the law?" I ask him.

"Well, I didn't say *I'd* be doing anything, now did I?" He gives me a wicked grin, and I feel butterflies slowly awaken in my stomach. Which terrifies me, so I decide to cut the bullshit. "Jared, you're funny, handsome, and I'm sure you can be very sweet, in your own unconventional way ..."

He gasps loudly. "You can't break up with me yet, babe. We've only just begun."

I burst out laughing again, wiping underneath my eyes.

"Man, you should really do that more," he says quietly.

"Huh?" I thank the waitress when she places our mugs down and moves to the table across from us.

"Laugh. You should definitely laugh more."

Oh. The smile wilts off my face as my cheeks start to heat. I tug my mug over to me, prepping it before blowing and taking a small, tentative sip. "Wow. This is amazing."

He takes a sip of his own. "Right? Best coffee in this damn city."

We drink in silence for a few minutes, and I start to fidget under his searching green gaze.

"It's your husband, isn't it?" he asks suddenly, looking at the diamond ring on my finger.

I almost choke on my coffee. "Excuse me?"

"Your husband. He's the one who's got you looking like you're barely scraping by." He then eyes my Gap t-shirt dress, my hair, and my purse. "Even if you have money."

"Funny you should say that. I grew up in this city in a tiny one bedroom flat—just me and my mom."

"No way." He whistles. "And Mr. Rich swooped in to save your ass? Cinderella style?"

I smile sadly. "Not exactly. We met in college, and I thought he was a rich prick until I finally gave him a chance. He grew up where we live now, Bonnets Bay."

Jared's eyes widen. "A Bay bitc—" He cuts himself off, a wee bit too late.

"A Bay bitch," I finish for him, rolling my eyes. "Yes. Though not all of us are bitches. Just FYI."

He simply smirks. "So Miss I have a perfect life, what's happened?"

I take a deep breath, not sure whether to say anything. We haven't really known each other that long. So I settle on something small. "Just … things between my husband and I have been, strained, I guess." I shrug as if it's not tearing me to shreds.

He leans forward again. "Well, just FYI … He's an idiot."

I can't help it; I start laughing again.

We finish our drinks, watching each other, me discreetly—though it's hard to be discreet when his eyes are constantly watching me. "Have you and your husband, ah, talked about it?"

I nod my head. "I've tried. He insists that nothing is wrong,

19

that he's just got a lot going on at work, and that he's busy. But I know something is definitely wrong. Nothing about how he's been acting lately has been right." I shake my head. "What am I even doing? You probably don't want to hear this."

He grasps my hand, gently squeezing it in both of his warm ones. I look down at them, unable to tear my eyes away from them. From the way they seem to shield mine protectively yet also hide the evidence of my wedding ring.

"Blondie, I wouldn't have asked if I wasn't interested. And in case you haven't noticed these past few weeks, I'm interested. Very interested in you."

A shaky breath leaves my lips as I raise my eyes to meet his heated gaze. "Why? You're probably six years younger than I am."

His green eyes narrow. "I'll be twenty-seven in a few months."

"Ho, wow," I breathe.

"What?" His thick brows pull in.

"I can't. It's not … It's just not something I ever thought I'd do. Besides, I just turned thirty-two, Jared."

His eyes widen a fraction. "I thought you were in your late twenties, max."

That makes me smile. "Flattering, thank you."

"It doesn't matter, you know. Hey, maybe you just need a bit of fun. Maybe, just maybe," he says quietly, tilting his head, "I can make you come so hard you'll forget you even have a husband."

Holy shit. Yep, my panties are officially damp, and my brain is screaming at me to run, run, *run*.

But I don't. I stay seated, shocked and turned on by his audacity.

He chuckles, running a finger over the top of my hand. "You haven't been fucked in a while, have you?" he asks with a deceptive softness in his voice that I feel all the way down to my bones.

"Jared," I hiss, glancing around to make sure no one heard him.

"Relax. I'll help you. Come on." He gets up, digging out a twenty from the pocket of his black jeans before holding a hand out to me.

I swallow over the boulder forming in my throat.

I can't do this. Why am I even thinking about doing this?

Shaking my head, I tell him, "I have to go. My children need to be picked up in a few hours." He takes my hand anyway, helping me up and passing me my purse.

I thank him but release his hand as soon as we step outside into the midday sun.

"I'll walk you to your car," he says.

When we reach my Range Rover, I dig my keys out and unlock it, opening the door and throwing my purse on the passenger seat. I turn around to find him right there. There's so little space between us that when I inhale, I can almost taste the coffee and the slight hint of mint on his breath. My eyes involuntarily land on his lips. *Thin, but tempting lips,* I think as I watch his tongue dart out to lick at the corner of them.

"Ummm …" I mumble shakily, having no idea what to do. Back my ass up into my car somehow, or tell him to back up?

I opt for the second option, but before I can get the words to leave my mouth, his lips are dangerously close to mine as he places a soft kiss right beside my mouth. Breath whooshes out of me when he pulls back and winks at me once more. "Later, Blondie."

I watch, trying to draw air into my starving lungs as he swaggers off down the sidewalk and disappears into the crowd of lunch goers who have filled the streets.

Chapter Four

"Hey, sorry I'm late," Lola says, a little out of breath as she takes a seat across from me.

I drag my eyes from the old couple huddled in the corner of the café. They would probably wonder why I keep staring at them if they'd bothered to look away from one another.

"Don't worry about it. Here"—I nudge her latte toward her—"I ordered for you."

She smiles. "Oh, I knew I dubbed you my best friend for a reason." She picks it up and takes a sip, closing her eyes and sighing contentedly as she visibly relaxes in her chair.

"So"—she puts her mug down, rubbing her palms together—"what's up? Your text had me worried."

I take a sip of my half-finished coffee, wondering if I should even say anything about it. A part of me thinks that maybe it's not a big deal and I shouldn't open myself up for judgment. But the other part of me knows better, and Lola won't judge—hopefully.

"The day before yesterday, I agreed to have coffee with Jared after our shift at the shelter." The words rush out of me in a whisper.

Her eyes widen. "Holy shit. How did that happen?"

I shift my mug around, staring down at it. "Um, well … he got under my skin a bit. Saying how I need a friend or whatever and that I reeked of heartbreak." I smirk, shaking my head at the memory. "He asked, and I said yes." I raise my eyes to hers.

"So what's the problem? It was just coffee, right?" She pauses. "Though I'd be pissed as hell if Trey had coffee with another woman, it could be worse."

"I …" I blow out a big breath. "But I enjoyed myself. I laughed. God, I laughed like I hadn't in months."

She smiles softly, and I see the pity in her eyes. Jesus, what has become of my life, that people feel the need to look at me like that? She reaches across the table to grab my hand with hers. "That's a good thing. But I'm sensing he did more than just make you laugh if we're here, talking about it …?"

I swallow, feeling tears sting my eyes and nod.

"Lia …" Her voice is quiet. "Did you …?"

I shake my head. "*No.* No, nothing like that. But I have thought about it." I sniff. "That's just as bad, right?"

She lifts a shoulder. "It's not good, no, but you've been a wreck and for so long now. So if you're looking for anger or a slap on the wrist from me, you won't get it, honey."

That has me sputtering out a laugh and swiping underneath my eyes as a few tears escape.

I lower my voice. "He said that maybe he'd make me come so hard I'd forget I even had a husband."

24

Lola's eyes bug out. She sits back, fanning her face dramatically.

"Oh, my God."

"You see what I'm dealing with here?"

"He said this over coffee?" she asks with clear disbelief.

I nod. "Yep."

"Sweet Mary, mother of …" She takes a deep breath. "Okay, what are you going to do?"

"I don't know. Keep ignoring his advances?" I ask meekly.

"Oh, nuh-uh. If you were ignoring them, you'd have gone straight home instead of having coffee with him."

The guilt hits again. "I know. It just feels good, you know? To have someone look at me again, want me again. I'm so sick of feeling invisible."

"I get that. But Lia, he sounds like bad news. The sexy but toxic kind, and if you think there's ever a chance of you and Leo working through whatever this is, then you need to stay away."

I bite my lip, knowing she's right.

"He kissed me," I admit.

"What?" she hisses, glancing around to make sure no one is suddenly staring at us.

"Yeah, just on the side of my mouth. He's … damn it, he's sneaky and calculating. It caught me completely off guard."

Lola eyes me as she sits back in her chair and rubs a hand over her cheek. "Shit, wow. Maybe you should stop volunteering for a while, just until he's finished his community service hours."

Again, she's right. I should, but I know I won't.

"Maybe," I mumble into my coffee mug and take a sip.

"Dahlia …" she warns with a frown.

"How're things with Trey? You mentioned that he was working hard with all the orders at the shop."

She grudgingly lets me change the subject. "Yeah, he's stressed out to the max at the moment. But he's hired someone to help him, finally, so the grouchiness should stop soon." She takes a sip of her coffee, lowering her voice. "It'd better. But shit, the sex is amazing when he needs to de-stress. He becomes an animal." Her cheeks turn a little flushed as she obviously thinks about it.

I laugh, but it's kind of forced. I miss sex with my husband, but most of all, I just miss him. I miss feeling close to him.

We chat about the party we dragged our kids to over the weekend, and how elaborate all the shit there was as we finish our drinks before saying our goodbyes.

"Make sure you call me, especially if you feel like doing something you might regret." She eyes me pointedly as we stop at my car.

I give her a weak smile. "Thank you. I'll make sure I do if I need to."

And I have an alarming feeling that I might just need to.

"You okay?" he asks, slowly thrusting in and out of me from behind. We're on our sides; his head is leaning down over mine, kissing and licking every inch of my shoulder and neck.

"Yes," I breathe. "You need to stop asking that. I'm

pregnant, not sick." I pant.

He chuckles roughly against my skin, his scruff tickling. "I can't help it." His hand drifts down to rest over my eight-month pregnant stomach, continuing until he finds where we're connected between my legs. I lift my leg higher as he gently circles my clit and fucks me with slow, lazy strokes. My eyes close as I feel myself hurtle toward pure bliss, breathing heavier and moaning as he stays rooted to the hilt inside me, then grinding.

"Leo …" I whimper.

"Come, beautiful. Let go."

And I do, as delicious, spine-tingling pleasure washes over me in waves down my entire body, making my toes curl as I moan long and loud.

He's right behind me. Thrusting and picking up speed until he stills, emptying himself inside me and biting my shoulder as he groans deep in his throat.

"I love you. Only ever, always you," he whispers hoarsely into my skin as he drags his teeth over it, evoking another shiver from me.

"I know," I whisper. He shows me all the time. I've been a hormonal mess for most of this pregnancy, but he's taken it. He's taken it all with a smile on his face and love in his eyes.

"I hope our boy is just like you," I say, reaching down to rub a hand over my swollen stomach.

"Yeah?" he asks quietly.

I nod. "Yeah. You're the best man I've ever known."

He withdraws from inside me, turning me onto my back to gaze down at my face. His blue eyes glaze over with something other than lust. No, it looks like tears. And it's then I realize that I've never seen him cry before.

He cups my cheek, rubbing his thumb over the apple of it.

"Some days … I can't believe how fucking lucky I am."

I give him a watery smile, nuzzling into his hand.

"You most certainly are," I joke with a laugh.

He grins, and I stare at his straight white teeth, reaching out to run my finger around the outside of his lips.

"I need to feed you," he murmurs.

I roll my eyes. "Soon. Stay here with me." I grab the back of his head, my fingers sinking into the disarray of his sandy blond hair.

He rests his lips over mine as we just stare at each other.

"Why can't we just stay in bed forever?" I whisper.

He sucks on my lip, releasing it before saying, "Because we're not in college anymore and real life awaits. But … you can." He moves away, and I reach for him. "No, come back."

He chuckles. "I know you, wife. You may be happy now, but if I don't feed you soon, you'll turn grumpy, or you'll start crying at TV commercials again."

He has a point.

I shamelessly stare at his taut ass. Muscles bunch on his back and arms as he bends, picking up his basketball shorts and walking off into the bathroom. He returns a moment later, shorts on and a washcloth in his hand that he uses to gently wipe between my legs.

It makes me giggle. "You're taking this whole caveman thing way too far."

He finishes cleaning me, his brows lowering as he looks down at me. "Lia, you're my heart and soul, and you're carrying my child. And shit, you have no idea what that does to me. So just let me do what I need to, okay?" He leans down to kiss my nose, and I melt into a puddle of hormones as he deposits the washcloth in the hamper before leaving our bedroom.

"Ice cream. I need ice cream!" I call out as I slowly sit up to get dressed.

"You'll get ice cream after you've eaten a decent meal."

I huff, smiling to myself as I stand, sliding my dress over my head and tugging it down over my stomach.

I pull into the driveway and turn the car off, taking a moment to collect myself as I stare, unseeing, at the garage doors in front of me.

Memories are funny things. Some are so palpable that you feel as if you're right there, experiencing everything all over again. The scents, tastes, the weather, the sliding of skin on skin, and the feelings that made your heart swell double in size.

Whereas others flit away, like cast off threads in your mind, feeling forever out of reach. Forgotten. Until one day, they decide to unravel from your conscience and knock you sideways by taking you back. Back to someplace you'd give anything to forget, or that you'd sell a piece of your soul to revisit just one more time.

This pain in my heart feels physical. Like I could march into my doctor's office and demand that they fix it. But I know there's no cure for this. There's nothing anyone else can do besides him. And maybe that's why I've allowed myself to sink even further inside myself, becoming someone I hardly recognize when I look in the mirror.

I can't keep waiting on him.

I can't keep hanging on by a frayed thread.

I think it needs to snap, once and for all. Let the pieces fall where they may.

Because if he won't do it, then the only person who can fix this pain and make me happy again is me.

Chapter Five

"**G**RETA! WHERE'S YOUR SCHOOL SKIRT? IT NEEDS TO be washed," I call out from the laundry room when I can't find it. She comes running in a few moments later, wearing her school skirt, a pink t-shirt, sunglasses, a sparkling scarf wrapped around her neck, and a pair of my Manolo black peep-toe heels.

"My, my, and what do we have here?" I ask her.

"I'm a Bratz doll," she declares with her hands on her hips.

I smile at her. "You look fabulous, poppet, but I need to wash that skirt. Can you go find a regular skirt to wear instead?"

"But it's not the same. I need it," she whines.

I give her my best mom glare, and she sighs, stripping it off and passing it over.

"Thank you." I toss it into the washer with the rest of the clothes and grab the laundry soap. I pour it in and close the lid before turning it on.

Greta waves like the princess she is and trots off out of the room in her underwear with my heels clopping against our expensive hardwood floor. I cringe, but let her go. Leo hates it and is always asking her to take them off. But once he catches sight of her pleading puppy dog eyes and her ridiculous outfits, he always gives in.

I hear my phone ringing in the kitchen and hurry from the laundry room to answer it. My mom's name flashes across the screen, and I can't help but feel a little nervous as I answer it. She doesn't know how bad things have gotten between Leo and me. She adores him, and she's so happy that I ended up with the life I did. It might cause her to worry.

"Hello?" I sing, trying to put some pep into my tone.

"Baby girl! How are you?"

"Good, how are you? How's Taylor?"

Funnily enough, my mother and Leo's mother are best friends. Well, if you can call it that. They're total opposites and used to hate each other when we first got together, but when Leo Sr. passed away four years ago, everything changed. My mother took one look at the bunch of fake friends at his wake and took it upon herself to help Taylor during that time. If not as a friend, then at least as something more real and not as forced as all the well-wishing but quick to disappear socialites who Taylor had thought were her friends.

Taylor didn't forget and never let her go. They travel together several times a year on Taylor's fortune. Even though my mom put up a fight, feeling like she couldn't possibly leech off her like that, Taylor didn't give her much of a choice. They're outrageous and kind of dramatic when they get together, but we love them. And I'm glad they've found each other.

"Oh, being her typical high-maintenance self. It took her

two hours to get ready yesterday morning. I'm telling you the truth. Two freaking hours, my girl. It's a record, I tell you."

I hear Taylor in the background. "Oh, shut your mouth. You're lucky I decided to get ready at all. I was having a terrible hair day, Dahlia!" she yells out to me.

Smiling, I lean forward over the counter onto my elbows.

"Do you know how much living you could do in two hours?" Mom asks Taylor. "We aren't getting any younger, you old bat."

"Renee, if I had shown myself in public with my hair looking like it did, I wouldn't want to live anyway," she says matter-of-factly.

"Ladies," I interrupt with a laugh. "Should I go and let you two finish this argument without me listening in?"

"Oh, we're not arguing, dear," Taylor interjects.

"Whatever gave you that idea?" my mom asks, sounding perplexed.

God. My hand dives into my hair as I try not to roll my eyes. I pull the phone away from my ear. "Greta! Charlie! Grandma and Grandma are on the phone," I call out, trying to wrap this up.

I hear them muttering to each other. "Look what you've done, Renee. She doesn't want to talk to us now."

"Me? It's not my fault. She's a busy woman; you can't hold her up with your incessant gibberish all evening."

Greta rounds the corner into the kitchen, hurrying to take the phone from my hand.

"Hi, Grandmamas!" Her sweet voice no doubt has them in smiling fits. They dote on these kids like nothing else. I busy myself with getting a salad prepped to have with our steak and potatoes. Getting the meat out of the fridge, I turn on the stove and watch Charlie sulk into the kitchen. I'm not fooled, though. He loves his grandmas; he just doesn't like to look too excited.

The kids finish talking twenty minutes later, and I say a quick goodbye, telling them that our dinner is almost ready and that I need to go.

After it's all finished, I place everything on the island in the kitchen. I'm about to sit down when I hear the telltale sound of Leo's Aston Martin as it rumbles into the garage. He's home in time to eat dinner with us for once. Huh.

"Um, okay, guys. Let's move this to the dining table."

Charlie grumbles. "But I'm too hungry to move."

I give him a raised brow, and he reluctantly grabs his plate, following us into the dining room. I return to the kitchen, grabbing the salad and another plate for Leo's seat at the head of our long oak dining table. He walks into the kitchen just as I'm leaving it, but I don't stop. He knows where we'll be.

"Daddy!" Greta sings when he enters the room behind me, taking off his suit jacket and laying it over the armchair in the corner of the room. He walks over to her, kissing her, and moving the sunglasses from her eyes to the top of her head. He scruffs Charlie's hair affectionately, who gives him a quiet hello. I watch it all out of my peripheral vision as I cut up Greta's steak for her and pass it over. He doesn't touch me, of course. But at this stage, I'd probably fall out of my chair in shock if he did.

He sits down, and I eat in silence as the kids tell him about their day at school and what their grandmas are up to on their vacation.

"Grandma Renee said she saw a real-life seal! In the ocean!" Greta says with awe.

34

Her father, to his credit, widens his eyes a little. "No kidding. A real one?"

He almost, *almost* smirks when she nods frantically.

"Who cares, you can see them in the zoo anyway," Charlie says to his plate.

I lower my cutlery, frowning at him. "Charlie …"

"What?" he mumbles and then glances at Leo's hard stare and shrugs. "Sorry."

We finish eating, and I head right to the kitchen to start cleaning up while the kids race to the living room after their father to watch TV and have dessert. When I'm done, I call them upstairs for their showers and tuck them both into bed.

"Mommy," Greta calls right when I'm about to head down the hall to take a shower.

I turn around and walk back into her room. "What's up?"

She smiles up at me. "I love you."

I tilt my head, smiling back at her and saying the words she wants to hear next. "Not as much as I love you. Good night, poppet."

"G'night." She rolls over onto her stomach, and I walk down the hall, grabbing some clean clothes and closing myself in the bathroom.

Once under the hot spray, I try to let it wash some of the tension away. I shouldn't be tense when my husband comes home. I shouldn't grow nervous every time I hear his car pull in. But I am, and I do.

This shit needs to stop. Lola's right. I can't keep doing this.

I turn the shower off and dry myself before getting dressed.

Resolved, I head back down stairs and find him in the living room, still in his work clothes as he flicks through his phone with the TV on some sports channel in the background. I tug out my kitting basket, grabbing my needles and the cardigan that needs finishing before trying to get comfortable on the opposite couch.

It takes about ten minutes, but I finally gain enough courage to ask, "Can we talk? Please?"

He taps away at his phone, not even so much as glancing up at me.

"What about?" he mumbles distractedly.

I clear my throat a little. "Well, us."

He doesn't even blink. I hear the email notification go off on his phone as he continues to stare down at it.

"Leo …" I warn quietly.

"What?" he snaps. "There's nothing we need to discuss. We've been over this."

I know, but fuck it, one last shot, right? Before I allow myself to completely give up.

"That's the thing, though. We haven't, not really. Can't you feel this?" I ask, feeling my heart try to climb up my throat when he continues to ignore me. "This isn't right. It's getting worse, and I don't know what else I can do, what I've done wrong, or how I can fix it. Not when you won't even look at me most days."

He rights himself on the couch, running a hand through his hair and making it stand on end in that sexy way it does. But he stays quiet, and I think he'll ignore me again until he says, "You know you haven't done anything wrong because there's *nothing* wrong, Christ. Stop trying to find something that isn't even there." He stands, and I watch as he leaves the room while growling at me, "I've given you two beautiful children, a beautiful home, and a beautiful life, what more do you want from me?"

You, I almost say. *I just want you.*

But feeling my heart slam violently against my chest, I shock myself by saying something else entirely. "I'm having an affair."

He freezes in the doorway. *Something,* at last.

I don't know what made me say it, especially when it isn't exactly true. But it could be. And I think I want him to realize that. To realize he could lose me. Because maybe if he does, he'll put a stop to this insanity.

He doesn't turn around when he finally speaks. His voice is quiet and as cutting as glass, slicing into my trembling skin. "Do whatever you want. We're not getting divorced."

Then he's gone, and I'm left staring at the wall as tears cloud over my vision before spilling silently down my cheeks.

Chapter Six

PULLING INTO THE PARKING LOT OF THE KIDS' SCHOOL, I park and jump out to grab their bags.

"Okay, don't forget to hand the permission slip in to Mr. Andrews, Charlie." I pass their bags over and then try to fix his messy brown hair.

"Mom, stop," he hisses.

"But did you even brush it this morning? It looks like you just rolled out of bed," I say as I try to smooth it back down again. It's cute how much it's like his father's, but it's not exactly sexy-sophisticated on a nine-year-old boy in a school where appearance is important.

Greta giggles at Charlie's annoyed expression behind her hand.

"Shut it, pip-squeak," he growls at her.

"Hey!" I admonish. "What did I tell you about speaking to her like that?"

"Sorry," he mutters.

I kiss them both and watch as they run inside as the bell rings. Then wave to Lola, who has to work today and is trying to drink her coffee while navigating the mass of traffic, all trying to leave the lot at the same time.

"Call me," she mouths.

I nod, turning around and about to climb back in my car when I spot Fiona standing next to it.

"Hey, honey," she says warmly. "Wanna grab a coffee?"

I groan. "Ugh, I wish. I could do with five of them this morning. But it's my day at the shelter." I wince in apology. "How about later this week? Come over to my place, maybe?" I feel like we haven't caught up much these past few months, but that's life. Always stealing time from you before you even realize it's happened.

She beams. "Okay, sure, but I'll hold you to it, Lia. I need girl time," she says dramatically. I laugh and tell her to text me before I climb in and start the drive to Rayleigh.

The sun is shining particularly bright through my tinted windows, and I find myself longing for winter if only to feel like I haven't wasted so much time cooped up inside my own head during what was supposed to be my favorite season.

I'm not doing that anymore. It's time to make me happy again. Somehow.

It's been four days since I told Leo about my non-existent affair. And nothing has changed. I wonder if he knew I was lying, or if he just thinks that I could never do such a thing. And that stupidly reckless part of me wants to rise to the challenge and bait him some more by actually having one. But I'm scared. And the scariest part isn't even the thought of being with another man. No, it's the fear of Leo truly not caring at all.

I flick my turn signal on, waiting for someone to pull out into the flow of traffic before taking their spot a few shops up from the shelter. Flipping down my visor, I fluff my hair and check to make sure no remnants of breakfast remain around my mouth. Satisfied, I flip it up and grab my purse, jumping out of the car to find a pair of amused green eyes watching me. Jared shifts from leaning against the back of my car. How the hell did I not notice he was there?

"Morning, Blondie." He moves in and smiles down at me. "No need to check yourself for me. You'd still be beautiful wearing a garbage bag."

My lips curve into a smile. "Morning, trouble. Let's go; I'm running a few minutes late, so I know that means you're even later."

I lock the car and drop my keys in my purse as he falls into step beside me.

"I love the way you worry about me, but Glenda loves me, so don't sweat it."

I roll my eyes. "You're so full of it."

He chuckles. "Come on. Places to be, mouths to feed." He opens the door for me, and we walk out the back to sign in.

"Jared Williams," Glenda huffs with her hands on her hips by the storeroom door.

Jared turns up the charm. "Morning, Glendie. Has anyone ever told you that purple is most definitely your color?" He gestures to her purple t-shirt.

She turns a little red in the face and waves her hand at him. "Oh, you sneaky thing. Get moving then, but be warned, I'll be watching the clock next time."

He beams at her. "Yes, ma'am."

"Were you late because you were waiting on me?" I ask as

we wash our hands.

He shakes his head, grabbing some paper towels. "Yes and no. Had some shit to check in on this morning."

Frowning, I wonder what he has to check in on before nine thirty in the morning.

"Like what?" I blurt as I tug my hair net and apron on.

He does the same. "My shop."

"Shop?" I ask.

"Yep." He pops the p then sighs before continuing, "I run a custom bike and car shop a few blocks from here."

Oh, wow. Though I don't know why I'm shocked. Just because he's had a run-in with the law doesn't necessarily mean he wouldn't have some kind of normal life outside of having to volunteer here. "What's it called?"

He snaps his gloves on then opens the fridge, bending to grab some vegetables. And yep, I end up staring as his jeans fall farther down over his boxer briefs. His shirt rides up, showing a sliver of skin. "Surface Rust," he says, standing and closing the door. A knowing smile on his face tells me he knows I was looking at his ass. I flush then realize what he said. "Wait, what?" A little snort escapes my mouth. "That's the name of your business?"

He shrugs, placing everything on the counter. "What can I say? Too many jaeger bombs and a good joint or two used to do wonders for my creative side." He grabs a knife and a chopping board. "Besides, the name hasn't turned away any customers yet."

I grab some gloves and pull them on. "How do you swing that? Working there and here?"

He stares down at the food. "I do what I need to." His tone lightens again as he continues, "Got a great team of guys helping out at the shop, too, so that helps."

Nodding, even though he's not looking at me, I grab the meat out of the fridge, and we work in comfortable, yet strangely charged silence for a while. I try to think of something to say to break the tension, but he beats me to it.

"Have you been thinking about my offer?"

Glancing around to make sure no one is within hearing distance, I whisper, "Shhh, and no."

He just grins down at the counter. "You sure about that?"

"I am," I answer. "Why wouldn't I be?"

He's quiet for a moment before finally responding. "I don't know. Maybe the fact that you instantly knew what I was asking you just now."

Swallowing hard, I avert my eyes back to the task at hand as my breathing turns choppy. I'm determined to ignore the curiosity and hurt that seem intent on sending me spiraling into something I shouldn't even be thinking about—let alone doing.

We're quiet again, but over the next half hour, he takes every opportunity to brush his arm or hand against mine, causing the tiny hairs all over my body to rise with awareness. He even goes so far as to brush his hand over my ass before he slips what I think is a piece of paper into my apron.

I keep preparing lunch, waiting until I go to the bathroom to read it.

Once I do, I open it to find that all it says is: *The Green, room twenty-two.*

My heart stills and almost stops beating as I piece together what he's asking me.

Holy shit. I toss it in the trash can and wash my hands before making my way back out to the kitchen. There's no way

I could actually do it.

Could I?

He finds me alone in the hallway and walks right up to me.

"What do you say, Blondie? Ready to let me make your legs shake?" he whispers as he gets close enough to tuck a stray piece of hair behind my ear.

My mouth dries; my body is feeling absolutely ready.

But my heart? It's pounding so fast, and I don't even know why. In excitement? Guilt? Fear? I think it's an unhealthy combination of all three.

"Live a little. What's the worst that could happen? It's not like anyone is ever going to know. Just you"—he runs his finger over the shell of my ear—"and me."

I close my eyes, taking a deep breath.

Don't do it, Dahlia. Do not do it.

Call Lola.

My head's nodding before I've even unraveled my thoughts. My conscience is screaming at me. But this stupid need for some form of happiness and vengeance, I don't even know—wins out.

"Just … just once, okay?" My voice breaks as I meet his heated gaze.

He nods, eyes darting between mine. "Sure. I'll meet you there."

As he walks off, I try my best not to run back into the bathroom and hyperventilate. I force myself back to the kitchen where I finish my shift with shaking hands.

Once the clock hits eleven thirty, I sign off, say goodbye, and make my way over to the run-down hotel a few streets away. I decide to leave my car out on the street instead of in the parking lot. Doing so makes me feel dirtier than even agreeing to this. But I told Leo I was having an affair, and he said to do whatever I want. He didn't do or say anything to stop me.

I take a deep breath and climb out, trepidation filling every step I take to room twenty-two. Jared opens the door before I even get there, and I didn't realize how much I must have dragged my feet until now. He grabs my hand and tugs me inside, locking the door behind me. I'd be scared if this were anyone else other than the man I've slowly gotten close to over the past month. But no, my gut churns for a whole variety of reasons instead.

He backs me into the door, tucking his face into my neck and inhaling deeply. The action causes my stomach to quiver.

"I've wanted you since I first laid eyes on you," he rasps.

I try to search for some bravado. "Well, now you can have … me," I stammer.

He chuckles, the sound huskier than usual. "I know you're terrified, but you can trust me." He lifts his head, and his eyes ask me to believe him. And I do. I know he won't hurt me. But that doesn't mean I'm going to be okay. Not at all.

"I'm going to kiss you now," he warns.

I try to talk, to say something, but his lips descend and land on mine before I can. My eyes close, and I try to adjust to the foreign feel of his mouth. He hesitantly parts my lips with his and licks at the underside of my top lip. My hands find their way into his hair as I tilt my head, allowing his tongue more access.

He groans. "You taste like heaven," he says into my mouth. "I bet you do everywhere."

A moan escapes me at the thought of his mouth tasting

me everywhere. He tastes like tobacco and spearmint. The vast difference from Leo should shock me, but it doesn't. It has me tangling my tongue with his as my body grows so heated that I feel as though I might burst into flames at any minute.

We're soon stumbling around the room, undressing each other while trying to keep our mouths fused together. "Just sex," I breathe as he stares down at my almost naked form with wonder in his eyes while I lie on the scratchy, threadbare comforter on the queen-size bed.

"Whatever you say, Blondie," he mutters against my skin as he dips his head to pull my lace panties from me with his teeth. I know this is wrong. That desperation mixed with a healthy dose of heartache could cause a recipe for disaster. But I can't bring myself to give a damn. Not when I've been starved for so long. Not when his rough hands are gliding down the insides of my legs, leaving goosebumps in their wake.

"So fucking beautiful. You've had two kids?" he asks in disbelief.

I nod. "There's evidence, so don't look too hard," I say jokingly as I reach for him. I need to stop reality from trying to enter this dimly lit hotel room.

He bats my hand away, tracing his fingers over the scar from my C-sections then some of the fine stretch marks around my hips and on the tops of my thighs. "Found them." He grins up at me.

He's taking too long. "Are we doing this or what?"

I need to do this. The longer we wait, the more I'm afraid that I might back out.

He tsks. "Let me look my fill. It's not every day a man comes across graceful looking curves of this perfection." He kisses my hip, moving in to dip his tongue into my belly button, making me giggle and arch off the bed.

"Stop!" I pant.

He does, and I open my eyes to see him leaning over me, almost nose to nose. "This needs to come off." He glares at my bra like it's offending him. "Show me those tits, Blondie."

The crass statement has me growing even wetter. I swallow hard, unclasping it and slowly pulling the straps down my arms. He leans on one arm to throw it across the room until it lands somewhere on the floor with my other articles of clothing. My eyes fall to the tattoos on his arms—the intricate shading of tombstones and roses. He couldn't be more different from Leo if he tried. And for some reason, I'm immensely pleased by this fact.

He leans down, making my hips buck from the bed and connect with his hardness as he takes a nipple into his mouth and sucks.

"Oh, God …" I gasp.

"No, baby, just me." He chuckles, and I slap his shoulder. "You're a turd."

He laughs quietly, shifting to rub his lips over my other nipple. "I've been called many things in my life, but I can honestly say that a turd is not one of them."

"Shut up." I laugh.

Lifting his head, he connects our mouths. His tongue slips inside and gently skims along mine. He leans on his side, dragging a finger around my breast before squeezing it and trailing his fingers over the dips of my stomach to the top of my mound.

That's when I start to shake; when reality decides to slap me upside the head. But he doesn't notice. His finger slowly parts me and trails through my wetness, eliciting a shiver and fogging my mind with pleasure once again. He drags the wetness around my clit, and I moan as he dips his finger inside, teasing me and making my hips rock as my need to come builds rapidly. Finally, he thrusts a finger all the way in, nipping my chin and thrusting in and out of me in a torturously slow rhythm.

"Feel good, Blondie?" he murmurs throatily with his lips now sucking at my neck.

I suck in a breath in response, and he picks up speed, circling his thumb over my clit. That's all it takes for the magic to happen. I come apart with a silent cry, my legs indeed shaking as they try to clamp around his hand and stars flash behind my closed eyelids.

When I open them, I find him grinning down at me. "That was one of the best things I've ever fucking seen."

I try to catch my breath, my mind starting to un-fog.

"It really has been a while, hasn't it?" He frowns.

I manage a nod, squeezing my eyes closed.

Holy fuck.

I just came on another man's hand.

I had an orgasm, courtesy of someone other than my husband.

And to make matters even worse, a sob escapes me. I move away from Jared to sit up, covering my mouth with a hand and looking for my clothes.

"Hey, hey …" He gently grabs my arm and pulls me back down on the bed. "Come here."

He wraps his arms around me, and I bury my face in his chest as I'm wracked by sob after embarrassing sob.

This can't be me; this can't be my life right now.

But it is. And I've gone and done it to myself.

"Shhh," he murmurs, kissing my head and stroking my hair. "It's okay, Blondie. I often have this effect on women. So good, they're guaranteed to cry happy tears every damn time."

I manage to laugh despite the hiccupping and sniffling.

"I'm so sorry." I wipe my tears, and what I hope to God isn't my snot, from his hard pec. "You gave me that, and ... and I just—"

He grabs my chin, tilting it up to make me look at him. I study the chiseled yet playful features of his face behind blurred eyes.

"Don't. I knew this might not go as smoothly as I'd hoped. And to be honest, I'm still shocked as fuck that you even agreed to it."

I give him a watery smile. "You're a good man, trouble. Not a lot would know what to do with a crying lunatic in your position."

He swipes a tear from under my eye with a smile that doesn't reach his eyes. "Nah, I just care about you, Blondie. Probably more than I should." His brows pull in adorably as he says it. Smiling softly, I lean on an elbow and use my other hand to smooth the crease from between his brows. He brings my head back down to his chest, and I tuck it into his neck as he runs his calloused fingers up and down my back.

I'm more than aware that I'm doing—that I have done— something I can't turn back from. But it feels too good to be cared for like this again for me to simply run out the door. Back to my cold house and even colder husband.

We lie in silence for a while, and I soon feel myself start to drift off to sleep before my eyes spring wide open. "Shit, the kids. I have to go before I'm late."

He releases me, and I grab my clothes, scurrying into the

shabby bathroom to dress. I try to fix my hair as best I can, hoping like hell that I have a brush in the car.

I'm about to leave the bathroom when I see it.

A hickey. Right underneath my earlobe.

My brown eyes look like they're about to pop out of my head as I look in the mirror.

Shit, shit, fuck.

With nothing to be done about it now, I move my hair around to make sure it's covered before racing back out to grab my purse.

"I'm sorry, so sorry. But I really do need to go. I'll see you next week?" I say to the room in general as I focus on getting out of here. Jared comes up behind me and halts the door from opening with a hand.

"Not so fast, babe," he says to my ear, spinning me around and bringing his mouth down to mine.

As soon as our lips touch, I pull away. "I can't. I shouldn't even be here …" I plead, backing myself up against the door. His lips tug into a tiny smile. Hooking an arm around my waist, he pulls me into his hard body.

"I know." He kisses my forehead. "Go."

I watch him for a second, feeling torn but knowing I can't and don't have the time to deal with that right now. He opens the door, and I run out to my car on the street. Climbing in, I check the time before I let my head drop into my hands.

Holy hell.

What have I done?

The pieces are falling, but now, I'm not so sure I want them to.

Chapter Seven

MY STOMACH HASN'T STOPPED TURNING SINCE I LEFT Jared in the hotel yesterday. Guilt has followed me around like a little black cloud, floating over my head. I'm so damn confused because if I'm being honest, I don't know if I should even feel guilty. But here I am, being dragged under anyway. I thought being with Jared would help, that it might wake me up a little from the bad dream that's become my marriage. But it's just made me feel worse.

And Jared …

Christ. I feel fucking terrible, not to mention embarrassed. What must he think of me? This wife, who has everything but is still miserable, and cries her woes into his lovely chest? *Oh, dear God.*

But I can't deny that any and all guilt disappeared the moment he made me feel important and cared for again. It's crazy how much you miss something you didn't even pay much attention to beforehand. Leo would always find excuses to touch me, kiss me, and show me in little ways how much he loved me. So having just a tiny bit of that back? Yeah, I can't stop thinking about it. About how much I took it for granted before.

I'd been starving, and Jared fed my weary heart in a way that I hadn't expected him to.

I lift the now finished cardigan up in the air to study it. It's tiny and peach in color, and it's going to look adorable on an infant. Rising from the couch, I lay it down on the coffee table to snap a quick photo with my phone. I'll upload it to my Etsy store later tonight.

I pull the lasagna out of the oven, serving some up onto the kids' plates after calling out to them. If Leo comes home while we're eating in the kitchen, so be it. He didn't come home for dinner last night, which I was thankful for. When he did get home afterward, I ignored him and barely mustered up a hello with how tumultuous I was feeling inside. I was scared my guilt would be written all over my face. Like a blazing yellow flashing sign above my head read 'guilty' with an arrow pointing down at me. I shake my head, laughing darkly to myself. I have no idea why I'm letting this tear me into even more pieces when he's made it very clear that he doesn't even give a shit.

Charlie comes in and takes a seat on a stool at the island, dragging his plate toward him and digging in right away. "Where's your sister?" I ask, placing a glass of water in front of him.

He shrugs, mumbling around a mouth full of food, "I dunno."

I wipe my hands on a dish towel before going to find her.

"Greta, dinner's ready!" I call out as I walk up the stairs.

"One minute!" she hollers, sounding a little panicked.

Frowning, I walk down the hallway, checking her room and finding it empty when I hear a, "Crap. Oh, no ..." come from our spare bedroom.

I walk in to find her in my silk and lace ivory wedding dress. The long gown pools on the floor around her small frame. My heart plummets painfully into my stomach when I see her staring down at the tattered, frayed skirt.

"I'm sorry. I just wanted to see how I'd look if I one day grew up and got married." She bites her trembling bottom lip. "I was trying to take it off, and I accidentally stepped on it, in your beautiful wedding shoes." She winces.

I grab the doorjamb and try to think, try to calm my emotions. It's not entirely her fault. I should've known that keeping it in the closet in here—and with her penchant for dressing up—that she'd one day find it.

"It's okay," I finally whisper, but I don't know if I'm trying to reassure her or myself.

She nods, her chin wobbling. "Can you fix it?"

I walk over to her, gently pulling her arms from the fabric and letting it fall to the floor as I pick her up and lift her over it.

"Maybe. I'll see what I can do." Though like many other things, I know it's ruined, and I shouldn't even bother trying. But she doesn't need to know that.

I help her out of my jeweled ivory peep-toe wedding shoes.

"Go wash up. Your dinner is in the kitchen waiting for you," I say quietly.

She goes to leave, pausing in the doorway as she watches me stare at the puddle of material on the floor.

"Are you coming, Mommy?" Her voice is hesitant, unsure.

"Yep. I'll just look at this and be right down." I give her what I hope is a reassuring smile then hear her run down the stairs to the kitchen.

Sighing, I sit down in front of my wedding dress and just stare at it for a minute. Looking at it, I can't help but think it's kind of symbolic, really. After everything that's happened, something that was once so perfect now sits ruined before me. When I think back to that day, where the sun seemed to bless us as it showered us in rays of warm light, I never would've pictured we'd be where we are now. But then again, my eighteen-year-old self never would have dreamed that the notorious player and captain of our college swim team would have set his sights on me for anything other than a one-night stand either.

"Go out with me," he says over the loud thumping bass of the music that blares from the frat house behind us.

I start to laugh, feeling a little lightheaded from the three beers I've already had. "For the third time, no."

He frowns down at me, and I feel kind of bad. He's determined; I'll give him that much. "Look, there are a ton of girls here who'd give you what you want in a heartbeat. And I'm sorry, but I'm not one of them." I watch Samantha Hall give me the stink eye before giving Leo a flirtatious smile when he glances over to see what I'm looking at.

He turns back to me. "I don't get it; I'm not trying to steal your virtue and bail—"

I start coughing, choking on the sip of beer I just took.

"Holy shit, you're"—he looks around and lowers his voice—"you're a virgin?" he asks as if he's never met one before.

And cue the eye roll because yes, I'm still a virgin. I've never had a boyfriend for longer than a few months, so I never got around to trusting them fully and giving it up.

"What does it matter?" I try to sound bored.

"Look, I'm not interested—okay no, that's a lie, I'm totally interested in fucking you." His honesty has me laughing again.

"Seriously, though, I just want to take you out, and keep taking you out until I devise a plan to make you mine. Permanently."

I guffaw. "A little presumptuous, aren't you?"

He shrugs, leaning in to tuck some of my blond hair behind my ear. "You can call me whatever you like. Just say yes."

Butterflies swoop violently in my stomach and cause my heart to flutter alongside them. The way he looks at me and the sincerity in his blue eyes is getting harder and harder to ignore.

He's a junior, the captain of the swim team and one of the most popular guys on campus. He and his friends stink of money and have no issue flashing it in people's faces. I came here on a scholarship, and I work two jobs, one as a tutor and the other a barista just to get by. Worse than all that, he could crush me and make me wish I'd never laid eyes on him.

But when he leans in to softly press his lips to mine, I don't move away, and I'm rewarded with a feeling I've never felt before. It feels like I've been sleepwalking for the past eighteen years, and I'm finally starting to wake up. It's a feeling so addictive that I surprise myself by rising onto my toes to wrap my arm around his neck and tilt my head, parting my lips to deepen the kiss.

He groans when I hesitantly skim my tongue along his, causing delicious shivers to rake their way over my entire body. We get lost in the slow exploration of the heat and curves of each other's mouths as if they're old friends who've finally reunited once again and have all the time in the world to catch up.

Until someone calls out, "Woo! Get it, Vandellen!"

I pull back slightly; our chests heave with our ragged breaths.

He gives me a crooked smile that I feel all the way down to the soles of my feet and tightens his arm around me. "You're mine now, Dahlia."

And I was. Despite courting me as he promised, from that night on, I was irreversibly his. I'd like to say that I wish I could turn back and shake my eighteen-year-old self and warn her of what's to come for us, but I can't bring myself to regret a thing. Not our years together and most definitely not our children.

We've had our ups and downs, as most couples do. We've never been much for bickering, no, we'd usually let it all out heatedly because we both knew what came after. That amazing, passionate, angry make-up sex. In the months after he started to slowly pull away from me, I tried to bait him. Tried anything to get that heated look back in his eyes. The one he'd get right before he'd lock us in a room and cover my mouth while he fucked the shit out of me.

But it didn't work. *Nothing* has worked.

I've often wondered what he'd do if I left; if I just walked out. But the kids … This is their home. Leo is their father, and despite breaking my heart, he's still good to them for the most part, just more absent than he used to be.

I pick the dress up, running my fingers over the smooth silk and spreading the skirt over my lap. I have no idea how much time has passed, but I feel him, standing in the doorway behind me. He doesn't say a word, just watches silently as I continuously run my finger over the fraying tear in the fabric. I feel his eyes on me for another minute before I hear him quietly walk away.

Chapter Eight

I LEAN BACK AGAINST MY CAR, LISTENING AS FIONA TELLS US about her latest fight with her husband.

"Over socks! I mean, can you even believe that shit? All I did was ask him to pick the filthy things up off the floor and put them in the hamper instead of in front of the damn thing."

"Ugh, Trey did the same thing, so I thought, you know what? Fuck him. And started leaving them there, unwashed. He's a quick learner, thankfully." Lola smirks, and we laugh.

"Thank God my cleaner does our laundry because there's no way in hell I'm touching them. Just seeing them lying around is bad enough." Fiona's eyes flick to me. "How's Leo? Has he been driving you mad? God, it feels like forever since we all hung out together as a group."

It has; the last time was at her and Dylan's anniversary party. Our husbands, even with their differing career choices, all get along really well, which is great when we all want a night out. I lift my shoulders in a shrug, deciding to dodge the question as best as I can. "I'm just so used to him now that I guess nothing fazes me." The lie slips past my lips so easily that Lola's eyes narrow on me.

But I don't want Fiona to know all about our dirty laundry, excuse the pun. It's not that I don't trust her, but the more people who know, the more chance of others finding out about our sham of a marriage. And if he refuses to divorce me, then I'm not about to make waves when I'll still be here to endure the fallout.

"Anyway, what's up with those new school hats they're trying to bring in? What the hell was wrong with the old ones?" I change the subject.

Fiona groans. "Right? Have you seen them? They'll all look like mini tennis players. Ridiculous."

Lola laughs. "I think they're kind of cute, but I definitely prefer the other ones. I swear, they're just bored and looking for ways to make us spend more money."

"You're not wrong there." Fiona sighs then her eyes zero in on my neck, and she steps forward, slapping my arm. "Oh, you little tramp, you still let Leo give you hickeys?"

Fuck. I quickly try to hide it with my hair. I almost forgot about it, and that makes me panic because if I haven't been careful, then maybe Leo's seen it, too.

"Uhhh," I stutter as Lola's eyes widen so much that I think she's about to fall backward. "Yeah, sometimes," I force out with a nervous giggle.

Fiona just grins, nudging me with her elbow. "You lucky thing. I can't remember the last time Dylan gave me a hickey, the bastard."

That has me frowning. I knew those two liked to fight more than what is considered normal, but she seems a little more upset with him than usual.

To deflect and because I'm curious, I ask, "Everything okay? With Dylan?"

Her eyes flit away for a brief second—so quick, I almost miss it.

"Yes, fine. He's just been in a mood thanks to his latest client at work. I can't wait till it's all finalized," she says before turning to look across the parking lot as the bell rings and kids start to pour out of the giant, old wooden doors.

Her husband works in marketing if I remember correctly. God, I've been trapped underneath my own problems for so long that I'm afraid I'll forget someone's birthday. I make a quick note of the date as the kids run up to us. Lola pinches my arm when Fiona turns toward her boys.

"Ouch. What was that for?" I rub my arm.

"You've got some explaining to do." She glares.

Damn it, I know. And there's no way she's going to believe what I want her to, that Jared didn't give me the stupid hickey.

"Okay." I sigh. "Tomorrow, though? I've got orders to send out on my way home." It's true. But I also want some time to wrap my head around what to tell her and prepare myself for the inevitable lecture that's coming my way.

Fiona turns and waves goodbye, heading over to her car.

"Right after school drop-off. My place," Lola says before opening the door for Sophie to climb into their car.

Sucking in a deep breath, I kiss both kids on the head, grab their bags, and help them into the car before making my way to the post office.

"Rupert said a naughty word today at recess, Mommy," Greta says solemnly after we're back in the car. My phone chirps with a text in my purse as I finally pull out of the parking lot and follow the long line of cars down the road. I ignore it; I'll check it when I get home.

"Shut it. It's none of your business, Greta," Charlie hisses.

"Is too!"

"Is not," he growls.

"Is too, is too," she sings.

"Okay! Enough." I flick my turn signal on before turning down our street. "What happened?"

"I can't repeat it," Greta gasps. "Then *I'll* get in trouble."

I see Charlie rolling his eyes in the rearview mirror. "He said his dad called his mom a slut. There. That's it. I said it," he huffs.

Oh, my God. I don't know whether to tug my mom cap down extra tight and give him a stern talking-to for repeating it or let out the shocked laughter that's begging to be set free.

I settle on a fucked-up combo of both.

"Charlie," I croak. "Thank you for … for …" For what? Repeating something he shouldn't have? But how else would he tell me? "Yeah, just don't say that word. It's pretty horrible, 'kay?" I pull into the driveway, waiting for the garage door to go up when he mutters, "Whatever. I wasn't going to, but you wanted to know."

"Thanks, smarty pants." I drive in and turn the ignition off.

"Is Rupert okay?" I turn around and ask.

He shrugs, taking his seat belt off. "I guess, he was just telling everyone about the fight his parents had last night. I think he thought it was funny." He climbs down and shuts the door.

"Hey! You forgot your bag," I grumble as he walks inside the house.

"He didn't seem sad," Greta says when I help her out. "Rupert just likes to tell stories. Henry, though, he looked a little annoyed." She gets her bag and runs inside.

Not my business, not my business, I repeat to myself as I grab my purse and Charlie's bag then head inside. Because yeah, I don't really want Fiona's boys describing their parents' arguments in detail, but I know if I say something, I'll either offend Fiona or embarrass her. Fine lines, I tell you. I unpack the kid's lunch boxes and bags before remembering I need to check my phone.

I almost drop it when I unlock the screen and see who the text is from.

Jared: Blondie, are you okay?

Jared: Don't freak out. I called myself from your phone while you were in the bathroom.

It's hard to believe it's only been two days since I ran out of the hotel like my ass was on fire. I don't know if it's a good idea for him to have my number, but I can't bring myself to tell him to delete it either. It's official—I'm a mess.

I tap out a response …

Me: I'm okay. Thanks for checking in.

I lock my phone, hoping that was sufficient enough to curb any more questions. It chirps again, and I bite my lip. Okay, apparently not.

Jared: You have amazing tits ;)

I burst out laughing in the middle of my kitchen.

"What's so funny, Mommy?" Greta comes running in, opening the fridge to grab a yogurt. I tuck my phone away in my purse, watching her peel the lid off and attempt to throw it in the trash can by the end of the counter. The yogurt underneath it makes it stick to the top of the trash can, though.

"Nothing. One of my friends just sent me a funny message." I kind of lie and grab a wipe to peel the yogurt lid from the trash can and wipe up the smear.

"I can't wait till I have a cell phone. I'm gonna send you funny messages all the time," she declares as she grabs a spoon and digs straight into the small tub. A bit dribbles over her lip as she says, "You have a nice laugh, Mommy."

She says it as if she's aware I rarely laugh—real laughter—anymore.

My brows lower as she walks out of the kitchen. I don't want my children to look back and remember me as some seriously sad woman who merely went through life, doing what she had to do each day.

My heart clenches painfully. That reminds me of my own mother.

I help the kids with their homework then clean up the living room and move a load of laundry from the washer to the dryer before we sit down and have dinner. Again, no sign of Leo.

I'm cleaning up after dinner, the kids already in bed, when I finally hear his car parking in the garage. I can't help but notice how long it takes him to get out of it and come inside. That stings—like he has to muster up the courage to come inside and see his own family. The people who love him.

I wipe my hands on a dish towel and pretend to browse

the contents of the fridge when he walks into the kitchen. He doesn't even kiss me on the head, one of the only ways he'll touch me anymore. Anger starts to drown out that ever-growing pool of hurt in my stomach.

"How was your day?" I ask bluntly, closing the fridge door and startling when I see him leaning against the kitchen counter, watching me—actually looking at me.

He shrugs. "Can't complain. Have you bought a dress yet?"

My brows furrow. "What for?"

He scratches at the stubble on his jaw, and I want so desperately to run my own nails down it. To touch him anywhere, everywhere.

"The charity gala is coming up next weekend."

Shit. "Oh," I reply dumbly. "Sure, I'll grab one next week."

"The kids in bed?" he asks, straightening his six-foot-two frame from the counter.

I nod. "Yeah, just before you pulled in."

"I have some calls to make, so tell them I'll be up in a minute," he says before leaving the room and turning for what I'm guessing is his office.

Ugh, I hate going to events in the best of times. Having to make small talk with pompous assholes and two-faced women is not my idea of fun. But it's even worse now. Now that I know my husband probably isn't going to help make it any more bearable for me.

Blowing out a breath, I head upstairs and tuck Greta in, letting her know that Daddy will be up soon. I then go into Charlie's room to do the same.

When he doesn't respond, I take a seat on the bed next to him.

"Did you hear me?" I ask.

He nods, staring up at the ceiling. "You and Daddy don't ever fight anymore."

My eyes widen, but what did I think would happen? That the kids wouldn't pick up on the tension and silence that now fills their once happy home?

"Um, well …" I try to think of what to say.

"Henry and Rupert's parents fight all the time lately, but you guys don't fight at all. You don't …" He stops and swallows. "You're just … different."

Tears gather in my eyes as I look down at my confused little boy.

"I know, buddy." It's all I can say. I can't lie to him—he knows better—and I have no explanations for him, not when I have none myself. I lie down next to him when he turns on his side, wrapping my arm around him and stroking his hair as he drifts off to sleep. Leo comes in a short while later but sees that he's asleep and leaves the room.

I kiss Charlie's head and leave to take a shower. Feeling emotionally drained and so damn over it all, I decide to grab my book and head to bed early. I run downstairs to grab my phone off the counter before turning off all the lights Leo won't be using.

Just when I'm about to go back upstairs, he calls my name from his office, which sits opposite the stairs.

"Yes?" I ask, pausing on the stairs and setting the alarm on my phone for the next morning.

His voice sends ice skating through my veins when he says, "Make sure you get rid of that shit on your neck before next weekend."

Chapter Nine

I TEXT FIONA THE NEXT MORNING, LETTING HER KNOW I'M busy today—yeah, busy getting the third degree from Lola—but that she's welcome to come over for a coffee tomorrow. She says she'll leave the boys at home with Dylan and be here at ten thirty.

I drop the kids off and wave to Trey, Lola's husband, who dropped Sophie off this morning before making the ten-minute drive to their place on the other side of Bonnets Bay.

Pulling over outside their gorgeous three-bedroom beach-style white cottage that Trey spent two years renovating himself, I grab my purse and climb out. Nerves take hold as I walk down the driveway to the front steps of their wraparound porch. I walk up them and knock, but Lola's already there, pulling open the door and grabbing my hand to drag me inside.

"Are you crazy?" she hisses, the door slamming closed as she releases me and marches into her living room. I follow her, feeling like a child who's about to be scolded and take a seat on the plush couch by the window next to her.

"It's from him, isn't it?" She reaches over and moves my hair aside to see the hickey that I remembered to cover with makeup this morning. She licks her finger and rubs it off.

"Ew!" I try to squirm away from her.

"Shut it, hussy. Stay still," she orders.

I do as I'm told, rolling my eyes.

"Shit, it's a good one. Has Leo seen it?" She sits back, her eyes bugging out comically as she drums her fingers over her mouth.

"Apparently. But he only warned me to cover it up before the charity gala next weekend."

My heart hurts at the memory of his cold, annoyed voice.

"Are you shitting me?" She breathes.

I shake my head then scrub my palms over my face.

"What a prick. He doesn't even care that you've been with another man?" She doesn't try to hide her anger or disbelief.

"It doesn't seem like it. But Jared and I, we didn't …" I trail off.

"You didn't have sex with him?" she finishes for me.

"No, we didn't. I couldn't do it." I sigh, leaning back into the couch and curling my feet under my ass. "But we kissed, and he, well, he made me, you know …"

"Oh, my God." She pauses. "I shouldn't be asking you this, but what was it like?" Her eyes light up with interest.

"Amazing. Well, it was until I … fuck, I feel like such a moron." I close my eyes briefly, "I started crying, Lola."

She tries not to laugh, but I see it there, the amusement in her eyes. "You're not exactly cut out for the whole affair thing after all, are you?"

"I don't know. I don't think so," I admit.

"Not when you're clearly still in love with your idiot of a husband." She sighs, relaxing back into the couch.

"I told him." I stare off at a picture of her, Trey, and Sophie on the wall. "I told him before it even happened that I was having an affair."

"What? Are you serious? But if you weren't …" It must click for her because she says, "Ohhh, you were trying to goad him into giving a shit, weren't you?" She laughs. "A little evil but clever."

I pick at my nails. "I guess."

"He didn't care when you told him?"

"No, just said to do what I want, and that we're not getting divorced."

"Holy fucking shit, I could kick him in the balls so hard right now, Lia. How the hell haven't you yet?"

I laugh, despite feeling like I want to curl up into a ball and sleep until this whole disaster is long behind me. "I have no idea."

She's quiet for a beat then asks, "So what did Jared do when you burst into tears? Hightail it out of there as quick as he could?" She smirks.

"Actually, no." I smile as I remember how sweet he was about it. "He held me. He comforted me."

"Seriously?" She frowns. "He's into you then? Wants more?"

The words make my back straighten. "Uh, well, he knows he can't have more." I think about that for a second, knowing I'm probably fooling myself. "So I don't think so. I think maybe he just has a thing for married women." I scoff. "The sneaky bastard sent me a text yesterday. He called himself from my phone when I was cleaning up my face in the hotel bathroom."

She slaps me on the shoulder. "Shit, Lia, delete it. It's bad enough that what's happened, has even happened *and* Leo knows. Don't let this go too far."

"Would you quit hurting me, woman?" I grumble and rub my shoulder.

"Sorry," she mutters sheepishly. "But seriously, what did he get all over your face that you needed to wash off in the bathroom?"

We both burst out laughing when my phone chirps in my purse, which is sitting on the coffee table. She dives for it, and I let her. Not really caring at this point.

"What the …" She drops the phone between us on the couch. I glance up to see her a little red in the face. "It's him," she whispers.

I can't help but laugh. "Oh my God, stop it. He's not going to reach through the phone and make you have sex with him."

I pick it up, shaking my head and laughing softly until I read what it says.

Jared: Can't stop thinking about the way you squeezed the fuck out of my finger. Makes me wonder how awesome it's gonna feel when you come wrapped around my cock.

PS: I don't like being ignored, Blondie.

I drop the phone, too. Dumbfounded and flushed as hell.

"I know this is going to sound bad," Lola says. "But my freaking panties feel damp."

My mouth is dry as I admit, "Yeah. Mine too."

"Fuck me, what are you going to do, Lia? That guy"—she points at my phone—"he wants you, *bad*."

I groan. "I don't know. I thought he'd be scared off after what happened on Tuesday."

She guffaws. "He's so far from scared it isn't even funny. In fact, it seems like he only wants you more."

Damn it. I rub my legs together, feeling frustrated and so confused. "Should I tell him to stop?" I bite my thumb nail. "I should tell him to stop, right?"

She nods, solemnly. "Right."

Sighing, I pick my phone back up and tap out a response, flashing my phone her way to show her what I sent.

Me: Jared, I'm sorry, but you need to stop. I think you should delete my number.

Lola snorts. "Oh yeah, real convincing."

Glaring at her, I ask, "What the hell am I supposed to say? He's been … good to me. I don't want to be a bitch."

She remains quiet, biting her lip as she stares at me.

"What?" I ask.

Her blond brows furrow. "You care about him. You *like* him, don't you?"

I roll my eyes. "What is this? High school? Wait till you meet him. You'll like him too. Trust me."

She snickers. "Yeah, but I know how to look and not touch, my lovely Lia."

My phone chirps again. "Ignore it," she practically growls.

I raise my hands in the air. "Fine," I huff. "Got any coffee? I need something stronger, but it'll have to do."

She scoffs, getting up and walking off to the kitchen. I follow her. "Do I have coffee? You should know better than to ask such stupid questions."

That has me smiling, thankful she doesn't hate me and that she's somehow trying to remain supportive through all this. Even if I don't deserve it.

That night, Greta sits next to me on the couch while we finish watching *Beauty and the Beast*. I'm a little more lenient with their bedtime routines on the weekend. Leo is out; he went to the effort to send me a text earlier to tell me that he's having dinner with a client and will be home late. But I don't mind. After he admitted to noticing the hickey on my neck last night, I would be even more anxious about what to do in his presence than I normally am.

God, I still can't believe I let Jared do that. But to be fair, I wasn't exactly thinking straight about anything, so desperate was my need to finally have an orgasm from someone other than myself. Yeah, I'm an idiot. I almost want to come clean to Leo, tell him that something happened but not what he might be thinking and that I'm not going to do it again.

But he either wouldn't give a damn, or he'd ignore me.

That has me remembering that I didn't read Jared's last text from when I was at Lola's house.

Once it hits nine thirty, I take the kids upstairs to brush their teeth and tuck them in before grabbing my phone and laying back down on the couch. I open it up to Jared's unread text.

Jared: You can't make me quit you, Blondie. So don't even try.

I'm tapping out a response before I can help myself. He needs to know that I can't do this.

Me: Please, Jared. I need you to stop. I shouldn't have let it go as far as I did. I'm sorry.

He replies right away.

Jared: I can't stop thinking about you.

Me: I'll change my number … and that's a pain in the ass. Don't make me do that.

Jared: Shit, okay. Friends?

I bite my lip, thinking about it. It's the best I can hope for at this stage really. He sends another message through, and I burst out laughing as I picture him singing the familiar song.

Jared: Why can't we be friends? Why can't we be friends?

Me: LOL. Okay … friends only. See you Tuesday.

Jared: ;)

I'm still laughing when Leo walks into the room, brows lowered as he looks down at me. I almost choke as I try to swallow down the panic.

"Hi," I squeak.

"What's so funny?" His voice is deceptively soft. He removes his cufflinks while his blue eyes dart all over my face.

I exit out of the texts and sit up. "Nothing, just Lola send-ing me one of those gif things." I'm a little shocked by how easily the lie slips past my lips. I'm getting way too good at it.

He stares at me for another second before finally leaving the room.

Of course. The only time my husband pays any attention to me is the one time I don't want him to.

Chapter Ten

Jared: Is it Tuesday yet?

I barely suppress a laugh, grabbing the sauce I was looking for from the shelf and moving my shopping cart to the next aisle. My phone buzzes in my hand again when I stop to grab some of Charlie's cereal and put it in the cart. I check the time and see it's just after nine thirty. Okay, time to hustle. I left the kids at home with Leo, who said he'd take them to swim practice this morning.

I glance down at the next message.

Jared: You will come on Tuesday, right? You're not going to try any avoidance shit?

I had thought about it, but really, I need to face him at some point. And besides, we agreed on just friends.

Me: Nope, it's Saturday, and yes, I'll be there. Don't worry.

Jared: I miss you … friend.

I almost groan with frustration.

Jesus, I have no idea what I'm doing. But I have a feeling this "friends" thing isn't going to work out.

Me: Jared …

Jared: Right, I get it. But it's true. You're kind of addictive, Blondie.

Me: I'll see you Tuesday.

I put my phone away and rush to finish grabbing the groceries. Fiona is coming over this morning, and I stupidly forgot until I'd already raced out the door. I speed walk to the checkout and figure if I've forgotten anything, it'll wait until I go back out on Monday.

Once home, I unload the car and quickly race to put it all away. I then clean up the living room, bathroom, and wash the breakfast dishes in the sink. I fix my hair and paint some lip gloss on. I'm just finishing up with some mascara when the doorbell rings. I cap it, chuck it in my makeup bag, put it in the cupboard, and head downstairs.

"Hey." I pull the door open to a smiling Fiona.

"Good morning. Here." She passes me some muffins. "Got them from that new bakery down the road because who has time to actually bake, right?" She laughs at herself, and I force one out too as I close the door behind her.

"Oh, God …" She breathes, running a hand along the gilded banister of our staircase. "Now I remember why I never like coming here. I always get severe house envy, you lucky bitch."

If there's one thing I appreciate about Fiona, it's her brutal honesty; even if it sometimes makes you feel a little uncomfortable.

"Shut up, your house is amazing," I say as I move past her into the kitchen and switch on the coffee machine. Her house is basically a mini mansion, marble flooring and sweeping staircases leading up to the eight bedrooms upstairs. It screams old money, but it's classically beautiful. Kind of like she is.

"You're right; it's fabulous. But you know what that saying is." She takes a seat at the island while I make our coffee.

"Milk and sugar, right?"

She nods. "Please, one."

"Always wanting what you can't have … that saying?" I ask.

"Uh-huh. Where are the children?"

I finish making her coffee and pass it over before turning back to finish my own. "Swim practice. Leo usually likes to take them if he's not working," I tell her.

Once done, I grab my coffee and place the muffins on a plate, taking both over to the island and sitting down across from her.

She raises a brow. "That's right. You said he was a big swimmer in college?"

I nod, taking a small sip from my mug. "Yeah, he was captain of the swim team. Still swims at least a few times a week, too."

She grins behind her mug, her green eyes flashing mischievously. "Ah, so that's why he always looks so damn good. How old is he now anyway?"

He does look good. If anything, he's even more attractive now than he was all those years ago when we first met. "He just turned thirty-four."

It was a quiet birthday, and I cringe just thinking about the way I threw myself at him that night. He stiffened as soon as I pressed my bare breasts into his back. I haven't tried since. That was two months ago.

"Shit, he'll probably turn fifty and still look as good. My Dylan is getting quite the gut on him." She smiles. "But then again, we do have a fucking great cook. Maybe if I fired her and he was forced to fend for himself, he'd lose a few pounds." She shrugs.

I laugh because she's insane. "Or he'd just ask you to cook for him." I raise a brow pointedly at her over my mug.

She gets wide-eyed at that. "Oh God, no. It's been so long. I don't know if I'd even remember how." She takes a sip from her mug, leaving a perfect lipstick smudge around the rim as she lowers it. "One time, Wendy, our cook, had the flu, and we couldn't get a replacement in for two nights. *Two nights.* Dylan and I whipped up some grilled cheese and soup, but it took us half an hour to get the settings right on the damn fancy stove that we just had to have." She rolls her eyes. "Breakfast I can do, but dinner? Never again. I have a spare chef on speed dial now."

I burst out laughing, not knowing if she's joking or being serious. But I know she's probably telling the truth for the most part.

"I cook all the time," I admit, shoving a piece of muffin

into my mouth.

Her brows rise. "Every night?"

I swallow before answering. "Sure. Unless we order in, which we usually do every week or two."

"You like to cook?" she asks, bewildered.

Shaking my head, I say, "I don't hate it, but no, I don't love it. I do like to eat, though, and after growing up having very little, it feels like a waste of money to pay someone to do something that I can do."

She cackles. "Oh, shit. Next, you'll be telling me that you clean your own house, too."

My hand, which is holding another piece of muffin, pauses halfway to my mouth. "Yeah, I do. We get someone in to do the windows and pool every so often, but I clean the house."

Her jaw drops open and hangs there comically as I smirk down into my mug.

"I've known you all this time, so why am I just finding this out now?"

I smile. "Because it's not important? Besides, if I didn't have something to do, I'd go crazy. Leo said he'd like me to stay at home, at least until the kids are in high school." I bring the muffin to my mouth. "I agreed."

"But ..." she stutters through her red painted lips, "he's worth millions."

Swallowing the muffin, I frown, well aware of this. "I know."

"Sorry, but shit, I just thought ... if you had that much money, then you'd barely have to lift a finger."

I brush the crumbs off my hands onto the counter and take a sip of my coffee. "Not always the case," I mutter.

"So, because you were poor, you don't like to waste money?"

That makes me laugh. "No, I love to spend money as much as the next person, but I'm just smarter about it because of my upbringing, I guess."

She pats my hand as if she feels sorry for me.

"Oh, and don't worry, Leo pays someone to come in and do the lawns every month, too," I joke, but he really does, though.

It's right then that I hear his car pull into the driveway and not even twenty-seconds later, the sound of the kids running in through the front door.

They stop in the entryway to the kitchen. "How was swimming?" I ask as they look around, probably searching for any sign of Rupert and Henry.

"Charlie won, again," Greta groans and walks over to wrap her arms around my waist.

"Congratulations, baby." Smiling warmly at him as he walks over, I pull him into my side to kiss his chlorine scented head then let him go. He immediately walks out of the kitchen with barely a wave at Fiona.

"And how'd you do, gorgeous?" Fiona asks.

"I don't race, just practice," Greta mutters. I rub her back. Swimming has always been Charlie and Leo's thing that they do together, and I think she's trying to find that something with her dad, too. Little does she know; she doesn't have to. Their bond is already pretty special. But she'll figure that out in her own time.

"Practice makes perfect. Here, muffin?" Fiona scoots the plate over, and Greta takes one before leaving the kitchen. I hear the TV switch on a minute later and cringe as I think about their wet pool hair dripping all over the leather couches.

I'm wondering where Leo is until he stops dead in the entryway to the kitchen a moment later.

Fiona turns on her stool. "Well, hello handsome, how've you been?" She beams at him.

He appears to be frozen, his tall frame stiff and unmoving. His top lip curls into a sneer, and his jaw is clenched tight as his ice-cold blue eyes land on her.

My own flit back and forth between them like crazy, watching the way Fiona visibly swallows as he seems to stare daggers at her.

He finally tears his eyes away, letting them skim over me. He clears his throat before turning around. "I'll be in the office," he mutters and disappears.

Fiona waits a moment before hissing, "Sheesh, what crawled up his amazing ass and died since the last time I saw him?"

She doesn't realize that I've been wondering the same damn thing for months now.

I feel my cheeks heat—how embarrassing. It might be forced, but he's managed to remain polite to most people. Especially our friends.

"I'm so sorry. I have no idea what's gotten into him today." I reach over and pat her hand.

"No, don't be ridiculous. He's probably just having a bad day or week. Dylan can be the same. I stay well out of his way when he gets irritable after a bad streak in the office." She waves her hand around. "Anyway, where were we …? Oh, you have *got* to finally tell me where you got those photo frames I saw in the hall …"

We spend the next half an hour chatting, and to her

credit, she acts as though my husband wasn't a complete ass to her. But I'm only half here. The other half of me is wondering if maybe something happened between the two of them. Because even though I don't think he's cheated on me or has been having an affair, my gut is rolling right now. So I'm glad when she decides to leave. I need to take five minutes for myself.

I lean over the kitchen sink, and rinse my mouth out with a glass of water in an effort to stop the bile from climbing up my throat at the thought of my husband with anyone, let alone my friend.

Coughing, I place the glass down and stare, unseeingly, out the kitchen window to the manicured gardens outside, just as it starts to rain. My eyes fall on the Dahlias Leo insisted we plant as soon as he bought the house. He went a little crazy. There's purple, pink, red—almost every shade you can find—as well as various shapes and sizes, including the huge Dinner Plate Dahlia's. They're spread throughout the beds in our front and back gardens.

My mom almost fell over when they finally all bloomed for the first time. Tears were falling from her eyes as she told me how lucky I was to find someone who loved me so completely. Who'd show it in ways that neither of us had ever thought possible.

I turn around and lean against the sink, drawing air into my empty lungs. Glancing up, I find him leaning in the doorway, watching me with what looks like remorse in his blue eyes.

He wouldn't have. Not her. *Would he?*

As if knowing where my thoughts have gone, he shakes his head subtly and straightens from the wall. "I'll go shower the kids."

My eyes stay glued to where he was standing as my thoughts tumble and tangle together, trying in vain to make sense of something that just doesn't make any sense at all.

Oh, what a fucked-up web we've weaved.

Chapter Eleven

Tuesday arrives quicker than I would have liked it to.

I walk into the shelter, kind of surprised Jared wasn't waiting for me this morning like he has been lately. I'm also a little concerned about the disappointment I feel over that.

"Morning, Glenda," I say as I sign in.

"Oh, good morning, Dahlia." She puts a box down that she was carrying. "Would you mind giving me a hand this morning instead of working in the kitchen? There's a new girl who's joining us for a little while to build some hours up for her college application, so Jared took her under his wing." She smirks, shaking her head and causing her gray bob to bounce around. "Let's hope he actually gets some work done." She laughs.

My stomach somersaults at the news. "Oh, okay. Sure." I force a smile and follow her into the storeroom where we spend the next hour reorganizing clothes, linen, and bringing in new donation bags to start sorting through.

"I'm going to hit the bathroom. Back in a minute," I tell Glenda who just waves me off as she goes over her checklist.

Feeling curious, I can't help myself and decide to walk by the kitchen. I don't see any new girl, though. Then I hear it. A giggle as I spot Jared's broad back. He moves to the side to reveal someone who looks like she's barely eighteen, slender and athletic with a pixie styled haircut. Her hand brushes his arm, and she beams up at him as he says something to her. I don't know what I feel more sickened over, watching them or the fact that I feel a little annoyed over seeing him with another girl in the first place. Girl. Right, because I'm a thirty-two-year-old woman with two children and a failing marriage. I shouldn't give a shit, but, oh fuck it … I just do.

I turn to leave, continuing down the hall to the bathroom where I do my business, wash my hands, and stare at myself in the mirror for a moment. I don't feel old. In fact, I've only seen a couple of random gray hairs on my head. But watching them, seeing the stark differences between me and her makes me feel ancient. I shake my head, telling myself to get over it. This is what I wanted, right? For him to move on and leave me alone. So why do I feel so annoyed about it?

I open the door, keeping my head low as I head back to the storeroom, but then a hand wraps around my bicep and tugs me into an old cleaning closet. I squeal, and Jared covers my mouth with his hand as he maneuvers me against a cold, cement wall and stands over me.

He removes his hand from my mouth, and I stare up at him with narrowed eyes.

"What are you doing?" I whisper-hiss.

He grins, his white teeth glowing in the dark room, and I

stare at that slightly crooked front tooth until his hands travel up my arms to cup my cheeks. My eyes lift to his.

"Where've you been?" He frowns.

"In the storeroom with Glenda, seeing as you apparently don't need any extra help in the kitchen today," I snap then wince. *Yikes.*

He only smiles wider. "Blondie, is something wrong?"

I close my eyes and sigh. "No, I'm being stupid. Don't worry about it."

Leaning in farther, he brushes his lips over my cheek. "God, you always smell so damn good."

"Jared," I warn, trying to push him away. "Friends, remember?"

He groans. "Yeah, yeah. Can I take you out after we're done here? Maybe another coffee?"

I shake my head. "No, I don't think that's a good idea."

He skims his finger across my exposed collarbone. "So stop thinking, Blondie. I'll meet you out front." He smiles again before opening the door and walking out without waiting for another response or even looking to see if the coast is clear. Of course, he wouldn't. He's not the one doing anything wrong here.

An hour later, I sign out and wave goodbye to Glenda before grabbing my purse and heading outside, thinking that I'll just get in my car and leave before he can trick me into anything again. But as if he knew my plan, there he stands, half leaning against my car. He's crossed his tattooed arms over his chest, and he's wearing a pair of Ray-Bans with a devilish grin to match. Combine them with his low-slung dark denim jeans, white t-shirt, and slicked back dark brown hair, and he's enough to make anyone's heart start pounding faster than it should.

He straightens, walking over to me then directing me back through the lunchtime crowd with a hand at my lower back. I don't ask where we're going because I'm too busy trying to figure out what happened to my sense of self-control. I'm also trying desperately not to inhale his tobacco and clean linen scent. But it's hard, especially with the warmth of his hand seeping through my black sundress.

After a few blocks, he finally stops in front of an old movie cinema.

"Time to hang out, friend." He grabs my hand and leads me through the paint-chipped doors to the stale smelling interior. It's dead quiet with no one around besides an old man behind the ticket booth who looks to be reading a weathered mystery novel as we approach him. "Hi," I say as Jared scans the choices above on the worn-out board. The man holds up a knobby pointer finger, a silent request for us to wait a minute. I glance at Jared who bites his lip and widens his amused eyes at me.

"Sorry," he finally mutters, putting the book down. "What can I get you?" He sounds tired but nice enough. Jared asks for two tickets to a new action movie that's just come out, some popcorn, and sodas. We wait as he gets them, Jared looking around at all the vintage memorabilia in the theatre.

"I love coming here," he randomly says.

I turn to face him. "Why's that?"

He shrugs. "Didn't have the best of times as a kid growing up on the streets, but me and my brother, we'd always sneak in here and hide out behind the seats. Some nights, we even slept here."

Well, shit. I knew he was from a rough part of the city,

but I'm starting to realize that there's still so much I've yet to learn about him.

"Where were your parents?"

He smiles, but it's not a nice one. "High, probably. We didn't even have a house. They just carted us from place to place, to whichever of their smacked-out friends would take them in next." He shakes his head. "Half the time, they didn't even remember us. We had to find them until one day, we just stopped trying."

"How old were you when you stopped trying to find them?"

"Twelve. We were thrown into the system soon after, and that was that."

We grab our food and drink from the old man when he hollers at us, before returning to his perch and his book behind the counter. Once inside the musty old theatre, I sit down and tell myself to forget about it. Not to ask any more questions when it'll likely only make things worse. But the burning curiosity gets the better of me.

"You have a brother?"

He nods, throwing a handful of popcorn inside his mouth and mumbling around it. "Yep."

"Does he still live in the city?" Even in the dim lighting, I notice his eyes darkening. His chiseled, stubble coated jaw hardening a little.

"No. He's in jail."

I almost choke on my popcorn. "For what happened? With stealing cars?"

He nods again. "Enough about me. How're things at home with ...?"

I notice how he doesn't say it. The word *husband*. But I

answer anyway. "The same, I guess." His eyes narrow on me and I turn to face the crackling screen as the movie begins. We watch in silence for a while then his arm is looping around my neck, and his hand is drawing soft circles on the bare skin of my arm. I should tell him to move it, to stop it, but I get lost in the feeling of being relaxed. His presence, despite not being the man I desperately want, is somehow soothing.

About halfway through the movie, I check the time on my phone, knowing I'll have to leave soon to pick up the kids on time. "You want to stay? I'm going to have to go back to my car in a minute." I shift in my seat to ask him.

He drags his eyes from the screen to me. "I'll walk you."

I give him a nod, grabbing my purse and drink as he rises from his seat. I follow him out of the aisle, and he waits, wrapping a hand around my waist before we start the walk down the steps of the abandoned theatre. Just as we near the bottom, I hear a moan come from the movie still playing above us. My eyes fly to the screen, seeing the male lead with a half-undressed woman as they make out heatedly. I swallow thickly, so aware of Jared's looming presence and his touch as we round the corner that goose bumps rise on my arms and a wave of heat overtakes me.

He must sense it because he stops, pulling me into the alcove right behind the closed doors to the theatre. He grabs my drink, tossing it in the trash can behind him before he moves quicker than lightning for my lips. I gasp loudly as his tongue instantly invades my mouth and touches mine, the taste of him overwhelming me beyond reason. He picks me up; my legs wrap around his waist, and my dress gathers around my hips as his hand snakes its way inside my panties.

My head rolls back against the wall with a moan as his

finger tests my wet entrance before sliding inside to his knuckle and twisting as his tongue and teeth travel over my chin and the underside of my jaw. My thighs quiver and my breathing picks up when he groans into my ear. "So fucking warm. You like that, Blondie?"

I whimper as he continues to fuck me with his finger, making my head spin faster and faster. Then he presses his thumb to my swollen clit. "Oh, my … yes," I croak.

"Coming so soon? And I thought we were friends, babe." He snickers then removes his hand, and I cry out from the loss. I was so close I could taste it. I growl, glaring at him. He just laughs, pecking my lips and dropping my shaky legs to the dingy carpeted floor.

Then my panties are gone, and he's on his knees, lifting one of my legs over his shoulder and swiping his tongue over my folds as he parts me with it.

"Holy …" My eyes slam shut, and I bite my lip to stop from crying out again when his finger re-enters me while his tongue flicks softly over my clit.

"Come on my tongue, Blondie," he demands.

And mere seconds later, I do. He grabs both my thighs to help hold me up as I throw my head back and get lost in the sensations sweeping over me from head to toe.

Placing a soft kiss on my mound, he rises and tugs my dress down. I grab his face, pulling his lips to mine and turning him into the wall. I'm rewarded with a groan as I rub my tongue against his, tasting myself on him. "Blondie." He pulls away, breathing heavily. "While I want nothing more than to bend you over and fuck you so hard you'll be feeling me for days … you gotta go." His words conflict with the desperation bleeding from his green eyes. But he glances away, and I take a step back.

Right. My kids. *Shit.* I run a shaky hand through my hair and look around for my panties. Jared grabs my hand, tugging me out of the theatre. Great, I hope the wind doesn't pick up, but a glance at the clock on the wall in the lobby tells me I don't have time to waste worrying about my undergarments. We race out the doors into the early afternoon sunshine streaking through the city avenues and skyscrapers. I don't let go of his hand. I don't even think about the fact that anyone could see me because my brain is still half mush thanks to his talented mouth and fingers.

Once we reach my car, he opens my door for me when I unlock it. I hop inside as he leans in, his arms stretching over the roof as he puckers his lips playfully at me. I laugh, grabbing his chin to gently kiss his lips. As I move away, his arms leave the car, and his hands weave into my hair. Tilting my head back, he slowly devours my mouth with his.

He pulls away, and it takes me a second to open my eyes. Once I do, I see him smiling softly at me. He reaches in to start the ignition and tug my seat belt on. My heart flutters crazily in my chest as he skims a finger over my kiss-swollen lips before closing the door and gently patting the roof. Slumping back in my seat, I try to catch my breath and clear my head enough to be able to drive. I glance into the rearview mirror just in time to see Jared's swaggering backside disappear into the crowd as he walks away.

What the hell is he doing to me?

Chapter Twelve

I t's Friday, and I'm doing the one thing I've been dreading all week—getting ready for the charity gala. I had to call in Clare, our sitter, which I haven't had to do in a while. Not since we last went out to Fiona and Dylan's anniversary party.

My phone chirps in my clutch, and my eyes dart to the en suite behind me as I hear the shower still going behind the closed door. Thinking I have enough time, I dig it out and read the message.

Jared: What are you doing tonight, Blondie?

I bite my lip to hold back a smile. He's toned it down a little with the texting. But I find myself looking forward to them now, even though I shouldn't. Leo's barely been home all week. When he does get home, I'm usually already in bed and pretending to be asleep.

Me: Not much. Might watch a movie with the kids. You?

For some reason, I don't want to make the differences between our lives any more prominent by telling him what I'm really doing.

I glance at the time, noting that it's almost seven. We need to leave soon to be in the city before eight when the event starts.

The shower shuts off, but his reply comes through right away.

Jared: Working. When can I see you again?

I knew the question might come, that I'd be a fool in thinking he'd be happy with only seeing me for a short time every Tuesday, but I can't think about that right now. Not when Leo opens the bathroom door and comes striding into the bedroom in just a towel. I put my phone away, slip my silver hoops into my ears, and watch his broad back through the mirror as he heads into our walk-in closet to get dressed.

I blow out a heavy breath, missing the days when he'd walk around naked in our room, teasing and taunting me with a crooked grin. I finish pinning my hair back off my face and rise from the stool at my dressing table, smoothing down the gauzy skirt of my lavender gown as I do. Doing a quick scan in the full-length mirror, I quickly adjust one of the off-the-shoulder straps. I then take a second to admire the way the bodice wraps tightly around me, accentuating my curves before flowing to the floor in a beautiful mess. I slip my feet into my strappy cream heels and bend over to lace them up.

Straightening, I find Leo adjusting his tie as he watches

me. I glance away and grab my clutch from my dressing table.

"Ready?" I head for the door, not waiting for a response. I walk downstairs to tell Clare that we should be back by eleven and make sure that she knows she can call me at any time.

"Mommy!" Greta gushes, running into the kitchen in her polka dot nightgown. "You look like a real-life princess."

She moves in to touch the soft material of my gown as I smile down at her. It's true, and it's one of the only perks of going to these events. I get to feel beautiful and spoil myself a little with getting done up for them.

"Greta," Leo admonishes gently. "Hands off, you were just eating dinner."

She steps back, smiling up at him sheepishly. He walks over to her and bends down to kiss both her cheeks and then her lips when she closes her eyes and puckers them up for him.

Charlie comes in, and Leo kisses his head, smoothing his large hand over our son's messy hair. "Be good and make sure you go to bed when Clare tells you to. All right?"

They both nod. Clare smiles at them, clapping her hands together. "Right. Let's go pick a movie and a board game." The kids run off, and she follows them, telling us to have fun over her shoulder as she leaves the kitchen.

Clearing my throat, I lift my gown and walk out into the garage, Leo following close behind and unlocking his car on the way. I climb in when he opens the door for me, a bit caught off guard by the act, then adjust my dress and clutch in my lap while he climbs in the other side.

I've always loved riding with Leo; the trust I have in him as he speeds around the curves and works the car to his every whim is implicit. Watching him drive, or do anything with his hands, makes my blood heat to a steady simmer in my veins. But tonight, I just stare out the window in the awkward silence and try not to inhale his familiar scent of expensive cologne and spearmint that's filling every inch of his Aston Martin.

"How's work at the shelter going?" he asks as we approach Rayleigh.

I'm startled by the question, by the interest, and I don't try to hide it as I straighten in my seat. "Um, good. Busy, as usual."

He nods and changes gears as we turn down the avenue that leads to the Hedgington Hotel, where the gala is being held.

"What about you? You've been gone a lot this week." I look over at him and notice the way his jaw subtly clenches.

"Yeah, got a lot of shit going on." He shrugs, but the visible tension in his shoulders doesn't allow them to move much.

We pull into the hotel and join the line for the valet. Feeling a lot braver than usual tonight, I let my eyes skim over his gray fitted suit. He's wearing a charcoal gray dress shirt underneath, but I notice that he ended up ditching the tie, opting to unbutton the first few buttons of his shirt instead. I bite my lip as heat gathers low in my stomach. But now isn't the time. *It's never the time,* I remind myself. Gone are the days when I could suffer through these events with a smile on my face. I'd mentally undress my husband all night, knowing that I'd be peeling his suit off him as soon as we got home. Looking at him now, though—well, it feels like a tease. A heart twistingly, unbearable tease.

He's my husband, yet it doesn't feel like I'm allowed to have him anymore.

I check my clutch and close it just as Leo gets out and

rounds the car to open my door for me. His hand is held out for mine, and I hesitantly take it, absorbing every inch of warmth that I can from the simple touch as he closes the door. He releases me but then tucks my arm into the crook of his elbow, leading me around the car and up onto the sidewalk to hand the valet our keys. *Right, appearances*, I think darkly to myself.

I blow out a breath, my eyes flying over to the valet when he says, "Sweet ride, man."

Leo merely nods, but my heart comes to a crashing halt in my chest as I take in Jared, dressed in a valet uniform, red vest and all. His green eyes are on me, and even though he winks, I'm not fooled. I see the way his corded throat swallows, the way his jaw clenches, the way his eyes dart back and forth between Leo and me before he stalks off to take Leo's car.

If Leo noticed anything, he doesn't make it known as we walk inside and join our friends and his colleagues for a few drinks before dinner begins. I'm both nervous and bored to tears but enjoying the delicious roast lamb, if nothing else, as Lydia Donald and her husband talk our ears off over dinner. When the auction begins, and everyone quiets, I'm petrified that the pounding of my heart is about to start echoing in the large room we're sitting in as I wonder where Jared is right now. I glance up at Leo, only to find his eyes are already on me.

"You look beautiful," he murmurs quietly. "Then again, you always do."

My heart warms, and I stare at his lips, his slightly plump, delicious to kiss lips. I miss them. But then he glances away, and I suddenly feel cold again.

After the auction finishes, I drag myself to the bathroom

for a reprieve and to text Clare to ask about the kids. I pause in the hallway on the way back out as her message comes through, saying they're fine and have just fallen asleep.

"Blondie." His voice is quiet but close.

Tucking my phone away, I turn around to find Jared at the end of the hall, leaning against the wall with his hands in his pockets. I look around quickly and spying no one else nearby, walk over to him, stopping a few meters away as his green eyes devour every inch of me.

"You look like you need a good ravishing, princess."

I smile, my cheeks flushing as my eyes fall on his mouth. His mouth that was between my legs just three days ago.

My teeth sink into my lip while I lean a shoulder against the wall next to me. "Shhh. You work here, too?"

"Sometimes they need the extra help for fancy events such as this, and the tips are nothing to sneeze at." He smirks.

"They … they let you? After your history with cars?" I can't help but ask.

His shoulder tilts into a half shrug. "What they don't know won't hurt them."

I watch him for a moment, noticing the way his eyes seem almost sad.

"What's—"

"Dahlia." Leo's deep voice cuts me off as it sounds from the opposite end of the hallway behind me. I turn and find his blue eyes like ice as they dart back and forth between Jared and me.

Looking back at Jared, I see him glaring at my husband.

Well, fuck.

"I'll see you on Tuesday?" I offer timidly to Jared, who finally drags his eyes from Leo long enough to nod at me with furrowed brows. I turn and walk back down the hallway, Leo falling into step beside me as we head back to our table. He's halted by Hugo, a work colleague, and I'm grateful for it. I excuse myself, needing a drink—or three—and head to the bar just as everyone starts milling around and the noise levels pick up again.

I sit alone for a while, enjoying the solitude and the champagne as my heart starts to finally slow to a normal rhythm. Matilda, one of the organizers' wives, comes over and joins me, and I hope I hide my wince well enough behind my glass.

"You look lovely, darling," she says, air kissing both of my cheeks. If the air kisses weren't enough to make me gag, the amount of Chanel no.5 she's smothered herself in definitely does the trick. But I manage to return the sentiment.

"Oh, don't I?" she gushes, smoothing a hand down the bodice of her midnight blue gown that would be better suited as swimwear, due to how little it leaves to the imagination.

"How are those babies of yours?" She bats her lashes, looking around the room distractedly and waving to a few people.

She always thinks they're still babies, and though I sometimes wish they were, it's been years of her asking the same question now. But I can't find it in me to correct her tonight.

"They're great. With the sitter tonight."

She hums. "And how's our dear Taylor doing, hmmm?" She tilts her head a fraction. "It's been a few years since she's graced us with her presence at any of these events."

Leo's mom. I force a big smile. "She's great, traveling and enjoying life as she should be." My tone dares her to say otherwise. Some of these people can get on my last nerve with their self-righteous bullshit. Taylor's donated and given enough of her money and life to them, so she deserves to do as she damn well pleases.

"Anyway"—I jerk my head to Leo who's approaching—"better get back to the husband."

She smiles thinly, saying goodbye and moving on to hassle someone else. I sink back into my seat, relieved that I don't have to move just yet and request a refill.

"Who was that?" Leo asks, coming up to my side.

I pretend to play dumb, "Who? Matilda?"

He shakes his head, his eyes searching the crowd of partygoers. "No, him. The valet."

"Oh, Jared?" I shrug, trying to act indifferent even as the alcohol and dinner threaten to travel back up my throat. "He works at the shelter."

Leo's gaze returns to me, studying and assessing, but I don't flinch or look away. I keep my eyes glued to his, daring him to ask the questions I see burning there. But he doesn't. My shoulders slump, and I tilt my glass back in a very unladylike manor, drinking down half of it and blowing out a gust of breath through my nose as Leo moves away to talk to yet another business associate.

We stay for another hour and a half before Leo finally says we're calling it a night, and we say our goodbyes. I'm glad because I'm feeling a little drunk and my feet are starting to hurt. He wraps an arm around my waist, almost possessively, as we step outside and wait for his car. But I don't see Jared. Not until Matilda sidles over to us, puffing on her cigarette and grinning like a devil as she gasps, "Is that a pair of panties in that valet's pocket?"

My eyes drift over to where she's staring, finding Jared who's smoking with his back turned to us and talking to someone. Then they land on the pink lace hanging slightly out of his back pocket. My stomach nosedives onto the cement beneath my expensive shoes.

Oh, hell.

They're my panties.

"Well, I hope whoever's been lucky enough to play with him hasn't done so in *our* car." Matilda giggles.

I think I nod, but I'm not entirely sure because my pulse is screaming in my ears as I glance up to see Leo with his eyes narrowed to thin slits on Jared.

A different valet finally brings our car around while I call myself all the names under the sun in my head as I thank God that it's not Jared this time and climb inside.

The drive home is silent as tension and anxiety fill the very air we breathe. But I can't bring myself to say anything.

And he doesn't ask.

Chapter Thirteen

WATCHING THE KIDS RUN OFF THROUGH THE SCHOOL
gates, I rub my tired eyes. Sleep hasn't come easily
to me since the event on Friday night, and Leo's
distracted yet still detached behavior isn't helping matters.

"Oh, you and I so need to talk," Lola says with a gleam
in her eyes Monday morning at school drop-off.

"Shush." I glance around. "I know."

"You saw him there? What the hell?" She gapes.

I sent her a text that night, telling her that Jared was
there, but despite the number of times she tried to call, I
didn't answer. Leo was home all weekend locked away in
his office, so I wasn't risking it. Though I don't know why
I'm trying so hard to hide it. I know he knows something's
up. I mean, I freaking told him as much. Okay, that was
technically before anything happened, but still.

Nodding my head, I lean back against the car and
sigh. "This is getting crazy. I have no idea what I'm even

doing anymore."

She waits until a few moms walk by and are out of ear-shot before replying. "What do you mean? Did something else happen?"

I scrub my palms down my face, exasperated with myself. "Yes."

So, I tell her about last Tuesday at the movies.

"I didn't mean for anything to happen, but then again, I shouldn't have even agreed to go. This whole 'friends' idea was doomed to begin with."

"You agreed to being friends? I told you to delete his number, you idiot," she hisses quietly at me. Not having a re-tort for that, I simply stare down at the ground, wondering what the hell I should do now. She's right. I'm being so stupid. But as much as I'm grateful to have a friend by my side who isn't afraid to call me out on my shit, it's all so much easier said than done.

She sighs loudly then leans next to me against my car. "Lia, can't you just end it?"

"End what?" I mumble. "I don't even know what *it* is."

She angles herself to face me. "You do. It's obvious the guy is either enjoying playing with you a little too much, or he's really into you."

Playing with me? I frown. Sure, maybe at first he was, but now … I remember the sad look he gave me in the hallway on Friday and the lack of text messages since then. I even caved and sent him one last night, checking that he was okay before I went to bed. He didn't reply, which kind of stung.

"I don't know. I don't want to hurt him, but he makes me feel …" I blow out a breath, stirring some of my hair from my face as I glance up at the sky. "*Good.*"

"I get that, I do. I'm just worried about the fallout, that's all," Lola says.

"Me too. I think it's just gone too far, too fast, and now I'm not so sure how to leave it alone. He's fun. And being with him, I don't feel like a wounded wife or a busy mother. I'm just me for a little while."

"Until you come back to your real life, Lia." She pats my shoulder and tears start to gather in my eyes.

"It's addictive, feeling that freedom," I whisper. "Even if you know it's fleeting."

Tires suddenly screech into the parking lot, and we look over to find Fiona's Escalade jumping the curb then flattening a flowerbed as it speeds down to the front gate entry to the school. The groundskeeper is walking over to close it as Fiona jumps out of the car, shouting orders to her boys. "Move it, let's go." She opens their doors and passes them their bags as they move unhurriedly toward the gate.

"Ma'am, you're gonna have to pay for replanting that flowerbed," Harold, the groundskeeper, says. He's around eighty years old, and from what Taylor and Leo have told me, he's worked here as long as they can remember. Even when Leo attended as a child.

"Yeah, yeah," she huffs, slamming doors and waving her arms around for the boys to hurry up and get to class. "Put it on the huge tab you assholes make us pay every semester."

Lola and I glance at each other, brows rising, before looking back at Fiona. She may be a little dramatic at times, but she's clearly more than pissed off about something today.

"Get your idiot of a father to call me, boys! Apparently, he's picking you up," Fiona hollers. Rupert just keeps walking while Henry waves meekly at her in response as they disappear inside the school.

Then she finally turns to us, eyes widening with her hands on her hips.

"Shit, ladies, I'm sorry." She moves her sunglasses to the top of her head, wiping underneath her eye. "I didn't even see you there." She laughs, but it lacks humor as she walks over to us.

"All good," Lola says. "One of those mornings?"

I watch Fiona, the way her chest slowly heaves and then gets faster and faster. "Oh, fuck it. Everyone's going to know sooner or later," Fiona blurts. "Dylan is leaving me. This weekend, he told me he wants a … a *divorce*." The word divorce is whispered as if she can't believe it's a word she needs to use.

Holy shit. I rush over to her, wrapping my arms around her as she bursts into tears with her head on my shoulder. Lola comes over and rubs her back. We stand here for a while, letting her cry in the middle of the school parking lot until she finally straightens, sniffling and wiping underneath her eyes. I run to my car, digging out my pack of wet wipes that I keep in there and pass her some for her to mop up the black streaks of mascara running down her face.

"Thank you," she mumbles, dabbing at her cheeks.

"Don't mention it. What happened?" I ask.

She takes a deep breath. "I don't know. He's been a miserable ass to live with these past few weeks." She sniffles again, folding up the black stained wet wipes in her French manicured fingers. "I suspect he's met someone. Probably one of the floozies at his office who work for him." She rolls her eyes. "Asshole."

Lola and I nod, agreeing. "What a dick," Lola says. "What are you going to do?"

Fiona shrugs. "I don't know. He thinks he's keeping the house and the kids." Scoffing, she says, "Over my dead body. But he's supposedly staying at a hotel in the city until I leave."

"He just left you there? With the boys?" Lola asks, her eyes bulging and her tone sharpening.

Fiona laughs then stops as she hiccups and starts to cry again. "Yep, he sure did."

"Jesus Christ," I mutter. "What do you need? What can we do to help?"

She gives me a watery smile. "You're so nice, but I don't even know myself at this stage."

If only she knew, I think to myself.

Lola chews on her bottom lip as she watches Fiona with clear pity in her eyes.

"Well, when you figure it out, you just ask. I mean that, too. Okay?" I say firmly. "Don't give us any of that too proud bullshit. We're here for you." I rub her back.

She wraps her arm around my waist, resting her head on my shoulder. "Thank you," she whispers croakily.

"I can't believe this. Is there anything you can do to work it out?" Lola asks.

Fiona lifts her head from my shoulder. "I don't think so. He was adamant that it's over. Was a total asshole about it, too."

"What, you don't even get a say? What about marriage counseling or something?" Lola's brows furrow as she puts her hands on her pink tank covered hips.

Fiona shakes her head. "No … no, I think we're beyond that kind of help."

We help her back into her car after she insists she's fine to drive and tell her to call us.

After watching her back out of the lot, I mutter, "Well, there's that."

Lola snickers, nudging me with her elbow. "Hey, at least you're not the only one with problems."

"Shut up," I mumble, shaking my head. I can't help but laugh, though. Because as much as I feel terrible for Fiona, it is nice to know I'm not the only one.

"Charlie!" I holler from the bathroom. "Where'd you put your swim trunks?" I dig through the hamper for the second time, but I still can't find them.

He walks into the bathroom, scratching at his belly. "I dunno." Then he promptly turns and leaves me here, bent over with clothes everywhere and no swim trunks in sight. Damn it. He has a swim meet again on Saturday morning. It's only Thursday, but after doing two loads of laundry, they still haven't shown up. I make a mental note to buy a spare pair.

"They're probably in Daddy's car, Mommy," Greta says from the doorway.

"Is he home?" I glance over at her.

She nods. "Just got here."

Sighing, I pick all the clothes up off the floor and carry the hamper downstairs to the laundry room. It all needs to be washed anyway.

The oven dings on my way through the kitchen.

"Crap." Dropping the basket and washing my hands, I turn the oven off and pull out the cupcakes I made for tomorrow's bake sale at school. After placing them on the cooling rack, I then continue hauling the clothes to the laundry and put them in the washer. Standing back up, I spot Leo's keys on the hook and grab them, wondering if he's already locked himself away in his office for the night. Probably.

I unlock it and search the trunk, not finding anything but his own gym bag. Cursing, I move to the back seat and dig around on the floor. Then I see the blue swim trunks on the leather seat right in front of my face. Of course, I laugh quietly to myself as I back my ass up to get out, then I see it. A piece of paper with numbers written on it on the floor. Huh. Bending farther, I snatch it up and hop out of the car, closing the door behind me and glancing at the messy scrawl.

Why the hell would he be keeping random numbers on a piece of paper? I'd think nothing of it, except for the little important fact that our marriage seems to be on the fast road to nowhere good. My pulse kicks up speed, ringing in my ears as I march back through the door and into the kitchen.

"Mommy, can I—"

Cutting Greta off with a wave of my hand, I mutter, "Give me a minute."

I storm through the kitchen and down the hall. Grabbing the handles on his office doors, I walk straight in before closing them and falling back against them.

Leo glances up from his computer.

"What are you doing?" I ask.

His brows pull in. "What does it look like?"

"Never mind." I march over to his desk and drop the piece of paper with the number on the mahogany wood below, watching as it flutters downward to land near his keyboard.

He scowls at it. "What's this?"

With my hands on my hips, I glare at him. "Why don't

you tell me? I found it in your car."

He shakes his head. "And you're searching my car for bits of paper … why?"

Oh, my God. I could slap him.

"Just answer the question," I growl.

He leans back in his chair, steepling his fingers together as his eyes study me for a moment. "And what do you want it to be?" he finally asks.

What? "What the fuck do you mean?"

He smirks, but it's not playful. No, it's full of arrogance and malice.

"I said," he leans forward, the leather chair creaking as he rests his elbows on the desk and stares straight into my eyes, "what do you want it to be, Dahlia?"

I blanch, rearing back. "I don't want it to be anything. What the hell are you playing at by even asking that, Leo?"

He merely shrugs, glancing back down to his computer and rubbing a speck of something off the desk with a long finger.

His head lifts as he sighs. "Are you finished?"

My face scrunches up. "Finished? I don't think so. I want to know whose number it is." I point at the offending piece of paper, quite aware of the fact that I probably seem a little crazy right now, but … so be it.

"Why? Would it make you feel better if you knew?" He raises a brow at me.

"Of course. It would if it's"—my throat bobs—"if it's nothing."

He nods. "It's too bad I'm not in the mood to make you feel better then. Sorry, but I've got shit to do." He moves the paper to the side, clicking away at his mouse and then resumes typing.

My jaw drops open. He's dismissed me. His own wife. Like I'm a fucking nuisance.

In a daze, I turn around, walking out and back to the kitchen. What did he even mean? Is it as bad as it looks, or is it nothing? Knowing I'll get no answers by stewing on it, I get the kids ready for bed then pack up the cupcakes for tomorrow before heading straight for my chocolate stash and the wine.

Chapter Fourteen

PICKING UP THE TUPPERWARE CONTAINERS, I MOVE THEM to the end of the table before squatting down to reach into a box underneath to grab the pack of napkins.

"Oh, my fucking God," Lola groans around a mouthful of chocolate mint cake. "It's like heaven has visited my mouth."

Lara Sparks and Melanie Trundle turn to glare at her as I rise and rip open the packet. I bite my lip, trying to stop the laugh from escaping. Lola notices and bugs her eyes out at them. "What?" she snaps. "There's no kids out here yet." She busies herself with separating some paper plates. "Give me a fucking break," she mutters under her breath.

"I wonder if Fiona will come," I hear Lara whisper, not very quietly, to Melanie a few minutes later.

"Ha! I doubt it. I mean, could you even imagine showing your face after that? God, I'd just die," Melanie declares rather dramatically.

A disbelieving laugh finally escapes my mouth, and

Melanie turns to glare over at me. "Something funny, Dahlia?" she snaps.

My shoulders lift. "Oh, no. Just that I remember you didn't seem to like it very much when everyone was talking about your husband's affair with your nanny." I tap my chin. "What was she? French? Seventeen?"

Lola gasps theatrically. "Yes, I remember that." She turns to Melanie. "Quite the scandal, wasn't it?"

Melanie looks like she's about to throw the bottle of juice she's holding in a death grip at our heads.

Lara clears her throat. "Yes, that was ah, interesting." She changes the subject back to Fiona. "How's she doing, though? She'd be heartbroken," she says with forced gentleness.

I shrug again. "She's doing as well as can be expected."

But to be honest, I don't actually know. I sent her a text yesterday, which she didn't return. I'll have to call her if she doesn't show today. But when I glance up a moment later, there she is, strutting over to us in her ... sweatpants, tank, and cardigan. Oh, shit. She normally wouldn't be caught dead in sweatpants, not even in her own house. I share a worried look with Lola quickly before Fiona arrives at the table and says, "Well, I'm here. Where do you want me?"

Melanie clears her throat delicately. "Did you bring anything?"

Fiona lifts her sunglasses to her head to give her the full power of her green-eyed glare. "Does it look like I did? Christ, you bitches are lucky I even showed up." She walks around the table to join Lola and me while Melanie and Lara stand there gaping at her.

"You okay?" I whisper then wince. "Stupid question, sorry."

She shakes her head; her brown hair pulled back into a messy bun that bobs around with the movement. "I'm fine." She grabs a cupcake and shoves half of it in her mouth then picks up a piece of caramel cake. "Holy fuck. I feel like I haven't eaten in years," She moans around the chocolate filling her mouth.

"Didn't you say you were gluten intolerant?" Lola asks her.

Fiona throws her head back with a loud laugh, her teeth covered in cake. "Yes, what bullshit. Just another way to say no to carbs." She rolls her eyes and snatches the juice from a still gaping Melanie before pouring herself a large cup full and draining it in three gulps.

"God, that shit would taste amazing with some vodka." She goes to grab what looks like a flask out of her purse that's still hanging over her shoulder. Lola grabs her arm and tugs her over to a box of custard tarts. "Could you help me put these out? Your eye for decorating has always been so much better than mine."

Fiona huffs. "Oh, fine." Then gets to work unpacking them and spreading them out over some trays just as the recess bell rings and the kids start racing out into the quad.

"Here they come," Lola mutters, snapping some gloves on and mentally preparing herself. Laughing, I do the same. We spend the next fifteen minutes selling almost everything to the children and teachers alike.

"Hi, Mommy," Greta sings, coming around the table to wrap her arms around my waist.

I take my gloves off to quickly fix her ponytail that's come loose.

"How's your day been? Have you seen your brother?" I ask.

"He's right here." Sophie giggles and I glance over to find Charlie busily sampling some of the treats still left on the table.

"Charlie!" I hiss. "We need to pay for them."

He glances up at me, chocolate coating his lips. "But you made some of them," he mumbles around the food then licks his fingers before going for another slice. Lola laughs as I swat his hand away and grab a slice with a napkin, passing it over to him. He gives me a chocolate-tooth-coated grin before running off to join his friends. I reach down underneath the table to grab a ten dollar bill from my purse and toss it in the ice-cream bucket.

"Where are Rupert and Henry?" Lola asks Fiona who's just returned from the bathroom, looking a little happier.

She waves her hand around. "Who knows. Their father dropped them off this morning."

My brows tug in. "Isn't he still staying at the hotel, though?"

She rolls her eyes. "Yes, he kept them there overnight. Says he doesn't trust me with them anymore." She shrugs. "Whatever that means."

"Shit, he can't just do that," Lola says, turning to me. "Can he?"

Wow. "I don't know. I don't think so."

I look over at the playground as everyone starts packing up. I notice Rupert and Henry with Charlie and Sophie over by the trees. The boys look okay, but wouldn't they want to come over and get a treat? Or say hi to their mom? I shake my head, not knowing the finer details, so it's pointless to try to understand the situation. I should know that better than anyone.

After handing the Tupperware containers back to

everyone, I take the bag of trash over to the dumpster by the side of the school before going to say goodbye to the kids then Fiona and Lola.

"You ladies want to go out? It's Friday. Let's shake what our mamas gave us before they get old and saggy ..." Fiona brushes some chocolate off her fingers. "Or fat."

Lola sighs. "While that sounds like fun, I'm pooped. I've got some work I still need to catch up on this weekend and having a hangover will make that impossible."

Fiona's gaze falls on me. "What about you, Lia? Feel like a bit of fun?" She shakes her ass for good measure.

I smirk. "No can do, sorry. Leo's going out to dinner with a client tonight, and I have no idea when he'll be home. It's too late notice for the sitter."

She pouts. "You guys suck. Oh well, I'll just have to grab a bottle of wine on the way home ... or three." She laughs loudly.

We force a laugh, too. "Yeah, just be careful. Call me if you need anything, 'kay?" I remind her.

She nods. "I'll be fine. Seriously, I feel free for the first time in years."

We say goodbye, and I make the short drive home. I'm just pulling into the garage when my phone rings from my bag. I lean over and dig it out, my stomach flipping at the sight of Jared's name on the screen.

I hit answer and climb out of the car. "Hello?" I say while shutting the door then almost tripping at the sound of his husky voice as I walk inside.

"Hey, Blondie."

I'm tempted to ask where he's been, why he didn't show up on Tuesday, and why he hasn't gotten back to me until now, but I stop myself because even with the questions begging to be unleashed, he's not mine to worry about like that.

"How've you been? Didn't see you on Tuesday." I dump my purse on the counter and walk into the living room, falling back on the couch.

"Yeah, had some shit I had to do, and I wasn't sure if …" He pauses.

"What?" I ask, probably too quickly.

"Nothing. I just didn't want to cause you any more trouble. But it seems like I just can't help myself, not when it comes to you."

I remain quiet, hardly breathing.

"I know you're married. I saw it with my own two eyes. But I can't … you're kind of all I think about, Dahlia."

The use of my real name is what jars me the most out of that admission.

"I'm sorry, trouble. I didn't mean for that to happen, for any of this to happen. But you've shown me what it's like to be wanted again, and as bad as this sounds, it's a feeling I've come to crave. But that doesn't mean …" I startle as the front door opens and slams closed. I panic, hanging up the phone and turning around just as Leo walks by and I hear him lock himself in his office.

"Fuck," I whisper, holding a hand to my chest, trying to get my heart rate to slow. What the hell is he doing home?

My gut tightens. Frustration and confusion have me rising from the couch. This is all becoming too much.

I walk down the hall and go to swing open the doors to his office, but he's locked them. What the …?

"Leo." I bang my fist on the wood. "What are you doing home?"

He doesn't answer me, but I hear him curse and something

smash on the other side, causing me to jump backward.

I wait a minute then two until I hesitantly knock again. "Is everything okay?" I ask through the door.

"Go away, Dahlia," he growls.

"No, not until you tell me what's going on," I demand. "Are you okay?"

He laughs sardonically but doesn't answer.

And still, I wait.

"Jesus, just leave me the fuck alone." His tone quietens.

Tears prick at my eyes as I back away from the doors, not knowing what to do. I scrub my palms over my face and take a deep breath before grabbing my phone and walking upstairs to lay on our bed.

My phone chirps with a text, probably Jared. I contemplate ignoring it, then grab it and look anyway.

Jared: What happened? Call me back.

Me: Leo's home. I'll see you on Tuesday.

I drop my phone onto the nightstand and stare off at the wall for a while. He doesn't write back, and I tell myself to be glad for it. I feel myself creeping closer to the edge of something. Maybe it's the tentative hold I've been keeping on my sanity or on my heart. I don't know. But whatever it is, it's dried the tears from my eyes and left me feeling strangely vacant inside. As if my reasons for giving a shit are slowly drying out like the autumn leaves scattering in the wind outside the bedroom window. Just one step, one wrong move, and the remains of my heart might crack and splinter into irreparable fragments.

Chapter Fifteen

M Y EYES STARE UNSEEINGLY AT THE TALL, IMPOSING brick structure of Bonnets Bay prep as I try to escape the confines of my tangled thoughts that are knotting and fraying together in my mind.

I had to take the kids to swimming on Saturday. Leo disappeared somewhere for most of the day and didn't come home until sometime late that night. He then stayed in his office again all day on Sunday.

"Hey, Lia," Trey, Lola's husband, says as he's walking back to his car after school drop-off.

"Hey." I snap out of my daze and offer him a small smile.

He walks over to me, waving to Sophie over his shoulder, who's throwing her arms in the air and grinning at him from the other side of the school gates. Charlie stands behind her, waiting with a bored look on his face for her to walk with him inside. I smile at him, and he gives me a small one in return.

"I tried to call Leo last week, but he didn't get back to me."

He shifts in his work boots, his hands moving into his cargo pockets. "Everything okay? Lola hasn't said much, just that things aren't going great … you know, at home." He looks a little embarrassed about asking, but he's Leo's friend, has been since he and Lola got together in our last year of college.

I avert my eyes to my cream-colored ballet flats. "Oh, you know. He's been pretty busy with work and …" Ugh, you know what? I shouldn't have to keep defending him. This is his friend, and it's his choice to shut people out with no explanation. "He's been distant, to put it mildly," I admit. "I don't know what's going on with him, but it started a while ago, and it's only gotten worse over time. I'm sorry. I didn't realize he was shutting other people out as well."

His dark brows furrow. "Did something happen?"

I fidget with my car keys for a second. "Not between us, no. I've been asking myself that same question for months."

He scrubs a hand over his bearded jaw. "I'll keep trying him then, or I'll pay him a visit during my lunch break one day this week." He moves to walk back to his car. "It's been too damn long since we've caught up, and hey, maybe he'll speak to me?" He shrugs and waves.

I wave back. "Well, let's hope so." Though I very much doubt it, I guess it can't hurt to try. But Leo's never been one for sharing anything too personal with his friends.

I climb back into the car and watch as Trey drives off before turning the ignition over and making my way to the shelter. I'm a little nervous, but mostly, I just hope that Jared shows up today. It's not like him not to—not to mention, it's also likely to get him in trouble with his probation officer.

Once I find a parking spot, I tie my hair back into a ponytail, grab my purse, and jump out. And there he is, leaning up against the brick wall outside, smoking and watching me with narrowed eyes. I tug up my skinny jeans and walk over to him as a real smile takes up residence on my face. He smirks as he continues to watch me, squeezing the cherry off his cigarette and flicking the butt into the trash can next to him before falling into step beside me as we walk inside.

"Sorry," I mutter quietly and pass him the pen. "About Friday …" About hanging up on you, I don't say. He takes the pen, his warm fingers skimming over mine, and I watch him sign his name in his messy scrawl.

"Don't mention it, Blondie. I know you'll make it up to me." He winks and nudges me with his elbow.

I smirk. "Oh, do you?"

He nods. "Morning, Glenda," he calls over to Glenda who's spinning around in a circle outside the storeroom, looking for something. She reaches up to pat her head and scoffs. "Idiot, there they are." She then tugs her glasses down and beams at us.

"Morning, you two."

I put my purse away, and we move into the kitchen to set up.

"Where's the new girl?" I wonder when the tension between us, once again, becomes too hard to keep ignoring.

He shrugs. "Glenda mentioned that she'd changed days. Tuesdays would interrupt her college schedule or some crap."

Oh. I chuck the celery back in the fridge and pull out some ground beef, taking it to the counter by the stove.

"Meet me after?" he whispers, coming up behind me and sending goose bumps racing down the bare skin of my neck.

I swallow. "Where?"

"Green. Same room," he says before getting called away

by Glenda to help her lift something.

I finish prepping lunch with one of the other women, Tilly, wondering if I'll actually go through with it this time. But I think I already know the answer to that, or else I wouldn't be going.

I wash my hands and freshen up in the bathroom before grabbing my purse and saying goodbye for the day. Walking outside to gray skies, I glance up to discover fat rain clouds floating threateningly across the city skyscrapers and pedestrians below. I race to my car and make the quick journey over to The Green, opting to use the carpark this time in case it rains. Also because the likelihood of anyone recognizing my car or giving a shit is slim to none, and I'm past the point of caring. Especially since I've only got a few hours before the kids finish school anyway.

Climbing out just as it starts pouring, I squeal, locking the car as I run over to the room where we met last time. The door is wide open, so I run straight in, only to be wrapped up in a pair of strong arms instantly. Laughing, I turn in his arms to face him. "How'd you get here so quick?"

"Bike," he mumbles into my neck, pressing warm kisses over my cold skin.

"You rode a bike that quick?" I rear back.

"Motorbike."

Wow, I've never seen him on one. He wraps his arms tighter around me, and as I place my palms on his dry shoulders, I realize how wet I am.

"Holy shit, I'm soaked."

He grins down at me. "Yeah? I knew it didn't take much, but shit, Blondie." He slams the door closed and moves me back toward the bed.

I slap his shoulder. "Oh, my God, you're impossi—"

He cuts me off with his lips, and I open mine right away, needing the warmth of his mouth as I shiver in my wet clothes. He swirls his tongue over mine then sucks my bottom lip into his mouth, slowly releasing it and pulling back to grab my blouse.

"Let's get you out of these."

I don't object and let him tug it over my head then his hands are unzipping my fly. I step out of my ballet flats and watch him bend low to tug the wet denim from my legs. Once removed and in a wet heap on the floor, he grabs the side of my panties. As he's slowly pulling them down my legs, I'm reminded of the event over a week ago when I saw him with my panties in his back pocket.

"Where are my panties?" My breathing quickens as he trails his fingers over my legs, kissing my thighs until he reaches the apex and licks a line over my folds then places a soft kiss on my mound. He stands, removing his clothes while he answers me. "You saw that, did you?"

I watch his abs contract as his shirt drops to the floor. His hands move to his jeans, un-zipping and lowering them over his impressive manhood that's tenting his black briefs.

I nod. "Me and probably countless others."

He smirks, walking over to me and undoing my bra. The straps slide down my arms, but his eyes stay glued to mine as he reaches up to gently untie my damp hair from its ponytail holder.

"Did your husband see?" he asks softly.

I frown as my blond locks fall around my shoulders and chest. He steps back, raking his gaze over every part of me as his teeth sink into his bottom lip.

"Yeah, I think so."

He doesn't bother to hide the delight in his eyes, which scares me a little. "Jared …"

"Shhh." He tugs me into his bare chest and kisses me. I wrap my arms around his neck, loving the feel of his warm skin pressed against my cool body. I bite his lip then lick it, enjoying the way he groans immensely. Pulling away, I shove him toward the bed.

"Sit down," I tell him.

He tilts his head, narrowing those green eyes, but does as he's told. I lean down onto my knees, grabbing the elastic of his briefs and tugging. He leans up to help me, and I pull them down over his feet, throwing them to the floor.

His fingers grab my chin, tilting it up to meet his eyes. "You don't have to …"

"Shhh." I grin then finally get my first good look at him.

He's long, thick—probably almost as big as Leo. The thought doesn't bother me. In fact, tingles dance their way down my spine as excitement courses through my veins. I wrap my hand around him and squeeze gently, earning me a hiss. He curses softly when I lean forward and take a long lick up his length before taking as much as I can of him into my mouth. His hands slide into my hair and gently tug on the tangled strands as I keep bobbing up and down.

"Holy shit …" His rough voice only makes me take him deeper as I pick up the pace. My hand wraps around the velvety base and then moves down to gently knead his balls. He curses again and pulls my head off him.

"What?" I wipe underneath my lip.

He just shakes his head, grabbing my arm and saying, "Get on the bed. I'm not coming in your mouth when what I really want is to get inside that sweet pussy."

My nipples tighten almost painfully at his words. I climb onto the scratchy sheets of the bed, and he digs into his jeans pocket for what I'm guessing is a condom.

Can I seriously do this? Have sex with him?

It's not a matter of not wanting to. My body is singing in desperation for it. But my heart thuds painfully fast as I think about the only man who's ever had me in that way.

Jared climbs back over the top of me, already sheathed and kisses his way up my legs. My eyes close as all thoughts of guilt and uncertainty float away into the deep recesses of my mind thanks to the feel of his lips and hands as he spreads my thighs open to lick up my center. His tongue spears my entrance, dragging the evidence of my arousal up to my clit where he sucks gently then swirls his tongue around it. He repeats the action, and I suddenly can't stand feeling empty anymore.

"Jared." I grab his hair. "Please …"

He lifts his head, moving over my body and staring down at me as I feel his hard length graze through my wetness.

"You're so beautiful." His nostrils flare, his eyes darting over my face then down to my breasts.

My brows lower. "Jared …" *We can't make this anything serious*, I want to say. It has to end at some point before one of us gets hurt.

He leans down to trail kisses over my collarbone and neck, working his way up to my ear. "That selfish fucker can't keep you. Not when I want you the way I do, not when I feel myself falling faster every damn time I see those brown eyes of yours."

A knot forms in my throat. I start to panic. "We can't …

this has to stay the way it is."

He raises his head to look down at me, his thick brows tugging into a severe frown. "Why?"

The door to the room bursts open and Jared instantly grabs the sheet to cover me. Bile fills my mouth when I see who it is. When I see Leo grab Jared and shove him off the other side of the bed before leaning down to wrap the sheet around me. Then I'm in the air and over his shoulder.

"What the fuck, Leo?" I screech. He ignores me, his grip around me tightening as he grabs my purse and stalks outside into the rain. I slam my fists into his hard back, mortified, ashamed, and so damn angry. "Leo, *what the hell* do you think you're doing? Put me down!"

He yanks open the passenger side door to his car and all but throws me in while growling, "Dahlia, this is your only warning. Do not say another fucking word or I'll make you watch as I kill him with my fucking bare hands."

He slams the door closed, and I sit frozen, staring out of the side mirror into the sheets of rain as he hunches over the back of the car. His hands hold him up as his head hangs down between them, toward the ground. After a minute, he finally climbs into the driver's side and speeds out of the parking lot. I barely catch a glimpse of Jared in the mirror, but I'm certain I saw him standing in his jeans under the awning outside the room. I don't dare ask about my car or my clothes. I just put my seat belt on and adjust the sheet over me, my mouth dry and my heart pounding so fast I fear it might stop dead at any second.

This can't be happening.

It can't. But it can.

It is.

My eyes, brave with a mind of their own, look over at Leo, who's thunderous expression stays fixed on the road ahead. His jaw is clenched so hard I swear I can hear his teeth grinding together. His hands white-knuckle the steering wheel so tightly I fear it's going to crumble beneath them.

Shit. I tug my eyes away to glance back out my window, worrying my bottom lip between my teeth. I've never seen him this angry before. It's actually frightening, so much so that I don't make a sound the whole way home. We finally pull into the garage, but I don't feel any sort of relief as he orders, "Get inside."

I take a deep breath, turning to him. "How'd you find me?"

He growls. "Lia, *fuck.*" His nostrils flare as he looks at me with so much anger in his eyes that I almost miss the hurt carefully veiled behind it. "Just get out."

So I do and run upstairs to put some clothes on, but I don't hear him come in. I don't hear him leave either, so I walk back downstairs, tossing the hotel's sheet into the trash in the kitchen just as I hear him roar and something break in the garage.

Shit. I twist my hands into my hair, not knowing what to do. Then I hear thudding as if he's punching the wall.

Chapter Sixteen

IS CAR RUMBLES OUT OF THE DRIVEWAY HALF AN HOUR later to go get the kids. At least, that's what I'm hoping. But I call Lola, just to make sure.

"Hey," she answers. "Jesus, it's pouring down."

"I know." I stare out the kitchen window to the rain blanketing the backyard. "Are you on your way to the school?"

"I've just parked. What's up?"

"Can you check that Leo's there?" I bite my thumbnail.

"Hmmm, oh, he's just pulling in now actually. What's he doing home?"

"Long story," I mumble.

"Lia, what's going on?" I look at the time, wondering if I can give her a quick rundown before the kids get out in two minutes. I decide to give it my best shot.

"He found me. He …" I squeeze my eyes shut. "He found me with Jared at The Green in Rayleigh."

Silence. I hear the rain tapping on the roof of her car as I wait, opening my eyes as a tear escapes.

"You and Jared, you had sex?" she finally asks.

I shake my head, even though she can't see me. "No, but we were about to."

"Holy hell, Lia," she whispers. "*What the hell were you thinking?*"

"I don't know. I wasn't." My fingers tug at my hair as anxiety tears its way through my body.

"What happened?"

"He just came in, threw him off me, and then grabbed me and left. I was wearing a sheet, for Christ's sake. Then he put me in his car … Mine's still there."

She exhales loudly into my ear. "How did he find you?"

"He probably hired someone. I didn't think he cared …"

She laughs. "Well, apparently he does."

I hear the bell ring in the background. "I'll let you go. I just wanted to make sure he was picking them up."

"Okay, call me if you need me, but Lia"—she sighs—"this is what you wanted, you know? I think it's obvious now that he does still care."

"But why show it in this way? Why wait until I potentially fuck everything up even worse to show me?" I groan. "Ugh, he's fucked with my head too much. I have no idea where I even stand anymore."

"Just … try to talk to him. One step at a time, 'kay? Call me."

"Okay, bye." I hit end call and toss my phone onto the counter. Then stare at it for a minute before picking it back up and quickly sending a message to Jared.

Me: I'm so sorry.

He replies right away.

Jared: You okay?

Me: Fine. I'll talk to you soon.

I exit the message, take my phone upstairs to charge it, and take a quick shower before the kids get home. Once under the hot water, I finally let it out. The sorrow, the fear, and the absolute horror of having my husband, the love of my life, walk in on me with another man.

After drying off and getting dressed in some pajama pants and a t-shirt, I come downstairs to the sound of the kids arguing.

"Hey." I walk into the living room to find them playing tug-o-war with the remote. I walk over and gently remove their hands from it. "What's going on?"

"I want the TV. Charlie always gets it when we get home from school." Greta pouts.

Sighing, I take the remote with me as I leave the room. "Well, no one is watching anything until their homework is done, so come on, let's do it."

They both groan but follow me into the kitchen and get started while I unpack their bags then put their lunch boxes in the dishwasher.

"Where's your father?" I ask, trying to act indifferent when inside, I feel like all my vital organs are twisting and knotting together.

"He's gone back out," Charlie says, chewing on the end of his pencil for a second, then pokes his tongue into his top lip as his eyes narrow intently at his sheet of math homework.

"Oh? Did he say where he was going?" I grab a knife and start cutting up some apples and oranges for them at the island.

Charlie shrugs. "Can't remember." He then scribbles something down on his paper while Greta watches me.

"He said he's going to see his friend Jim."

I pause mid cut. "Jim?" I frown over at her.

She holds her hands out and shrugs. "I dunno. I'm just the messenger."

She goes back to doing her homework, and I finish chopping the fruit. Then it clicks. His favorite bourbon—Jim Beam. He's gone to get drunk? Well, he has enough reason to. But what the hell? He doesn't even want to try to talk to me? Not that we'd get much of that done with the kids awake. It's not exactly the kind of fight we can have within earshot of them. But I still thought he'd want to, I don't know, *do something*. Why go to all that effort of finding me and hauling me out of there buck ass naked only to ignore me all over again?

I chuck the fruit into a bowl and put it between them. I try to distract myself, and we discuss their day while I clean up the counter and the knife before putting it away.

An hour later, Trey is knocking on the front door with the keys to my car and an awkward smile on his face. I glance outside to see my car in the drive, and Lola waving at me from hers. She then motions with her hand for me to call her.

"Uh, thanks," I mutter, feeling my cheeks heat.

"Hey, I'm not judging. He didn't tell me what was going on. But he sounded pretty, um … upset." He scratches at the back of his neck. "I'm supposed to meet him at the bar. Don't worry. I'll get him home safe."

"Thank you, Trey. I'm sorry you two got dragged into this."

He shrugs. "Don't worry about it, honestly. Shit happens."

With a wave, he runs off through the rain to climb into Lola's blue Mazda.

I close the door and stare down at my keys.

Shit happens indeed.

My life has officially become one big clusterfuck.

And I'm one of the main reasons why.

I wake to the sound of the sink running in the bathroom. It keeps going, and I start to get worried that maybe I accidentally left it on when the en suite door flies open, and Leo stumbles over to the bed. Ripping his white dress shirt over his head, he tosses it to the hamper then discards his pants before sitting down on his side. His head falls into his hands, his palms rubbing over his face and through his hair.

I turn over, staring at the smooth ridges of his back as the moon shines in on the shadows of our bedroom through the cracks in the curtains.

"Where've you been?" I ask quietly.

I don't think he's going to answer, but then he laughs darkly. "You have the audacity to ask *me where I've been?*"

The venom in his voice stings and causes my eyes to glaze over with tears, but I keep trying. "We need to talk … I just want—"

"How many times?" He cuts me off.

"What?" I whisper, but I think I know what he's talking about.

"I said how many times. How many times did you ..." He blows out a loud breath. "Did you *fuck* him?"

I sit up. "I didn't ... we didn't."

He spins around, his blue eyes shooting more venom at me. "Don't lie to me, Lia. *I fucking saw you.*"

"I didn't." I shake my head frantically. "That was the first time we were going to. We hadn't before then, but we've done ..." Like a coward, I can't even bring myself to say it. To own up to what I have done.

He laughs, the sound breaking off abruptly into a drawn-out groan as he curses and stands. "You know ... I thought you were joking when you said you were having an affair. I never thought you'd actually go and do it," he says roughly.

I stare up at him, pleading with my eyes for a little understanding even if I don't deserve it. "You shut me out. I felt like—"

"Like what?" He snarls at me. "You felt like you needed to get fucked, and I wasn't giving it to you, is that it?"

"No, well, kind of, but it wasn't just that ... not at first," I admit with a whisper. "When I said that to you, I never thought I'd actually do it either."

He shoves his hands into his hair, and even with the lack of light, I see his features contort with pain. Pain that I put there.

"Leo, please." Tears start to run down my cheeks. "I didn't know what was happening. You wouldn't talk to me, touch me ... It's been months since we felt like us. I didn't know what else to do."

"So you do *this?*" His voice cracks with emotion.

"I've needed you—for so long—and you just …" I sniff and swipe at my nose with my hand, "you just left me."

He stares at me for a heartbeat, and I see the way his eyes flash with something. "But I've still been here. I haven't fucking left you. I'd never leave you." He growls the words at me, and my heart crumples in my chest.

"You were here, but you haven't truly been here at all." Why can't he see that? Or is he buried too far beneath whatever has changed him that he just can't?

He pinches the bridge of his nose. "I can't … I can barely stomach being near you right now."

"No." I scramble across the bed. "I still love you, Leo. But you've been breaking my heart for too damn long."

He sniffs. "Yeah?" He rounds the bed to grab his pillow before walking toward the bedroom door. "Well, now you've gone and broken mine, too. Fuck you, Lia."

I flinch. He opens the door then closes it behind him with a quietness that would only have been for the sake of keeping the kids asleep.

But he may as well have slammed it.

I fall back onto my pillow, silent tears still streaming down my face. My hand reaches over to touch the cold, empty space where he was sitting just a minute ago.

What have I done?

Chapter Seventeen

THE NEXT MORNING, I GO THROUGH THE MOTIONS AS IF I've just woken from a bad nightmare that I can't shake yet. My vision is clouded with everything that I can't bear to admit. That my marriage is in an even worse place than before. That it might be truly over. Some dark voice is whispering that stupid saying on repeat in my head, be careful what you wish for.

But I don't have the luxury of falling apart. Not when two little souls are relying on me to keep my shit together. And none of this should burden them; none of this should trouble their fragile hearts any more than it might have already.

"Let's go, guys!" I call out as I grab my keys and purse off the counter and walk into the garage.

Their shoes slap against the tiles of the kitchen behind me then come to a skidding halt, Greta's face colliding with my ass when I stop dead inside the garage.

"Ooof." She grunts. "Mommy, you're lucky your butt's soft

or I might have broken my face." She giggles.

Charlie stops beside me and stares at the opposite wall where my eyes are fixed. "Mom … why are there holes in the wall?" he asks quietly, a hint of fear in his voice that puts yet another crack in my already broken heart.

"Hey, wow. Did Daddy do some painting?" Greta asks. No fear at all as she rounds my car to the wall on the other side.

I walk over to find paint cans on the ground. The noise I heard Leo making in here yesterday. There are obvious holes from his fist, but it also looks like he's launched the paint cans at the wall. Gray paint runs down the bottom half of it onto the cement floor below, forming a gray puddle that's probably still wet.

I close my eyes and force myself to breathe.

Just breathe.

In and out. In and out.

I count to ten then open my eyes.

"I'm not sure what he was doing, poppet, but we've gotta go." I move to the trunk and open it for them to toss their bags in. "Come on," I encourage when I see Charlie still frowning at the mess.

Greta opens the passenger door, climbing inside. "Maybe he got mad when it fell and spilled everywhere." She shrugs and closes the door.

"Maybe," I mutter as Charlie finally puts his bag in and gets in the car.

Greta talks my ear off about both of their grandmas coming home from their holiday tomorrow, and the big sleepover they're all going to have this weekend. I'm grateful for her chatter, not only because it seems like I've forgotten—yet again—about something else, but I also need to keep busy. I need to try to think of anything other than this debilitating fear and heartache that's vying for my attention every second of every minute.

Charlie's noticeably quieter than usual when we pull into the school. I get out and pass Greta her bag, kissing her head then watch her walk off.

"Hold up, Charlie," I say when he grabs his bag and is about to walk away, too.

He halts, chewing on his bottom lip and looking so much like a little Leo that my heart hurts even more.

I bend down in front of him. "You okay?"

He shrugs, averting his gaze to the car for a few seconds before asking, "Dad wasn't mad at the paint, was he?" His eyes narrow on me.

Damn it. I shake my head. "No, he wasn't. But you know it has nothing to do with you guys, right? He loves you both."

He stares at me for a minute, his blue eyes studying and searching my face. Aware.

He finally nods. "When will things go back to the way they were?"

Tears blur my vision, and I roll my lips between my teeth, trying to keep them at bay. "I'm not really sure, buddy. But just know that we're working on it, okay?"

He nods again and I stand, wrapping my arms around him and whispering into his hair, "If you need to talk, to me, Daddy, your grandmas … anyone, make sure you do. Okay?" I kiss his hair and step back. "Love you." I smile softly at him.

He gives me a small one in return. "Love you, too." He runs off to join Sophie who's waiting for him at the gates.

My eyes stay glued to him until he disappears inside the

school doors then I move back to the car to grab my sunglasses. I slip them on as Lola walks over and pats my back. "Hey, you okay?"

I give her a weak smile. "Not really." I exhale a shuddering breath at the remorse in her eyes. "My fault, though, right?"

She frowns. "Yes and no. Hey, you told him. You've tried. He can't keep shutting you out and expect you to just deal with it."

She's right. "What if it's really over now?"

She looks away for a moment. "Trey said he was a wreck last night. Would hardly say a word to him, just kept staring down into his drink like he was waiting for it to talk to him or something."

The sad part is that doesn't really surprise me.

Lola sighs. "Look, I can't promise you anything. But personally, I think now is the time to really try to sort through this with him while his emotions are running wild."

She has a point. "Yeah, I guess."

"What are you going to do about Jared?" she whispers.

I have no idea. I haven't thought that far ahead yet, not with my emotions so entwined around everything going on with Leo.

"I need to talk to him, but I just don't think I should yet."

She smiles, but it's full of pity. "Be careful."

I nod. "Have you seen Fiona?" She hasn't been at the school since last Friday's bake sale.

Lola shakes her head. "No, but I'm kind of worried. She seemed a little …" She scratches at her cheek. "I don't know. She doesn't seem to be taking the separation well, though."

"I might go over there today to check on her," I say.

"I'd come, but I need to get a crapload of stuff done at

home. Call me and let me know how she's doing?"

"Sure. I'll talk to you later."

We say goodbye, and I make the short drive home, deciding that I'll clean the kitchen up and put a load of laundry on before I go over to Fiona's.

When I get out of the car, I stare at the holes in the wall and the paint, not knowing what to do about it. I guess there isn't much to be done. I'll have to call someone to come repair it. Tearing my eyes away, I walk inside and load the dishwasher, starting it before cleaning the kitchen. I head upstairs, collecting the dirty clothes from the hamper in the bathroom then walk down the hall to our room to check ours.

Putting the basket down, I walk over to our hamper and grab the few items in there then make my way back downstairs. I shove them all in the machine, but then I find Leo's dress shirt he was wearing yesterday. It needs to be washed separately, so I put it on the ground. After I've put the liquid in and turned the machine on, I pick it up, laying it over the top of it so that I remember to wash it. I go to leave when I finally see it. Brown smudges on the cuff of his shirt. Frowning, I pick it up and rub my finger over it. It looks like blood. Like dried blood.

The tap running for ages in the bathroom last night.

My face drains of color as I realize what he might've done and race to my phone.

Dialing his number, I pace the kitchen, listening to it ring out before hitting redial and trying again. On my sixth walk through the kitchen, he finally answers, "Blondie."

He sounds like he's half asleep.

"Jared, shit. Are you okay?"

He laughs, the sound husky with sleep. "You mean did

your husband and his friend find me last night?"

"So they did?" My eyes widen.

"Yeah, but look, it's not a big deal. The other guy, he just watched while your husband got his hits in. Only intervened to pull him away when I'd had enough and started fighting back." He yawns. "I'm fine, had worse."

Shit. Holy shit.

I pinch the bridge of my nose, struggling with disbelief and my inability to keep up with all the dominos that keep falling.

"Dahlia?" he asks.

"I'm here. I'm so sorry. Fuck …"

"It's fine. I deserved it, I guess. That's the only reason I let him do it. Fair is fair, right?" He snickers.

"No, it's not fair. He shouldn't have touched you. How the hell did he find you anyway?"

"Probably the same way he found us. I was at the Westbrook bar, waiting for a buddy of mine when he found me, and we took it outside."

"Why the hell are you so calm over this? My husband beat you up!" I almost yell before stopping myself.

He laughs. "Nobody beats me up unless I'm severely out-numbered or I let them, Blondie. Like I said, I deserved it, so I let him."

I lean back against the counter. "How hurt did you get?" I feel like getting in the car and going to check for myself, knowing he's going to downplay it.

"Jared," I snap when he doesn't answer me.

He sighs. "Just a shiner, bruised nose and jaw."

"Just?" I laugh like a madwoman. "This is *insane.*"

"It's not. You're his wife. If you were mine, I'd have left the guy half dead."

God, this is all so crazy. "I'm sorry," I repeat.

"No need to be. Just tell me when I can see you again."

I start choking on a laugh. "Did he injure your brain? We can't …"

"No, we can. I don't give a shit about him," he says heatedly.

I can't do this right now. "I have … baggage, Jared. You can't possibly still want me."

"You have kids, Blondie, and a dickhead for a husband. Nothing I can't handle." His tone lightens. "Besides, I love kids."

I burst out laughing, wiping a few tears from underneath my eyes. "You're a good man, trouble."

"I'm sensing a but coming, and I'm gonna ignore it. Take a chance on me, Dahlia. You won't regret it."

I know I wouldn't. But I would because that dickhead I have for a husband? I still love him with every fractured piece of my heart.

"I have to go," I finally say.

"Wait, just … promise me you'll think about it?"

The desperation in his voice is hard to ignore, and it makes me feel like the biggest bitch in the world.

So like a coward, I lie—yet again. "I'll think about it, but you know—"

"Stop," he says roughly. "I'll speak to you soon, Blondie."

He hangs up, and I scrub my palms over my face. What a mess. What a great big stinking mess. I used to listen, gasp, and watch as drama unfolded for other people and their families. Which in this town, happens a lot. And like a fool, I never thought it would happen to me. To us. But I guess that's what everyone thinks.

Never me. Thank God, it's not me.

Until the other shoe drops, and suddenly, it's your turn.

I head to the pantry and reach up to the top shelf, grabbing a block of my favorite milk chocolate. Then, tucking my phone into my dress pocket, I grab my keys and make my way over to Fiona's place. We can be miserable together.

Pulling up outside her mini-mansion by the bay, I can't help but notice how quiet it is as I step out. How the only noise to be heard comes from the shrieking of the gulls flying overhead, heading out to the ocean. The two cream-colored cement lions who sit on either side of their porch steps seem weathered and fragile now, instead of imposing. I use the knocker and wait. When I don't hear anything, I try the doorbell. Okay. Worried, I lean in to try to see through the frosted glass that sits on either side of the huge double doors. But it's too blurred to make anything out.

I turn around, thinking I'll just go home and try to call her later to let her know I stopped by.

But then I remember last Friday. Not only what she wore, but how she behaved. The attitude that screamed of imminent self-destruction.

Fuck it. I turn the handle, not surprised to find the door unlocked, and walk inside. I close it gently behind me, calling out, "Fiona?"

I hear music coming from somewhere and walk down between the sprawling black staircases, making my way to the kitchen. Which is destroyed. Dishes, pots, and pans are everywhere. Flies buzz around food-crusted utensils and plates in the sink. I have no idea how long they've been there, but the smell is pretty bad, so I leave and walk down the hallway that I remember leads to the living room.

And that's where I find her. Sprawled out in a pair of panties and a t-shirt, sound asleep. I round the corner and take a seat on the opposite couch, looking at her usually perfectly styled brown locks that now fall in a greasy heap over half of her face. I chew my lip, unsure of what I should do. Pulling the chocolate out, I put it down quietly on the coffee table then lower the volume on the TV. Deciding to let her sleep, I go back to the kitchen. May as well make myself useful.

I grab a trash bag and toss out the pots and plates that look beyond saving and fill the sink to soak the rest while I grab some old food from the refrigerator to chuck in the trash too. After I've scrubbed everything, I put it all in the dishwasher and start it before wiping down the counters and making us some coffee.

While the coffee cools on the counter, I take the trash out through the laundry door to the side of the house where the trash cans are. They're overflowing. Damn it. I don't know if I can lift it, either. I remove some bags and hold my breath from the smell as I quickly rush it out the side gate and down the driveway to the curb. Then I grab the other bags and take them down, trying to squash them in. I end up taking one that won't fit back up to the house so that the animals don't tear it apart over her front lawn.

I'm washing my hands at her kitchen sink when she finally wakes up. "Dahlia?" she asks croakily from behind me.

I turn around, grabbing a dishtowel to dry my hands, and give her a weak smile. "Hey, sorry to barge in. I was worried."

She shakes her head. "No, no." She looks down, realizes she's half naked, and cringes. "Shit, I'm sorry."

I scoff. "Don't be. If I had the house to myself, I'd prance around in my pajamas all day long. Makes sense to do what you please, I guess." I try to make light of it.

She spots the coffee. "Oh, you're a gem." She picks hers up and takes a sip while eyeing the kitchen. "Seriously, you cleaned this disaster?"

"It didn't take long," I lie.

She laughs. "Don't be stupid. It probably took you forever. I'd hug you, but I don't know when I last showered." She frowns. "God, I'm a train wreck, aren't I?"

"Kind of, but hey"—I glance at her legs—"at least you're a hot one."

She laughs, and we move into the living room to finish our coffee. She dives for the chocolate, moaning while she chews. "You know, I don't know what I'm so upset for really. I still have money, and I can do whatever I want."

But her eyes glaze over with sadness anyway. I see it and ask, "Have you seen the boys?"

She shakes her head, her brown hair falling into her face. She leans forward and snags a hair tie from the coffee table. Tossing her head forward, she throws it all up into a messy bun and sits back. "Not since last weekend." She rolls her eyes. "He's giving me supervised day visits with them. How dumb is that?"

My nose scrunches with confusion. "So, what, they're staying with him at the hotel?"

She nods. "He's waiting for me to move out." She grabs another piece of chocolate. "Good luck with that, douchebag," she mumbles around the chocolate.

"Have you talked to him about it? It doesn't make sense that he'd just make all these decisions and cut you out." I know Dylan. Not overly well, but I've known him long enough to know that this isn't him. He wouldn't treat her this way. The man I know is a workaholic, but he's also a family man who loves his wife and boys.

She sinks back into the couch. "Tell me about it. None of this makes any sense to me."

We finish our coffee, and I grab our empty mugs to take them to the kitchen.

"I need to go. I have to get the kids in a little while. Will you be okay?" I walk back into the living room to find her still sitting there, staring at the TV screen that's playing music videos. She leans forward to grab the remote and flips through the channels.

"I'll be fine. Just going to try to wake up a bit more before I take a shower. I think it's time I get in touch with my lawyer."

I nod in agreement. "Sounds like a good idea. I'll lock the door behind me."

"Thank you, Dahlia." She finally looks up at me. "You're a good friend."

As I drive home, I realize that maybe we're all a little broken.

Some of us are just better at hiding the missing pieces.

Chapter Eighteen

"**O**KAY, I'LL SEE YOU GUYS TOMORROW," I TELL MY mom.

"Tell my son that he'd better be home!" Taylor orders in the background.

"Yell in my freaking ear next time, why don't you?" my mom grumbles at Taylor.

"Well, you never share. Serves you right," Taylor remarks.

"Okay. Bye, ladies." I laugh and hang up.

God, tomorrow should be interesting. They've only seen us a few times since our marriage took a long nosedive into failure. And despite knowing that something isn't quite right, they haven't meddled. Yet.

Leo got home late again last night, took a shower in the main bathroom, and went to bed in the spare room—again. Which hurts so damn much. We've never slept apart unless he's been away for work. Not since we first moved in together in my second year of college.

I head to the living room, intent on working on the blanket I'd started making a few weeks ago before Lola comes over. I spoke to her briefly at school pick-up and told her about my visit to Fiona's, but thanks to another bout of rain, she said she'd come over today so I can fill her in.

Pulling my basket out, I sit down and get comfortable on the couch just as my phone starts ringing again. Damn it. I get up and make my way back to the kitchen, missing the call by a second. I see Jared's name come through on my missed call notification and chew my lip. I can't bring myself to call him back. I don't know what to do about him, really. I care about him, probably a lot more than I should, and yes, obviously, I'm attracted to him. But I can't make any more waves for fear of the aftermath that's still to come. I know I'll have to break it off with him regardless, though. Not only was it not right to begin with, but my heart just isn't in it. Not when it's always belonged to Leo.

If there's anyone who could make me forget that, though, even for a little while, it's Jared.

But even after everything that's happened, I don't want to forget. I still don't want to let go. Not just because we have a life together, but because he's the only man I've ever wanted. It's a shame it's taken all this to realize that will never change. I'll take the torment and the heartbreak in hopes that we can find our way back to who we used to be. Whether that makes me weak or not, I don't care; love doesn't just remove its hold on you because you want it to.

A knock sounds on the door, and I lift my head from staring at my phone, shaking it before walking out of the kitchen and down the hall to let Lola in.

"Hey." She shuts the door behind her and passes me a

takeout coffee cup.

"Oh, you're amazing." I take a sip. "Thank you."

We move into the living room, and I put my basket away then take a seat. She removes her purse from her shoulder, placing it on the ground and sitting on the opposite couch.

"So …" She takes a sip from her coffee. "How was she?"

I roll my lips together as I think about how to answer that. She winces. "That bad?"

Giving her a nod, I sink back into the couch and tell her everything.

"Wow. Really?" Her eyes widen when I finish.

"Yeah. What do we do?" I ask. "I'm actually pretty worried."

Lola looks down at the dark wood of our coffee table, seeming lost in thought. "I don't know. You're right, though. It doesn't sound like something Dylan would do. She mentioned a lawyer?"

"Yeah." I wrap my hands around my cup to warm them.

"Well, it's bad that she has to resort to that, but good if it means she's starting to do something."

"Maybe we should take shifts? We can both go over there once a week to check in on her. She seems a bit … lost."

Lola sighs. "Not a bad idea. But …" She crosses her legs, turning to face me fully. "I know what you're doing."

My brows furrow. "What?"

"Leo. You're trying to distract yourself." She holds up a hand when I go to interrupt her. "Now, I know this is something you'd do anyway, but it still makes me worry—for you."

I wait, kind of stumped by where she's taking this.

"You need to allow yourself to feel, Lia. You're a wreck inside. Quit trying to suffocate those emotions. Have you spoken to Leo again?"

My face scrunches because I didn't think I was doing that. I shift, tucking my legs underneath me. "No, but not for lack of trying. He came home late and went to bed in the spare room. He was gone when I woke up this morning."

She scowls. "Asshole. Maybe he just needs a few days."

"Well, our moms are coming tomorrow to take the kids for the weekend."

Her blond brows rise. "They're back?"

I nod.

"Hey, this could be a good thing. You two could use the time together to fix this mess once and for all."

I try not to roll my eyes. "There's just one problem with that," I say. "You can't fix a damn thing when the other person doesn't want to."

"I think you've shaken him awake with what happened with Jared. So don't go assuming things just yet." She arches a brow while taking a sip from her coffee.

I'm not convinced that's true, though. If he's stopped arguing and smashing things, and if he's not home, then I'm afraid that once he is, he'll just go back to how he was before. And the only thing worse than his anger is his indifference.

"I know he said he wouldn't let you guys divorce. But after everything, do you think that if things don't get any better, you might separate?" Lola asks hesitantly.

I pick at a thread on my red sweater. "I don't want to. You know that. I never really did. I'm in this, whether he's an asshole or not. And I'm going to make sure Jared knows that whatever we had, it's over now."

She smiles. "Oh wow, getting a little fight back aren't you, honey?"

"One of us has to. And I'm sick of trying to make him see me. It just backfired and got way out of control, anyway. So hopefully when he realizes that I'm here, and that I'm not going anywhere, he'll finally start to see me again."

"Mommy, can I take my makeover set to Grandma's place?" Greta asks while lying in bed. I tuck her in and kiss her cheek.

"Of course. You'll save Grandma Taylor loads of time by doing her makeup for her." I wink, laughing softly to myself as I stand. Taylor is liable to have a conniption, but she'll put up with it. She adores Greta, and she'll suffer through anything just to show my mother that she can. They're both so damn stubborn.

"Love you, Mommy." Greta yawns and rolls over.

I switch off her light. "Love you more."

I walk into Charlie's room only to find Leo's already there, lying down next to him with Charlie's head resting on his chest. He's still in his work clothes, which reminds me of the blood stain I found yesterday from when he punched Jared. My stomach turns, but I tell Charlie good night and walk down the hall to take a shower.

When I get out, I find Leo rummaging in his drawers until he digs out a pair of red and black checkered pajama pants and a gray t-shirt. He walks past me into the en suite without even looking at me and closes the door. I close our bedroom door then get dressed in my yellow flannel pajama pants and a tank top. Taking a seat on the bed, I flick through my phone and wait until he's done in the shower. My phone rings just as the door opens, and he walks out shirtless in a cloud of steam. I look up from Jared's name flashing on the screen and rake my eyes over Leo's broad chest that tapers into slim, defined hips. His abs and muscles bunch tauntingly as he pulls his shirt over his head, evidence of how hard he works to keep himself in top physical condition. Ever the athlete.

"Is that your boyfriend?" he sneers, causing my eyes to snap from his chest to his face.

"What?" I gape.

"You heard me." He goes to walk out the door, and I run for it, slamming it closed and standing in front of it.

"Talk to me," I pant, raising my eyes to study the light brown stubble, the slight dip in his straight nose, and the tiny, faint freckles that you can't see unless you're this close to him. It's been so long since our faces have been this close together that I take in every detail I never knew I'd miss so painfully. Like the perfect symmetry of his sculpted cheekbones and the long dark brown lashes that fan over his ice blue eyes. Eyes that flare wide at our proximity. He takes a step back.

"Move," he rasps.

I shake my head. "I saw the blood, Leo. I know you went to the Westbrook and found Jared."

His top lip curls. "You would know, playing phone tag with each other like you have been."

Glaring at him, I say, "No, I know because I found the blood on your shirt, you asshole. And yes, I called him to make sure he was okay. I won't lie to you."

He throws his head back with a humorless laugh, his biceps expanding as he lifts his arms to scrub his hands roughly over his face. "Shit," he breathes. "My fucking wife had to call her boyfriend and make sure he was okay," he says to his hands.

A growl rips from my throat. "He's not my boyfriend."

"Oh, yeah?" He drops his hands, taking a step closer to me.

I hold his gaze, not backing down from the anger and disbelief clouding over his eyes.

"A fuck buddy? Lover? What the fuck do you call what you've been doing with him then, *wife*?"

"Trying to feel like me again!" I yell and watch as all expression falls from his face. "Yeah, I've fucked up. But …" I point a finger at him. "I never lied to you. I fucking told you I wanted a divorce, and then I told you that I was having an affair."

"I thought you were taunting me!" he yells.

"I was!" I yell back, my voice breaking. "I was," I finish quietly.

He averts his gaze, rubbing at the stubble on his chin. "Please, just move."

My chest heaves up and down at the same alarming rate as my heartbeat. And despite wanting to have this out, I know taking it any further tonight might just make things worse. So I reluctantly step aside.

"Don't forget, our mothers are arriving tomorrow to take the kids," I tell him before he shuts the door without saying another word.

Chapter Nineteen

AFTER DROPPING THE KIDS OFF AT SCHOOL THE NEXT morning, I make my way to the local shopping plaza to grab some groceries for tonight. Nerves set my emotions running in all different directions when I think about having to play happy family with my mom and Taylor. Especially with how Leo and I left things last night.

I woke up this morning and heard the shower running, so I assumed he'd stay for breakfast with the kids as he normally tries to make time to do. But he didn't. By the time he was dressed and I was making breakfast, he was kissing the kids goodbye and walking out the door. Greta even asked me why Leo didn't say goodbye to me. I didn't know what to say, so I simply told her that he must've forgotten about me. Then tried not to laugh at how ridiculous that must have sounded even to a seven-year-old's ears. Charlie was quiet; he's getting too quiet. I think when they get home on Sunday, it's time Leo and I sat down to have a talk with him and see how he's doing.

I flick my turn signal on and pull into the parking lot, waiting for a car to back out before I drive into the now vacated spot. I jump out, reaching over the console to grab my purse then shut the door and adjust my baby pink lace sundress and cream cardigan. Walking through the automatic doors, I stop quickly at the butcher before making my way into the supermarket to grab the rest of the ingredients for tonight's dinner, as well as some other things we need.

I get a cart and make my way through the aisles, grabbing milk, butter, vegetables, and some fruit before my phone rings in my purse. Stopping at the end of an aisle, I tilt my bag off my shoulder, digging through it and pulling my phone out.

Jared.

Christ, I can't do this now. Not here. Can I? I'd planned on talking to him on Tuesday. But I guess I can't keep ignoring his calls until then, especially with the way Leo reacted last night. Mind made up, I hit answer just before it goes to voicemail.

"Hey," I say, moving into the next aisle and grabbing some cereal.

"Blondie," he breathes. I hear a horn and the noise of the city from his end of the line. It sounds like he's walking somewhere.

"I'm sorry. I couldn't talk. Things haven't been great at home," I admit quietly.

"What's he done? Are you okay?" The worry is evident in his tone, despite the noise surrounding him.

I tuck some hair behind my other ear, eyeing the contents of my cart. "Yeah, I'm okay. I was hoping to talk to you on Tuesday."

He's quiet for a moment. "Have you thought about it? About us?"

"I have." Because I kind of have, but I've always known, and I've always told him this could go nowhere. "You know my answer, trouble."

He sighs. "Shit. Don't break my heart, babe." He laughs, but there's no humor in it.

"I never wanted to." My eyes widen because he can't mean that. "You don't. You're not …" I can't even bring myself to say it.

"In love with you? And why can't I be?" His tone turns colder.

I glance around nervously. "Because it was only a few weeks, Jared, and you know why," I whisper-hiss. "I told you from the start that it couldn't go anywhere."

He chuckles. "Relax, Blondie. I'm not that far gone."

I swallow. "Okay," I breathe. "Okay then."

And I don't feel stung by his admission at all, only relieved.

"Um, can we talk on Tuesday?" I ask hesitantly when he stays quiet.

I hear him exhale as if he's smoking. "Sure, Blondie. We can talk on Tuesday." He hangs up as soon as the words leave his mouth.

I pull the phone away from my ear and stare at it. Okay, so that went well. I snort to myself. I'm a thirty-two-year-old woman. A wife with two kids. And I think I just had to dump my fling—or whatever he was—over the phone. If someone had told me a year ago that I'd be here, that this would be what became of my life, I'd think they were fucking nuts. I put my phone away and make my way through the rest of the aisles, grabbing what I need. Stopping just before the last aisle to grab some chips from the end display, I hear a familiar voice.

"I don't care what she says. This is fucked. I just went

around there with the appraiser, and she wouldn't even let them in the door." I move forward, peeking into the last aisle and finding Dylan Fitzgerald—Fiona's husband. Or soon-to-be ex.

He grabs something off the shelf and tosses it into the basket hanging over his suited arm. "I don't care. I want the house on the market. It's fucking tainted," he snaps into the phone held to his ear. My brows furrow at his words, and I start to back away. Now probably isn't the best time to talk to him. But then he turns, his brown eyes falling on me as he looks over his shoulder and says, "Gotta go. Just send the paperwork through to my office asap." He hangs up, turning on his heel and approaching me.

"Dahlia, hi." He stops in front of me.

"Hey." I wave awkwardly.

"How've you been?" He drags a hand through his blond hair.

"Um, good. How about you? I saw Fiona the other day …" I trail off.

He nods, averting his gaze for a moment. "Yeah, it's been difficult, to say the least."

"How are the boys handling it?" It's hard to judge with the few times I've seen them at school.

"All right, actually. They think staying at a hotel is awesome." He chuckles.

I force a smile, feeling a little uncomfortable, what with the state I last saw his wife in and all. "I went to the house on Wednesday, actually. Fiona doesn't seem to be taking it too well," I admit, for all the good it might do. Which probably isn't much and he likely already knows exactly how she's handling it.

His eyes widen. "What? You've been …" He blows out a heavy breath. I frown and something stirs in my gut at his baffled expression. "Look, for what it's worth, tell Leo I'm sorry. That I had no idea, I never would've. Christ, you're still friends with her? I'm sorry, but shit, it just doesn't make sense."

I'm so confused, and it must show because realization dawns on his handsome, clean-shaven face. "Holy shit, you don't even know, do you?"

"Know what?" I shake my head.

His throat bobs as he swallows, running a hand through his hair again and leaving the short strands standing in a neat disarray.

"The reason I left her. I found the tapes."

My grip tightens on my shopping cart. "Tapes?"

"Fiona and Leo …"

No. No, no, no. I start backing up, needing to get out of here. I don't want to hear it; I don't need to. It's written all over his face.

"Stop, please. I have no idea why you don't already know, but you deserve to."

I close my eyes as he says the words. The words that I know are going to destroy me. But what he says, what actually comes out of his mouth, destroys me in a completely different way than I could have ever expected, "The night of our anniversary party after you'd left and we'd passed out … She raped your husband."

My eyes fly open. Raped my … *"What?"* I gasp when I finally find my voice.

He nods. "I couldn't believe what I saw myself, but she's done it before, to others, by the looks of it. I found five tapes, and one of them was of her and Leo." He scrubs a palm down his face. "She drugged him. I don't know, but he was practically passed out the whole time. And the stuff she did ..." He stops when he sees my face paling.

I feel bile rise up my throat. He curses, grabs my cart, and directs me to the checkout line. I don't say a word as he puts my groceries through, pays for them, and helps me get them to my car.

"Shit. I'm sorry. Are you okay to drive home? I can call the office, maybe sit with you for a while until someone comes?"

Coming out of my daze, I finally focus my eyes on his worried face. "Uh, it's okay," I mumble and quickly grab a hundred-dollar bill from my purse. "Here, for the groceries."

He waves me off. "It's fine. The least I could do, really. But are you sure you're okay?" He frowns.

I have no idea what I am, but I manage to say, "I'll be all right."

"Okay, tell Leo to call me, anytime. If he still even wants anything to do with me."

After saying some kind of goodbye, I hop into my car. And sitting here with the door closed in the silence, everything finally starts to click into place.

All the changes in Leo these past months.

Since that party.

The change in his personality.

The distance.

The way he'd flinch or reject my advances, hell, even my touch.

The silence.

I bury my head in hands and let the tears fall.

Chapter Twenty

"LEO, STOP." I GIGGLE INTO HIS NECK AS HE PALMS MY ass underneath my yellow cocktail dress.

"No, let's just go to a hotel and pretend we're in college again while Clare has the kids."

I kiss his throat, inhaling his scent and feeling my legs grow weak. "So we can lay in bed and fuck all night?" I whisper.

He groans. "God, I love hearing that word from your mouth, and yes. All night." He kisses my neck, nipping my chin and finding my lips. "And morning," he says into my mouth before dragging my bottom lip into his and sucking.

"What are you doing?" Our lips break apart at the sound of Greta's voice from the doorway, but he doesn't release me. She stands there, hands on her hips in a Disney Frozen costume and Santa hat, a curious smile on her face.

"Just showing Mommy some love. What are you doing?" Leo eyes her ensemble with a grin, releasing my ass and moving his hands up to my waist.

"Just getting ready for dinner. Can I borrow your red lip gloss, Mommy?"

"Sure." I smile at her and give Leo a gentle push so he'll release me. He grumbles low in his throat but lets me go.

I head into our en suite, grabbing it and bending down low in front of her to apply a little bit to her lips. At least if I do it, I know she's not going to get it everywhere. Leo adjusts his black dress shirt while watching us through the mirror at my dressing table.

I rub and smack my lips together, making a kissy face. She copies, making me grin. "Perfect. Now, go start on your dinner, and we'll be down in a minute to say good night before we have to leave."

She gives me a huge smile, displaying the gap from her latest missing top tooth and hikes up her dress to skip out of the room.

I cap the gloss and return it to the bathroom. Leo walks in behind me, kissing up and down my exposed neck, thanks to doing my hair in a tight bun on top of my head earlier.

"We need to go." I laugh and fix my mascara quickly before turning around in his arms.

He sighs dramatically. "All right."

Placing a kiss on my forehead, he grabs my hand and tugs me back into our room.

"Hold up. I need my purse." I run back to grab it. "Oh, and the present …"

"It's already in the car," he says, standing by the door.

I slip my feet into my nude pumps. We walk downstairs to say goodbye to the kids and Clare before making our way out to his car in the garage.

He opens the door for me, and I climb in, carefully gathering the puffy skirt of my dress into my lap. Leo gets in, and we back out onto the street before making the short drive over to the Fitzgerald's home for their ninth wedding anniversary party. His warm hand finds mine between gear changes as I look out the window at the beautiful blur of homes.

Once there, I stare up at their huge house from the street as Leo helps me out of the car. The lion statues that sit either side of their porch are giant and look as though they've recently been cleaned because you can see every last detail.

"Don't look too closely, Trey thinks one of them has a camera in its eye," Leo whispers, linking my arm through his as we walk up to the looming double doors.

I draw in a breath. "Don't be ridiculous. They wouldn't." I think about it for a second. "No, maybe they would."

Leo chuckles, kissing my cheek and ringing the doorbell.

"Hello!" Fiona beams, opening the door wide and waving an arm to welcome us in. "You two look amazing."

"It's all her, I'm afraid," Leo says, letting go of me and air kissing Fiona's cheeks. I blush as Fiona winks at me and mouths, "Swoon."

Leo and Dylan pat each other's backs when he comes into the entryway. I give them their gift, and we exchange hugs and congratulations before the men walk off into the house, laughing loudly at something as they go.

Fiona closes the door, linking her arm through mine. My eyes roam over her tight black floor-length gown that shimmers under the light of the overhead chandelier. "You're the one who looks amazing." I pat her arm and glance down at her dress. "That has got to be the prettiest black dress that I ever did see."

She laughs, the sound a tinkling echo in the large space as we walk between her spiraling staircases to the hallway behind. "Isn't it? I almost died when I saw how much it cost, but I just had to have it and that was that."

"Hey!" Lola grins when we walk into the kitchen, a champagne flute already in her hand. "You look hot!" She winks at me.

Laughing, I tell her the same. And she does, wearing a peach-colored sleeveless cocktail dress, the skirt swinging with every move she makes in her white heels.

"Where are the men?" I ask, thanking Fiona when she passes me a flute of champagne.

She waves her hand around, taking a sip from her own. "Entertaining as men do. I forgot the game was on tonight."

"Not for a few hours yet, so don't stress. We'll get bored of them by then anyway," Lola teases.

"You're so right." Fiona raises her glass, and we all clink in solidarity.

Fiona leaves to talk with a few more guests while Lola and I hang out in the kitchen. Where the chocolate-covered strawberries and champagne are, of course.

"Do you think we should go be social?" I ask, grabbing another strawberry from the tray.

Lola pretends to think about it. "Nah."

We both laugh when Leo and Trey walk into the kitchen.

"There you are," Leo says, wrapping an arm around my waist.

Lola holds a strawberry up to Trey's open mouth, giggling as she tries to stop the juice that's escaped his lips with her thumb from running down into his beard.

Leo turns me into his chest. "Ready to go yet?" His blue eyes heat, and I start to feel a bit lightheaded. Maybe it's the second glass of champagne that he removes from my fingers and places on the counter behind me. But I know better. He's had the same effect on me since I first laid eyes on him in my freshman year of college.

"More than ready. We can't, though." I kiss his shadowed jaw and go to move away. His hold tightens, and he leans in to place a soft kiss on my lips.

"Delicious," he whispers to me.

"It's the strawberries, or the champagne."

He nudges his nose against mine, shaking his head from side to side. "It's you. Always you." He kisses my nose and pulls away.

"And people say we're bad with the PDA." Lola smirks over at us.

Trey chuckles. "Yeah, they're so much worse. Let's go see where the food's at and if we can convince Dylan to put the game on after." He slaps Leo on the back, leaving the room.

Leo's lips curve into a soft smile as he stares down at me. "Later, beautiful."

I melt into the counter behind me, wishing I'd taken him up on his offer to go to a hotel instead.

"Ugh," Fiona grumbles, coming back into the kitchen and grabbing another glass of champagne. "You'd think hosting parties would be fun by now, but it's a total drag having to make sure you don't get too sloshed in your own home."

Lola quirks a brow at her. "Poor baby."

Fiona slaps her arm playfully. "Shush, give me a strawberry."

"Yes, ma'am." Lola passes her the tray, and Fiona grabs the smallest one on there.

"Did you see what Dylan's cousin is wearing?" she whispers

conspiratorially to us, eyeing the doorways to the kitchen.

Lola and I glance at each other. "Uh, we kind of haven't left the kitchen yet," I admit.

Fiona laughs. "Oh, my God, come on, you've got to see this …" She walks back out of the kitchen, and we both shrug before following.

We spend the next half an hour chatting with some of their family before we all sit down on their huge porch outside to have dinner. But the food is so fancy that I barely even pick at it.

Leo chuckles into my ear. "It won't bite you, Lia."

I scowl at him. "I'll bite you in a minute, Mr. I'll Eat Anything."

He wraps his hand around mine on his lap, stroking his thumb over my skin. "You know you're welcome to bite me anytime, beautiful."

My cheeks start to burn, so I stare back down at my weird looking crab dinner.

After dinner, I remain outside, chatting and drinking with the girls until I check my phone and see that it's almost eleven o'clock. The men have long since gone inside to drink and watch the game in Fiona and Dylan's theatre room. I scoot my chair back. "I'm going to grab Leo; we need to get home so our sitter can leave. She's got an exam to study for this weekend."

Fiona pouts. "No, stay."

"I can't, I'm sorry. But we should all go out for a girls' night soon," I offer instead. "Now, let's see if I can tear my husband away from the TV." I shake my head with a laugh.

"He's welcome to stay, you know we've got the room."

I bite my lip, not sure if I like the idea of that.

"Or he can get a cab later with Trey?" Lola suggests. "I'm

going to get going soon too, and already told him he could hang out a while longer."

I nod, digging my phone out to quickly call a cab. "Okay, I'll go talk to him."

Lola walks me inside after I say goodbye to everyone. I finish calling the cab company and find Leo in the theatre room, sprawled out on the couch with his eyes glued to the game on the TV. They all shout and cheer when their team scores, startling us. We laugh and move into the room, getting annoyed glances as they try to see the TV around us.

"I'm going to go. Clare needs to get home soon," I say, leaning over him. He grabs my hips and tugs me onto his lap. I feel him grow hard beneath me, and I giggle, a little embarrassed. "Leo," I hiss quietly.

His hooded eyes glaze over from alcohol and lust. He bites his lip, staring up at me. "Can you wait a little while? I wanna finish watching this." He tugs my head down, whispering, "But I don't want you to leave."

I place my palms on his chest and push myself back up. "I can't. We told Clare we wouldn't be too late. You'll come home straight after?" I lower my lashes. "Because ... I'll be waiting."

He growls quietly, bringing my lips to his. I taste bourbon, but I also taste him, and it's enough for me to forget all the people around us for a few heartbeats. Until he groans, his tongue entering my mouth. I pull back. "Don't be too long." I wink and climb off his lap as he reaches for me lazily with a huge grin on his perfect face.

Fiona comes over to him, passing him a drink. He thanks her and returns his eyes to the game as she walks me outside. I climb into the cab that's thankfully already there and wave goodbye to her and Lola through the window. Once at home, I thank Clare, give her some money, and watch as she drives off in her beat-up Toyota before I close the front door.

Climbing upstairs, I check on the kids quickly then kick my heels off as soon as I walk into our room. My dress goes next; I lay it over the hamper and walk to the shower in my bra and panties. After I'm done, I pick out Leo's favorite, a black lace thong and plain black t-shirt. He's got a thing about seeing my c-cup breasts bounce freely behind a short-cropped tee. I don't know why, since he rips it off me in five seconds flat anyway. I brush my hair out then brush my teeth before climbing into bed and picking up my book to read while I wait.

I must have fallen asleep because a glance over at the clock says it's now after four in the morning. When I last looked, it was almost twelve. I pick my book up off my chest and sit up, placing it on the nightstand as I hear the noise again. The one that woke me up.

Thumping. Or falling. Then the bedroom door opens and Leo flinches from the dim light of the lamp that's still on. "Ugh …" He moans, his shirt is in his hand, and he chucks it to the floor by the hamper. Then he falls over trying to tug his already unzipped pants down his legs. I bite my lip, not wanting to laugh at how wasted he is. I don't think I've ever seen him this drunk, not even in college. But I'm also annoyed. He promised he'd be home hours ago and didn't even call or text to tell me otherwise.

"Leo," I whisper-hiss when he rolls over on the floor, kicking his pants off and using the wall to help himself get up. I don't think he even heard me. Hell, I'd be surprised if he knew who I am or where he was from the way he's acting. He uses the wall to assist with his walk to the bathroom, closing the door behind him. I lay back down and roll over to face the en

suite, my eyes slowly drifting closed. Then I hear him vomiting. It doesn't stop for what feels like forever, so I move to get up and check on him but then the toilet flushes and I hear the shower turn on. Thinking that he's probably a little more sober now, I lie back down and let my eyes close once again.

Chapter Twenty-One

FLUSHING THE TOILET, I STAND ON SHAKY LEGS AND MAKE my way over to the sink to rinse my mouth out then brush my teeth. I feel like I've entered some weird twilight zone. My stomach churns again as Dylan's words play on repeat in my head.

She raped your husband …

My mind refuses to process them. Struggles to wrap itself around the fact that she'd do such a thing. I take a deep breath, rinsing my toothbrush and putting it back in the holder before walking downstairs to finish prepping tonight's dinner. I pick up the kids from school half an hour later, thankful that Lola isn't here. I'm not sure I can handle talking yet. And I need to keep this mask on my emotions until the kids leave tonight with my mom and Taylor. They come running out as soon as the bell rings, excited to see their grandmothers and climbing straight in the car while I put their bags in the back. I wave to Trey as he drives out of the parking lot with Sophie making faces out the back window.

"How was your day?" I ask when we finally escape the line of cars all trying to leave at once.

"Amazing," Greta sings. "I got a ten out of ten on my spelling test."

"Well done, poppet. That's so good."

"Rupert bought in this cool robot for show and tell. It speaks three different languages," Charlie says with clear awe.

"Oh? That sounds interesting," I mutter as I flick the turn signal on and turn onto our street.

"Yeah, can I get one?" he asks.

"Um, maybe for your birthday." Though I am glad he's interested in toys again. Even if it is a freaking robot.

"Yes! It's only one month away." He punches the air in excitement.

One month? Oh damn, it's almost October. Time sure flies when your life is in shambles.

I pull into the garage, grabbing the kids' bags as they race inside. I close the car doors and walk in behind them. "Your bags are packed, so if there's anything you want to take, make sure you grab it. Just not too many things!" I call out when I hear them race each other up the stairs. I unpack their stuff and put their schoolbags away in the laundry room. Once they're in front of the TV with afternoon snacks, I quickly run the vacuum through then head upstairs to take a shower. Just because I feel like falling apart doesn't mean I can look that way. My mom is already likely to see beneath the tower of lies we've constructed since she last saw us.

After I've dressed in one of my favorite purple maxi dresses and a lilac cardigan, I brush and straighten my hair before putting on some mascara. Swiping some nude gloss on,

I head downstairs to set the table in the dining room for to-night. We won't eat until Leo gets home, but our mothers are a whirlwind of action and distraction as soon as they enter the house, so I want to be prepared to prevent them from leaving too late with the kids.

Once I've done everything I can, I check the clock on the microwave to find that it's almost five o'clock. They knock on the door not even a second later, opening it up and letting themselves inside.

"Yoo-hoo!" my mom calls.

"Where are my grandbabies?" Taylor sings, her heels clip-ping on the floor as she trots down the hall. I exit the kitchen just in time for my mom to engulf me in a hug. She swings me side to side then pulls back, her arms gripping mine to study me. "Beautiful dress, baby girl."

I try for a soft smile, and her brows tug in a fraction. So I move my eyes to Taylor as the kids run to her, wrapping their arms around her.

"Oomph." She laughs and gets flattened to the wall.

"Quit being such a hog, and you guys, you told me I was your favorite." My mom points to her chest and forces an out-raged look onto her softly lined face. The kids giggle, coming over to give her a hug, too.

"Mommy said I can bring my makeover kit to your place," Greta informs Taylor, clapping her hands together.

My mom looks at Taylor, who's trying hard not to show her displeasure. "Oh, Grandma Tay is going to *love* that." My mom snickers.

Taylor scowls at her then catches Greta watching so she paints a big smile on her face and nods her head. Her dark blond hair swishes around her shoulders. Not a gray hair in sight. My mom, however, has embraced it. Half of her blond hair is now streaked with it. But it looks rather lovely, and I've always hoped that mine will do the same.

I make them a cup of tea and we walk into the living room, taking a seat as they tell us all about their cruise and then their stay in Europe for the past two months.

"Then she lost our luggage …" my mom says to the kids with a serious face.

"Really?" Charlie laughs, and my heart warms at the sound.

"Oh, yes." She nods. "She'd lose her head if it wasn't screwed on, but we already knew that, right?" She nudges him gently in the shoulder, causing another round of laughter.

Taylor merely rolls her eyes, sitting back with an arm around Greta and taking a sip from her tea. "You're hallucinating. You know it was your fault." She looks down at Greta. "She tried this new fruit over in France." Taylor shakes her head solemnly. "Hasn't been the same since." Her and Greta's eyes widen comically at one another, their lips pressed thinly together.

"It wasn't a new fruit. It was a tomato," my mom interjects.

Taylor points a finger at her. "And there you go, it's a damn vegetable."

My mom rolls her eyes. "It's always been a fruit."

And here we go again.

I zone out, thinking that it's probably a good thing that they live separately so they can have a break from one another. Who am I kidding, though. I know they still see each other almost every day or talk on the phone to ask each other random, silly questions. They're cute, and I'm happy that they have a real friendship, even with their teasing and brutal honesty, but Christ, when they're together, it's best to see them in small doses.

I get up to check on our dinner in the oven, pulling it out just as I hear Leo's car drive into the garage. I almost drop the tray of baked vegetables. I put them down and bend over the counter, taking a few deep breaths. There's nothing I can do. Not yet. If I'm going to tell him that I know, it's obviously going to have to wait. I turn around, grabbing some glasses and the water jug out of the fridge. Turning again, I find him leaning in the doorway, watching me. I can't even bring my-self to say hello, for fear of the wrong words spilling out of my mouth instead. So I try for a smile, hoping it doesn't look like a grimace, and get back to the task at hand.

I finish bringing the food out, hearing him say hello to the kids and our mothers in the living room while I wash my hands then dry them on a dishtowel as I walk in to get them.

"Oh, smells divine, dear," Taylor says, taking a seat.

"Yes, well, she learned everything she knows from me." My mom grins and takes a seat beside me. Greta sits on her other side, between her and Leo, who's taking off his suit jack-et and draping it over the back of the dining chair.

"Is there gravy?" Charlie asks, sitting between me and Taylor.

"Psh, is there gravy ..." my mom mutters, winking at him while nudging the little jug closer for him. Charlie grins, pick-ing it up and almost drowning his meat and vegetables with it.

"That's enough, buddy," Leo says, taking a seat and rolling up his sleeves.

Charlie huffs but puts it back on the table for my mom to pick up. She puts some on Greta's plate then her plate before passing it to me.

I look down the table at Leo, watching him take it from his mom and drizzling a little over his dinner before putting it down to grab the salt and pepper. His eyes flit over everyone at the table before he takes a bite of his food.

"You ladies glad to be home?" he asks after he chews and swallows.

"Yes," my mom says while Taylor says, "For a little while. God, you two really need to do it. Travel, it's exhilarating and so much fun."

Leo's lips curl into some semblance of a smirk as he looks at his mom. "Yeah?" he asks.

She nods eagerly, chewing some food.

"Yeah, until you lose your luggage, get third degree sunburn, swindled by a seventy-nine-year-old man in the airport, and food poisoning while you're on a cruise," my mom grumbles.

Taylor scowls at her. "Oh, don't be such a bore, Renee. You weren't even the one who got sunburned." Her eyes turn to me. "Oh, but that was terrible. My skin peeled for weeks." She mock shivers.

My mom snorts. "Yeah, but I was the one who had to slap aloe vera onto your flaking skin while you whined ungratefully at me. Every damn day. For two weeks," she deadpans.

A laugh escapes me, and I feel Leo's eyes on me as I cut into my meat and take a bite. My stomach revolts, and I quickly grab my glass of water, chugging half of it down.

"You all right, dear?" Taylor asks.

My mom reaches over, thumping me hard on the back. "Probably went down the wrong pipe." I flinch, trying to shove her hand off me.

"I'm fine," I croak.

"Really, Renee. If someone saw you doing that in this day and age, you'd be locked away for child abuse," Taylor informs her.

"For trying to save my choking daughter's life?" My mom guffaws. "I'd like to see them try."

Taylor laughs. "As would I."

They both laugh with each other, and I remove my gaze from them to find the kids still eating, their eyes darting to and fro between their grandmothers and then I finally look at Leo. He's watching me again, his brows tugging in to form a tiny crease between them. My eyes stay glued to his as I struggle to understand why. Why he wouldn't tell me, why he chose to deal with this all alone, for so damn long. He swallows, but I didn't see him chew anything, and he averts his gaze back to the conversation carrying on around us.

Clearing my throat, I excuse myself to prepare dessert. I dig out the wine from the fridge, opening it and taking a hearty swig and then another before recapping it and putting it away to bring the cheesecake out.

After dessert is done, I take the kids upstairs for a shower before they leave. We're quiet, listening to Taylor and my mom talking as they help clean up the kitchen downstairs. I don't know where Leo is when the kids are in their pajamas and we're walking back down with their bags, but he needs to come say goodbye to them.

"Ready?" my mom asks.

They nod their heads eagerly then Greta yawns.

"We'll watch a movie and get you two in bed, I think," my mom says as Taylor hangs up the dish towel behind her.

They'll stay at Taylor's place for the weekend as they usually do when they take the kids for sleepovers. I think they handle them a little better when they're together. Plus, Taylor's house is even bigger than Fiona's. Her face flashes through my mind and I cough.

Oh, my God.

"You all right?" my mom asks quietly, coming to stand beside me.

I nod. "Yeah, just not feeling too well." It's not a lie.

She frowns, rubbing my back. "Well, you put your feet up and just relax for the weekend, okay? You need to take care of yourself."

I force a smile onto my face, walking them all outside and helping them get the kids into Taylor's Mercedes.

"Be good. No fighting," I warn them as I kiss their heads.

They both nod, distracted by the iPads in the back of the headrests.

"Love you both." I blow them a kiss and step back.

"Love you, too!" they call out.

Leo finally emerges from the house, leaning inside the car to kiss them goodbye.

I thank my mom and Renee for taking them, telling them to call me if they need anything.

"We'll be fine," my mom insists. "Besides, the queen over there has a cook and a butler that we can always hand them off to if we need to sneak away for a smoke break." She laughs.

Taylor scowls. "We will do no such thing. Come on, let's go." She climbs into the car as my mom winces playfully at me. I kiss her cheek and stand back, trying not to put too much distance between Leo and I, for fear of him disappearing as soon as Taylor's car is out of sight.

Which is exactly what he tries to do, but I run after him.

"Leo," I call down the hall once we're back inside. I flip the lock on the door, slamming it closed behind me.

He doesn't answer me, but I hear his feet moving around upstairs. I walk up them and head down the hallway to find him in our room, snatching clothes out of drawers and tossing them onto the bed.

My pulse starts ringing in my ears. "What are you doing?"

"What does it look like I'm doing?" He walks into our wardrobe and reemerges with a duffle bag, stuffing the clothes inside then walking to the bathroom.

"You're leaving?" I take a seat on the bed, my hands starting to shake.

"You think I'm going to stay here with you all weekend?" He laughs, putting his body wash in the bag. "Not fucking likely."

My eyes squeeze closed at his cruel words. "Why tell me I could do something when you didn't actually want me to do it?"

He sighs, and I open my eyes. "We've been over this. I didn't actually think you'd do that to me, to us." We stare at each other for a beat, and I bite my thumbnail, not knowing how to spew the words out now that we're finally alone. But knowing I need to before he goes.

He tears his eyes away and zips the bag up, making his way to the door.

"Wait …" I say quietly.

He doesn't, just continues out into the hall.

So I inhale and let it all out with a ragged breath, "I know, Leo. I know what she did to you."

Chapter Twenty-Two

I HEAR HIS FOOTSTEPS STOP IN THE HALL.

"I saw Dylan today at the grocery store." I laugh a little, but there's no humor in it at all. "He couldn't believe that I didn't already know. That I was still friends with a woman who …" I trail off when I look up to find Leo in the doorway, his face bleached of all color.

"What?" he rasps.

"A woman who sexually assaulted you." I meet his eyes, unflinching. Daring him to try to deny it.

He inhales sharply, and I stand. "Why didn't you tell me?"

He doesn't answer me. The duffel bag slips from his fingers, but he still doesn't answer me.

"*Why?*" I scream the word at him, my chest heaving as my eyes fill with tears. "All you had to do was tell me …" I suck in a breath, my fingers finding their way into my hair and twisting, "You let me, oh God, I feel sick." I drop my arms, glaring at him. "You just let me do that to you when all you had to do was open your damn mouth and talk to me," I finish with a whisper.

He closes his eyes, leaning heavily against the doorframe. I grab a pillow off the bed and throw it at him. "Talk to me, damn it. *Tell me why!*"

His eyes flash open as the pillow collides with his chest then falls to the floor next to him. "Because I couldn't!" he roars then his voice softens. "I just … couldn't."

My brows pull into a frown as I sniff. And looking at his pained expression, I suddenly get it. I don't agree with it, but I understand a little better. He's always seemed so untouchable. A powerhouse of vitality and wealth. He embodies strength in every facet of his life. He exhibits control in everything he does.

Except for this.

Except for this inexcusable violation that's not only fucked with his head, it's also tainted everything.

"Because you're worried about what others might think of you? You're worried that I—"

He cuts me off, his top lip curling. "Would look at me the way you're looking at me now?"

My head shakes frantically, but he keeps going. "I don't want your pity, Lia. I can't fucking handle that shit. And I didn't want you to think …" He pauses, scrubbing his hands down his face.

"What?" I ask softly.

"That I betrayed you in some way." He drops his hands, staring at the carpeted floor. "I didn't want to let it become some kind of big deal. I thought I could just ignore it."

I chew on my lip. "But it wouldn't let you."

His head snaps up, and he stares at me for a moment then

shakes his head.

I walk over to him, stopping when he takes a step back.

"I'm so sorry," I whisper. "I never would have done it. I never even meant to …" His eyes darken as he keeps them on me. Hesitantly, I reach out and grab his hand. He surprises me by letting me. I stare down at our hands, turning his wedding band over and rubbing my fingers softly over every inch of skin he's allowing me to touch. "I've only ever wanted you. And when I thought you didn't want me anymore, I was desperate for you to see me again."

He lets a sigh loose. "I see you, Lia. I've always seen you." I look up at him then, my heartbeat kicking up speed in my chest. "Even in my darkest moments, you shined so fucking bright. Bright enough to keep me going." He pulls his hand away. "Until you broke me even more and left me alone in the dark." He steps back, bending to grab his bag before walking out of the room.

And all I can do is watch as he goes. Watch even after the door has slammed closed and I hear his car take off out on the street. I hear it all before being engulfed in the dead silence that now radiates through every air particle in this big house. And suddenly, I can't breathe.

I never knew silence could be so suffocating.

I refill my wine glass and head upstairs to climb into the bath I've run for myself. Stripping out of my dress and cardigan, I throw them on the floor. After sinking down into the bubbles, I take a sip from my glass and place it on the corner of the bath next to the bottle of bubble liquid.

It's funny, really. That you sometimes find yourself wishing for a moment of solitude, just a little time for yourself, only to finally get it and hate everything about it.

I sink farther down into the water and close my eyes to try to keep the tears from falling. It's not like I expected us to get anywhere tonight but to know that this chasm between us is only widening is terrifying me to the point of shaking. And what's worse is I can't tell anyone. I can't call Lola and spill all my problems to her this time. I can't betray him like that. I've already betrayed him enough.

I sniff, wiping my nose, then I pick up my glass and down the rest of its contents before throwing it at the wall and watching it shatter on the tiles in front of the shower. In a daze, I stare at the mess, wondering why, when there's so many missing pieces, so many irreparably broken fragments, you would even contemplate trying to piece it all back together. It'd be a misshapen cluster of desperation. A warped memory of what it once was, never to be the same again.

When the water cools, I decide I've had enough and climb out. I dry myself, walking back into the room and falling onto the bed on my stomach with the towel still wrapped around me. I close my eyes, wondering where he went, where he might be staying for the weekend. But even if I knew, would it do me any good?

My eyes open, landing on his nightstand where a photo sits of the four of us together. We were sitting outside the aquarium in Rayleigh. Greta was only four years old and Charlie six. They look so small, but it's not them that snags my attention. It's the way Leo and I are smiling at each other with a child sitting on each of our laps, instead of the camera.

A love like ours isn't only beautiful, it's rare. I know that. Yet I was so eager to potentially ruin it with my anguish and recklessness. So much so, that I might have actually succeeded. I lean over, grabbing the black framed photo and pulling it to me. Lying on my side, I swipe a finger over the two faces that have no idea of what's to come, of the heartache and hurdles they have yet to face.

But I know now. And I guess the only thing left to do is decide.

I need to decide if I'll give up and continue to let the pieces keep falling, or if I'll fight for what's left of my heart, for the other half of my soul, and try to knit them all back together somehow. Placing the frame down on the bed next to me, I rest my head on my arm. He needs me—has needed me all this time. He just didn't know how to ask for help.

And if he can't ask, I'll just have to try to give it to him anyway.

Chapter Twenty-Three

SUNLIGHT FILTERS INTO THE ROOM IN STREAKS OF blinding gold when my tear swollen eyes flutter open the next morning. I yawn, stretching my arms over my head when I feel it. A heavy arm draped over my waist. My stomach flips when I turn my head, finding Leo sound asleep behind me. I lie still, afraid he might disappear if I make my presence known, and just stare at him. His handsome face is rumpled from sleep, but the severity of everything he tries to hold inside is absent from his features. His lips are parted slightly. His long brown lashes rest on top of his sculpted cheeks. His sandy brown hair is in its usual disarray with a few pieces sprinkling down to rest on his forehead.

Where did he go? And when did he come back home? My eyes flit to the photo frame, which is now back on his nightstand.

The need to touch him is so strong that I bite my lip to sti-fle the urge. I slowly turn, his arm falling from my waist to the bed as I rise. Then I realize I'm naked, spying the towel I'd put on last night hanging over the side of the bed. Padding quietly across the carpet, I grab my robe from the back of the door and tie it around my midsection before going to the bathroom to do my business and brush my teeth. I pause in the doorway when I see the glass on the floor but ignore it. I'll get to it later. I gargle mouthwash after brushing my teeth then make my way downstairs to grab the broom and dustpan, flicking the coffee machine on before going back upstairs. But when I walk into the room, it's empty. I find Leo standing inside the en suite with his toothbrush in hand as he stares down at the mess on the floor. His eyes move to me.

"Hi," I say dumbly.

He stands back, allowing me entry. I hear him brushing his teeth as I bend down, sweeping up all the pieces of glass into the tray. I shake out the bathmat over the tub to check for any more, but it seems okay, so I hang it over the side after I'm done. Bending back down, I pat the ground and look closely for any more glass.

"Don't do that," Leo says, spitting and rinsing his mouth out. "You'll cut your hand if there are any small pieces."

Rising, I take the dustpan over to the little trash can by the sink and empty it in.

"What happened?" He turns around, leaning against the sink to look at me.

I shrug. "I just got a little cranky about everything, I guess."

Deciding to change the subject, I say, "Coffee? I'll make us some coffee." I go to leave, but he follows, grabbing my arm before I get through the doorway of our bedroom and spinning me around to face him.

"You and your … that guy …" His Adam's apple bobs as he swallows. "It's nothing? It's over?"

I fidget with the dustpan in my hands, nodding my head. "I promise. It wasn't like that, not for me."

His eyes squeeze closed for a second. He reopens them and nods. "Okay." He blows out a breath. "Coffee sounds good."

With my heart thudding hard enough to rattle my bones, I smile. Probably looking a little crazy with the tears that are stinging the backs of my eyes as I leave the room.

Putting the dustpan away under the sink, I busy myself with prepping our coffee, trying not to get too far ahead of myself with the feelings coursing through my bloodstream. He said he wants coffee, not a red-eye flight to Vegas to renew our wedding vows. But still, it's a start. And maybe that's all we need right now. To start somewhere.

I head back upstairs when he doesn't come down and find him sitting on his side of the bed, flicking through some emails on his phone. I put his mug down on his nightstand and move over to my side, taking a seat and a big sip of coffee. He puts his phone down, picking up his mug and leaning back against the headboard. Crossing his pajama clad ankles, he takes a sip and thanks me while staring at the wall.

"Where'd you go?" I glance down into my mug. "Last night."

I tuck my bare legs beneath me, taking another sip and waiting for his answer.

"I was going to stay at the Hedgington, but then I just sat in the car for ages before calling Trey."

My eyes widen. "He knows?"

He stares at his mug. "Yeah, as little as possible, but he knows."

"How'd it make you feel to tell him?"

Taking a sip of his coffee, he swallows before answering, "I didn't know if I could, but I did, and yeah, I guess it helped some."

Trey's not like a lot of the men in Leo's world. He's a little more down to earth and easier to talk to, not interested in appearance and power plays. "He wouldn't tell anyone."

He looks over at me then. "I know."

"I haven't …" I shake my head.

"I know you haven't."

"What time did you get home?" I ask.

His eyes drop to my chest, and I look down to find half of my breast is hanging out, thanks to the robe. I quickly adjust it.

"About one in the morning," he says quietly.

"Well, thank you … for coming home."

He nods, and we finish our coffee in silence. It's a silence that both hurts and comforts because he's here, and I think that means he's trying.

"I'll go make us some breakfast," I finally say when my stomach grumbles then get up from the bed.

He doesn't say anything, just remains sitting there while I leave the room. I quickly whip up some toast and fruit. I'm spreading some strawberry jelly on Leo's when he finally comes into the kitchen and takes a seat at the island. I put his plate in front of him and pour him a glass of orange juice before getting my own toast from the toaster and spreading some butter onto it. He taps the stool next to him when I remain standing and take a bite. Smiling, I move around and sit beside him while we eat. I laugh lightly when he finishes, brushing crumbs off his hands onto his plate.

"What?" He smirks at me.

I lean forward, noticing the way he tenses as my hand hovers over his face. He nods his head subtly, and I swipe the jam from around his top lip with my thumb. Moving my hand away, I'm shocked when he grabs it and brings my thumb to his mouth. Heat spreads throughout my body as his blue eyes hood while watching me. His hot mouth sucks the digit, swirling his tongue around it before slowly releasing it. He doesn't let go of my hand, though. Tugging on it, he pushes his plate back and grabs my waist, lifting me to sit on the island in front of him. He spreads my legs, running his hands up my thighs and evoking a full body shiver.

"I do love you, Lia. More than my own life."

My heart thrashes inside my chest at finally hearing those words. Tears gathering and spilling down my cheeks at the sincerity in his rough voice.

"What did she do to you?" I shock myself by asking.

He winces, looking away but keeps his hands on me.

I gently grab his chin, turning his face back to me. "You don't have to tell me now or ever. But it might help, and I want to help." A shaky breath leaves my mouth. "I also want to kill the bitch."

He smiles at that. "There's my inner-city girl."

I wait, and he lets go of my leg to run a hand over his mouth.

"Look, I don't remember a lot of it. Just that after you left that night, she gave me another drink. It wasn't long until I was just lying there on their couch, feeling all sorts of fucked up. I kept passing out. At one stage, I woke up to find most of the guys had gone. One or two of them passed out on the couch. Including Dylan."

He exhales heavily, his whole body shuddering with it. I grab his hand, holding it and imploring him with my eyes to continue, that I can handle it.

"She came into the room, told me to just go upstairs and sleep it off. She said she'd call you to come get me." He shakes his head, smiling sadly. "I believed her." And of course, he would because she was our friend. "So I let her help me up the stairs. I don't know where, but when I was finally able to leave, I remember seeing toys and blue painted walls. One of their boy's rooms, I assume." My stomach lurches, the toast I just ate threatening to make an ugly reappearance. "Anyway, I passed out again as soon as my head hit the pillow. I came to once or twice, but whatever she gave me … I was struggling to stay with it. She was … my pants were gone, and she was doing …" He stops, closing his eyes and taking a deep breath. "I don't remember much of that, thank fuck. But when I really started coming around, she was riding me." He swallows, meeting my gaze, as silent tears stream down my cheeks. "I kept telling her to stop, but she didn't hear me, or maybe I just wasn't making any sense. Not that I think she would've given a shit. And then she was making me …" He averts his eyes to the refrigerator. "I couldn't control it. Could barely move my hands to get her off me," he whispers croakily then his eyes close. "I'm sorry."

It's then I realize that the shame from his body's natural reaction has messed him up just as much, if not more, than the heartbreaking violation itself.

I gently grab both sides of his face. "Open your eyes."

He does, tears escaping and running freely down his

cheeks. I lean in, kissing them and licking them up one by one. "I love you," is all I say.

It's all he needs to hear. He hooks an arm around my waist, grabbing me and holding me tight to his chest. I continue kissing his face as he stands, carrying me back upstairs to our room. I wrap my legs around his waist, and he takes a seat on the bed with me in his lap. His arms constrict around me as he shoves his head into my neck and lets it all out. I wrap my arms around his back, kissing his neck and trying to stop my own tears from falling. It's no use, though, because they keep coming anyway. It's hard to stop them when my husband is holding onto me for dear life, his big body shaking with the force of his torment.

He keeps repeating the same thing. "I'm sorry. I'm so fucking sorry."

And so do I. "It's not your fault. I love you."

After a while, he finally pulls back, and I use my hands to wipe some of the wetness from his face. "Why don't you hate me?" he rasps.

Smiling sadly, I lean in to kiss his nose. "I've wanted to, believe me. But I won't hate you for this, never this."

He rests his forehead against mine. "Don't fucking break my heart again, Lia. I won't survive it."

"I'm sorry, so damn sorry. I won't. Never again." I hope he hears the truth and the conviction in my voice. "But please, don't leave me. You can't shut me out like that again."

His eyes soften, and he leans in, skimming his lips over mine. I sigh, my whole body relaxing into the familiar feel of them. It feels like coming home after being locked outside for too long. I tilt my head, tentatively opening my mouth to take the kiss deeper. He groans, opening my robe wide and causing the satin material to slide down my arms as he skims his hands up my bare back. Goose bumps rise in their wake then he squeezes my ass, licking my top lip and causing my breathing to pick up.

"I didn't think I could touch you," he says into my mouth. "Or that I could let you touch me."

My fingers pause in their exploration of his thick hair as I pull back a little. "We don't have to," I say quietly. I want this, more than I've ever wanted anything in so long, but I won't push him.

He shakes his head. "No, I want to. I *need* to," he declares.

I stare into his eyes, into the silent fear that lurks there. But behind it, I see the longing, that quiet desperation that's fighting for dominance, and I make my decision. I move my mouth back to his, gently kissing his bottom lip and letting my fingers sink into his hair.

He exhales heavily, his chest heaving up and down as his hold on my ass tightens and his tongue dives into my mouth. Our lips, teeth, and tongues dance a familiar rhythm, our hearts pounding against each other's chests. He tears his lips away, turning me until I'm on my back in the middle of the bed and then stripping out of his clothes.

I watch, hoping that he's ready for this, and that we're doing the right thing. But when his body covers mine, his arms flexing as he holds himself above me and looks down at me with love burning brightly in his blue eyes, I don't know how this could ever be wrong.

"I've missed you," he says, raking his eyes down my body. He leans on one arm and softly, hesitantly, trails his fingers over my breast. Then leans in to kiss my nipple with a gentleness that sets my emotions into orbit and ignites a burn between my thighs. I lie still, letting him look and touch, watching him kiss a path over my stomach until he reaches my mound. He spreads my legs roughly, nostrils flaring as he looks up at me from between them. And I see it, that recognition, the anger that someone else touched me there.

He covers me with his whole hand, glaring up at me while I try not to shake from the intensity of my shame, of my betrayal, and this burning need to finally have him again.

"This is mine, Lia. Don't fucking test me on that again." He nips the inside of my thigh, making me yelp and causing wetness to pool at my center. He smiles, but it's cruel. "You like that, don't you?"

He removes his hand and leans down on his elbows to spread me open with both hands. He tilts his head. "I think you do. Did he touch you here?"

"Leo." I whimper when he keeps his eyes pinned between my legs and slowly trails a finger from my clit down to my entrance, teasing it before dipping his finger into his mouth. "Fuck," he rasps then his mouth is on me, and my back is arching off the bed as his tongue laves at my entrance. Moaning loudly, I reach down to grab his hair. His tongue moves up to my clit, flicking it softly as his finger enters me, and he slowly fucks me with it.

"Leo …" I pant his name again when I feel myself creeping closer to the edge. But he doesn't stop, just flicks his tongue harder, swirling it around and hooking his finger inside me. I explode, shaking as bright lights flash across my vision. My legs wrap around his head, and I grind myself into his face.

"Mine." He tears my thighs from around his head and takes a long lick up my center, causing an aftershock that echoes throughout my entire body. Then he's climbing over me, his head going to my neck to suck and kiss a path up to my ear. "I was tested," he says before his biceps bunch next to my head, and he thrusts inside me.

"Oh, fuck," I hiss. The invasion is more than welcome, but it's been so long, I need time to adjust.

"Shit." He stops once he's seated to the hilt and lifts his head. "I'm sorry. I wasn't thinking …"

The madness in his eyes dulls some as he looks down at me. I shake my head. "No, take me." I wriggle my hips, winding my legs around his waist. "Please."

His eyes blaze again, and he growls, stealing my lips in a kiss that's every bit as savage as it is sweet while he pulls out then slams back home. He does it slowly a few times, but I can tell he can't hold back whatever is driving him right now. So I curl my arms around his neck and kiss every part of his lips and jaw I can reach until he rips his mouth away, hooks one of my legs over his shoulder and fucks me harder than he ever has before. I take it, though, knowing he needs this. And with each thrust, I feel those tiny shards, those splintered fragments of my heart start to meld back together. It might not be perfect, or the same as it once was—but it's enough. Being loved by him will always be everything.

It doesn't take long before I feel my walls start to clench tight as he keeps hitting that perfect spot deep inside me. He watches me as I start to fall apart again. "No one else will ever have this but me," he pants between thrusts. "No one, Lia."

I nod, biting my lip as the pleasure, the look in his eyes, and everything about this moment becomes too much. "No one else. I'm yours, only ever, always yours. Every part of me."

He leans down, untucking my lip from my teeth with his own and demanding, "Keep your eyes on me. I need to see you come on my cock."

And holy hell, I almost scream as my second orgasm takes me higher than the first.

"Fuck yes," Leo rumbles, stilling and grinding his pelvis into my clit as he empties himself inside me. The action has me moaning as the pleasure slowly rolls over me from head to toe, rendering me a trembling mess as I cling to him after he collapses on top of me and shoves his nose into my neck.

I don't care about his weight crushing my lungs, in fact, I never want him to get off me. He must feel the same because we continue to lie there for some minutes with only the sound of our heavy breathing filling the room while he remains buried inside me.

Until I blurt out, "Holy fucking hell, I missed you."

His body shakes with his laugh, and my heart warms. Kissing the side of my neck, he rolls onto his back, wrapping his arms tighter around me and pulling the covers over our rapidly cooling skin.

Chapter Twenty-Four

WITH MY HEAD STILL RESTING ON HIS CHEST, I ASK, "What made you decide to come back?"

His fingers that were running up and down the indents of my spine stop moving. But his warm hand remains resting on my skin. "I don't think I would've stayed away, but when I talked to Trey, he said something ..."

I hum. "Oh?"

"Yeah. He said that I can either walk away, let it be over, or I could fight and find my way back to you—back to us."

"That's all I ever wanted," I admit, "was for you to come back to me. But the way I went about it, what I did ..." With my arm draped over his chest, I squeeze him. "I never meant to take it that far."

My head rises with his chest as he sighs. "I can't say that I'll get over it quickly, but I love you too much not to forgive you. I need you too much to walk away. And I know ..." He pauses. "I know that I'm just as equally to blame in all this. It never would've happened if I had just tried to talk—"

I shift to lean over him, cutting him off with a finger against his lips. "Shhh, we'll never get anywhere with what-ifs. And I love you too … only ever, always you."

His breath leaves him in a shuddering whoosh. He pulls my mouth up to his to kiss my lips tenderly. "Did I hurt you?"

My brows furrow. He knows he's hurt me, but he's talking about the sex. I shake my head, leaning in to bite his bottom lip. "I'll take you any way you'll let me have you."

"Lia." His brows lower. "Don't. I'm here, which means I'm not going anywhere. I never was."

I swallow. "Okay."

He reaches a hand up to tuck some hair behind my ear. "Did you tell him it's over and that you won't be seeing him again?"

Oh, shit. Jared.

Not being able to talk, I settle for nodding my head. His eyes narrow on mine. "When?"

My tongue comes unglued. "Friday. He called me, and I told him. I've always told him, I just …" I blow out a breath. His hand falls from my face as I admit, "I really was lying, Leo. Though his interest in me had been clear before that, I never planned on doing a thing about it. He was just a friend, but then it turned into what I think most people have affairs for." He remains silent, waiting for me to finish even though I feel him tense beneath me. "To get that connection again, that feeling that's missing from their lives. I know this sounds horrible and I hate myself for it, but I wanted it back, so I …"

"You just gave in," he finishes coldly.

"Yeah," I say truthfully, not removing my eyes from his. He deserves my honesty. He gave me his. And if this is going to work, we need to share the hard truths. The soul crushing admissions. Then try to find a way to forgive, to work through it together.

"How'd you find me? And why didn't you say anything before then?" I think I know, but I want to hear him say it.

"A guy I know. I wasn't certain until he did some digging for me. But the hickey, the valet that night … that's when I contacted him." He averts his gaze to the window with a low growl that I feel reverberate through me.

Placing my hand on his stubbled jaw, I turn his head back to me. "I was weak. I'm still weak, but I'm determined to be stronger, to try to leave that broken part of me behind." I beg with my eyes for him to believe me.

He swallows hard. "You're not weak, Lia. You're so strong that it scares the shit out of me. I never would've thought you'd have the guts to tell me face to face that you wanted a divorce." He chuckles hoarsely. "Fuck, you stunned the shit out of me. For a split second, I almost thought to hell with it, that I needed to finally tell you. That something's gotta change before I lose you." He closes his eyes briefly. "But I didn't know how. Every time I heard you cry. Every time I thought I could tell you, my fucking throat would close up. Besides, I never thought you'd walk away from me. I thought you were just fucking with me as some desperate cry for attention."

I flinch from his words, my heart cracking a little. That he thought so little of something that took weeks for me to dredge the courage up to ask hurts. It hurts like hell.

He winces, his eyes softening as he cradles the side of my face and removes a tear that I didn't even realize had escaped. "I'm sorry." He pulls my face to his, kissing me. "So fucking sorry."

I melt into his body as his tongue slides against mine, his hands gliding up and down my back until they rest on my ass. Grabbing a cheek in each hand, he grinds me over his hard length. "Again?" I whisper with disbelief.

He reaches between us, aligning himself with my entrance. "We've got a lot of time to make up for." He bites my lip. I lift my hips and slowly sink down on him, his cum from earlier seeping out and causing us both to moan as he fills me so completely.

"You like that, don't you? My cum filling you up," he rasps into my mouth.

I nod, whimpering out a garbled, "Y-yes."

He smacks my ass, grabbing my hips and shifting me up and down while his lips stay attached to mine.

"Dirty girl." He pulls away, chuckling darkly. "Then I'll just have to keep filling you, won't I?" He nips my jaw and sits up, leaning back on an arm and using the other to maneuver me over him. His words and his actions elicit a loud moan from me.

"Answer me," he demands roughly.

And he's back. This is the Leo I've been craving. The filthy mouthed, sweet, bossy animal in the bedroom. He owns my heart every day, anywhere, anytime. But when we have sex, he owns parts of me that I never knew existed before him. I've missed it so much that I don't hesitate to bring my lips to his, staring deep into his eyes as I tell him, "Fill me and never stop."

His nostrils and eyes flare at my words, his arm leaving my waist to travel up my back and hook around my shoulder, causing my knees to ride up his sides as he seats himself so deep inside me that it almost hurts. "Fuck." He ducks his head to my shoulder, nipping and sucking my flushed skin. "I can't believe I ever thought I could do without this, without *you*."

"Never again." I grab his head, bringing my forehead to his and moving up and down in time with his controlling hand that's drifted down to my hip. "Promise me," I whisper heatedly.

"I fucking promise." His eyes flash before sealing it with his lips on mine. Then he's flipping me over, pulling me up onto all fours, and entering me from behind. He leans forward, gathering my hair into his fist and tugging, causing my back to arch as I meet his powerful thrusts. With emotions only heightening the pleasure, that familiar sensation is soon washing over my skin again.

"Leo, I'm … gonna come."

He lets go of my hair and his thrusts slow as he wraps an arm around my waist and leans back on his knees until I'm almost sitting on him from behind. His other hand squeezes my breast, teasing my nipple between his fingers as he growls into my ear, "Come, I want to feel you shake as your pussy milks my cock." He sucks my lobe, grinding and thrusting into me from below. His hand creeps down my stomach, gently rubbing my swollen clit and causing me to cry out as I shatter into a million pieces while he holds my trembling body. He kisses my neck, gently rubbing me to draw out the pleasure as his thrusts slow and he stills, emptying himself inside me once more.

"I love you." His lips graze a path from my shoulder over to my neck and back again. "So fucking much, Lia."

I swallow, trying to catch my breath as I breathe out, "I love you, Leo. Always."

He kisses my shoulder one more time before slowly

moving me off him and helping me into the shower, where he proceeds to wash every inch of my body before I take the loofah and do the same to him. I expect him to flinch, to shy away from my touch now that we're out of our bed, but he doesn't. His eyes watch my every move, but he only smiles when I meet his gaze. We dry off, Leo deciding on ordering pizza for lunch and watching a movie in bed.

I don't know if it's healthy that we're not leaving this room, but we're a thousand steps ahead of where we were last night, so I'm not going to say a word. Opting instead to just soak in the happiness of being wrapped in his strong arms as I sit between his legs and he feeds me, laughing as I dribble sauce down my chin.

That night, I'm lying on his chest again, tracing the dips and ridges of his abs with my finger when I decide to ask, "Do you think Charlie's doing okay?"

He stares off at the news playing on the TV. "I think he'll be okay, but he's like a sponge, absorbing every detail of everything going on around him." He sighs. "There's no doubt in my mind that he's not dealing with how things have been between us very well, but I'll talk to him. Hopefully, he'll see for himself over the coming weeks that things are getting better, and it'll help."

My finger trails up and around his pec. "I'm still worried. He knew it was you, the mess in the garage."

He curses. "Really?"

I roll my eyes. "He's nine, Leo. He's not going to ignore something just because we want him to. He's well aware of what's been going on even if he doesn't know the details." I look up at him. "He knows whatever it is, it's not right, and it's messing with him."

His eyes dart back and forth between mine, observing the worry in them. Brows furrowing, he says, "It'll be okay. Like I said, I'll talk to him." He moves some hair off my face. "Do you think he needs to …?"

"Talk to someone?" I cut in, and he nods. "I don't know. I guess we'll see how things go."

"You're not alone, and I'm sorry if I made you feel that way." He pulls me farther up his body, pushing my face into his neck. His hand winds into my hair at the back of my head. "We're in this together. Like we used to be, like we always should've been," he says sternly.

"Okay," I answer, my heart swelling with so much relief that it feels like it's going to burst all over him. He strokes my hair while he watches TV, and my eyes soon close as I drift off into the most restful sleep I've had in a long time. Wrapped in his arms, I feel warm and loved, my worries held at bay as I inhale his scent every time I breathe.

Chapter Twenty-Five

STRETCHING MY ARMS UP OVER MY HEAD, I FEEL A delicious ache between my legs. A smile curves my lips as I remember the orgasms Leo drew out of me yesterday morning. Rolling over, my heart stills in my chest as I find no sign of him. His side of the bed is unmade and cool when I rub my palm over it. I sit up, looking around the room and listening for any sign of him. Taking a deep breath, I tell myself to calm down as I remember everything that we talked about yesterday and last night.

He's back. He's come back to me.

Throwing the covers off my legs, I make my way to the bathroom, doing my business and then brushing my teeth. Looking in the mirror as I brush the tangles out of my hair, I see something. The change written all over my face. The light surrounding my brown eyes as I apply a bit of mascara. The pink tinge to my cheeks as I decide to ditch putting some powder on today. And the redness to my lips from kissing

Leo's. Smiling to myself, I put my stuff away in the cupboard before heading back into the room and dressing in a pair of black leggings and a long sleeved, red cotton dress.

Walking downstairs, I head into the kitchen and busy myself with getting everything ready to make pancakes before hearing something clang in the garage. Frowning, I go check to see if Leo's in there.

"Leo?" I call as I walk into the doorway of the garage.

He's over by the wall on the other side of my car. He turns around at the sound of my voice, a putty applicator in his hand. "Hey, woke up early and thought I'd fix this before the kids get home."

Indeed, he has. The holes have all been patched up, except for one. He turns back around, finishing the last one while I stand against the doorjamb and watch. He's still in his pajama pants, a white t-shirt hugging his upper body tightly.

"I was going to call someone," I finally blurt out.

He steps back, eyeing the wall before bending to put the lid back on the tub then checking his hands as he straightens. He looks over at me. "Yeah, I'd rather not have to explain why I lost my shit and destroyed my own garage to a complete stranger."

Ouch. My brows tug in, and I decide to go finish making breakfast. His hand grabs mine from behind, stopping me in the doorway to the kitchen then tugging me into his chest. He kisses my head, resting his cheek on it as he wraps his arms around me. "Sorry, beautiful." He sighs. "But really, it's okay. I didn't mind doing it myself."

"Breakfast?" I mumble into his chest, pushing away slightly.

"Sure." He releases me with a soft smile.

We eat at the island again, and it almost feels like it used to, only better. I stuff a piece of pancake into his mouth when he pulls me into his lap, giggling as he smears syrup on my nose and then leans in to lick it off. "Delicious," he murmurs. His eyes turn from playful to heated, taking my lips with his and rendering my mind empty of everything but him. I suck the syrup from his lips while his hands make their way underneath my dress. I pull away, breathing heavily and kiss him on the nose before climbing off his lap and finishing my pancake as I start to clean up.

Walking up behind me at the sink, he whispers, "Where do you think you're going?" His arms wrap around my waist, melding me into his hard body. He's hard and poking my lower back through his pants.

"Leo, I'm still recovering from yesterday." I grab a plate and rinse it, putting it on the dish rack to go in the dishwasher.

He groans into my ear. "Later then." Kissing my jaw, he releases me with a smack on my ass. He opens the dishwasher, loading the plates and cutlery inside. So many questions blaze a trail through my mind as I finish wiping down the counter, but I bite my lip, not sure whether to push or not. His hands fall to my hips, and he spins me around, crowding me into the counter behind me. He gently untucks my lip with his finger, staring at me intently.

"What's wrong?" His eyes flick back and forth between mine.

He can still read me then, despite how long it's been since we've communicated as we once used to. Sighing, I put the wipe down and reach up to brush my finger over the crease between his brows. It smooths out at my touch, but still, he waits.

"About what I said, last night with Charlie and how you asked if he should talk to someone …" His eyes widen a fraction, and he rears back a bit. Okay, he knows where I'm going with this then, but I continue anyway. "Do you think that maybe you should talk to someone? That it might help?"

He snorts, running a hand through his hair. "A professional?"

I nod.

"Yeah, no," he says. "I don't think it'd help." He leans in again, bracing his arms behind me on the counter and smirking. "Besides, I think I only ever needed you. I just wish I'd realized that months ago."

My brows furrow as I stare at his chest.

He tilts my head back up. "What?"

"I just think that maybe you should try it. Just a few times and see if it helps. What she did, what happened to you … it's pretty fucking messed up, Leo. You're allowed to acknowledge that."

His blue eyes narrow, and he snaps, "Don't you think I know that? Christ, it felt like a joke, like I couldn't treat it as anything other than a sick fucking joke."

I hold his gaze, my heart clenching tightly in my chest.

"Sorry," he says quietly. "Really, though, I just want to move on and forget about it. And for the first time in months, I feel like I can finally do that. *With you.*" His teeth sink into his bottom lip. Giving him a small smile, I refrain from saying anything more right now. It's still so fresh, so new for me, that I don't know where to tread. But I do know that I don't like it. The way he blatantly refuses to even think about talking to someone. Because while being together again and loving each other how we used to might go a long way in healing him, I know it might not be enough.

"Let's go for a drive. I want to take you out for lunch." He kisses my nose and walks out of the kitchen. I stare down at the floor for a moment, wondering if I should be doing anything else. But I guess, other than just being here, supporting him, and taking it day by day, there's not much else that I can do.

We pull up outside the small Italian restaurant at the plaza, and I wait as Leo rounds the car to open my door for me. He grabs my hand to help me out with a mischievous smile pulling at his lips.

"What?" I ask as he closes the door. He pushes me back against his car, leaning down to peck my lips. But a peck quickly turns into his tongue rubbing against mine. My arms wrap around his waist and any soreness between my thighs evaporates as heat engulfs me.

He pulls back, framing my face with his hands. "So fucking addictive. I don't know how I survived for so damn long without it."

I laugh. "My mouth?"

He beams down at me, his white teeth blinding in the midday sunlight. "You. All of you."

"Oh," I breathe.

"It feels surreal. As if this past year has been a nightmare, and I'm just now waking up."

I've never wanted to inflict bodily harm on someone the way I want to with Fiona. God, just thinking her name has my vision hazing over with red. What a crazy fucking bitch.

"Hey." He arches a brow at me. "What is it?"

"I want to kill her. She's made us lose so much time," I whisper.

He frowns. "Yeah, she has. But that's partly my fault and the way I've handled it."

I shake my head. "Will you report her?"

That has him rearing back. "Why?"

"Because it's the right thing to do. Attractive woman or not, she deserves to pay for what she's done to you. And others, too." I straighten from the car.

He glances around briefly. "Dylan has probably already put things in motion in order to gain full custody of their kids."

"But won't you need to—"

He cuts me off. "Lia, please. Let's just drop it for now, yeah?"

He grabs my hand, and I reluctantly let him lead me up the curb and inside the restaurant where Margo, the manager greets us with a smile. "Hey, you two, it's been a while. The usual?" she asks as we take our seats across from each other. We both nod eagerly, and she brings us our drinks before taking our order to the kitchen.

"I wonder if the kids have been behaving," I think out loud.

Leo snickers, his hand fiddling with my fingers and my wedding ring. "They're probably giving Robert hell." Robert is his mom's butler, and he hates children. But he's loyal to the Vandellens. He's been working for them since Leo was born, so he puts up with them. I smirk just thinking about what they're up to.

As if thinking the same, Leo asks, "Remember that

time Greta tried to get him to pat the frog she found in the backyard?"

I burst out laughing. "Yes."

He chuckles. "She cried because he called it a slimy disease-ridden enemy of the garden. Then she told him it was just a little old frog …"

I continue for him, "And he said it was a toad, didn't he?"

He nods. "Then she said that the only toad she could see was him." We both laugh quietly at the memory of his mother laughing and telling Robert that Greta had a point and to leave the poor thing alone.

Our food arrives, and I dig into my carbonara right away. Leo does the same with his spaghetti and meatballs. We eat in silence for a little while, but it's not uncomfortable. It's perfect, and makes me realize how much I've missed this. Just being with him. I think it would kill me if he ever took this away from me again. But I'm determined not to let that happen. I'll fight harder next time, love harder, and make sure he knows that whatever he's going through, he's not alone. That I'm not going anywhere.

That afternoon, I'm quickly cleaning up and putting the kids uniforms away, ready for school tomorrow while Leo returns some calls he's ignored over the weekend in his office. My phone rings from the kitchen, and I hurry downstairs to grab it, in case it's my mom or Taylor. They should be back any minute now. But it's not them; it's Lola. I hesitate for a moment before deciding to answer. "Hello?"

"Jesus Christ, you have so much to tell me, it's not even funny," she hisses into my ear.

I cringe, not knowing whether she knows or not, therefore not knowing what to say. "I do?" I settle on.

She laughs. "Oh no, you don't. Fiona, *what the ever-loving hell?*" she screeches.

I pull the phone away, rubbing at my ear before putting it back. Okay, so she knows.

"How'd you find out?"

"I overheard Trey talking with Dylan about it on the phone earlier. Shit, it all makes so much sense now."

Well, I'm glad she thinks so. "Shit. He doesn't want anyone to know, Lo."

Lola huffs. "As if I'd tell anyone. Trey's been acting weird, so I hid around the corner and listened in when he disappeared on the phone for too long. I cornered him after and demanded that he explain or I'd think he was having an affair." That has me laughing as I imagine her doing exactly that.

"Anyway," she says. "How're you handling it all? God, it makes me sick."

Taking a seat at the island, I idly trail my finger over the marble countertop. "I don't know. I'm glad I know even if I want to go to her house and kick her ass." She laughs. "But he's …" I glance behind me, making sure Leo is still in his office. When I don't hear anything, I continue, "It's like a switch has flipped, and he's back to being the same old Leo."

"That's good, though, right?"

Sighing, I answer, "Yes and no. I mean, I'm happy. So damn happy and relieved. But a few rounds of hot sex and some deep conversations with me won't miraculously fix things."

203

"We'll get to those juicy details later, but what do you mean? You think he needs some help?"

"Yeah, I do," I say. "I know he's a guy, and being the way he is you can only imagine how much he doesn't want anyone to know. He sees it as more of an embarrassment. A weakness, I guess. But something terrible happened to him, and he knows that; he's just hoping it'll fade away. That I'm enough to finally help him through it."

She hums into my ear. "That's tough, Lia. I don't know. I'm happy things are looking up for you both, but I see what you mean." Resting my elbows on the counter, I lean my head on a fist and stare out the back window, watching the breeze stir some leaves from the tree before they float slowly to the ground. "Just see how he does. I think that after everything that's happened, not only with that crazy bitch, but with the both of you, you might be onto something, though."

"Exactly what I was thinking," I agree. The front door opens, and I hear the kids race down the hallway. "Gotta go; the kids are home. I'll talk to you tomorrow."

We hang up and I turn around, jumping down from the stool and sweeping Greta into a hug when she runs into the kitchen.

"Grandma Tay got me a Furby! It snores!" She pulls away, shoving it into my chest. Lifting the pink ball of fluff into the air, I almost drop it when it moves and mumbles something to me. Leo grins, walking into the kitchen with Charlie hanging over his shoulder. "What's that freaky sounding thing?"

"A Furby. It's so annoying," Charlie grumbles when Leo sets him down. I gather him into my chest for a hug, kissing his messy head of hair. "Were you guys good?" I ask.

He steps away but leaves an arm around my waist as my

mom enters the room. "Yes. They were fantastic." She stops beside me, pinching my cheek. "Looks like this weekend did you some good." She winks, and I flush when I see Leo grinning at me as he stands by the kitchen sink, holding the Furby while Greta animatedly explains everything it does to him.

"Where's your robot?" Taylor asks, coming into the kitchen and kissing my cheek before looking down at Charlie.

"Oh, shoot! I left it in the car." He races off to get it.

"You got him that robot?" I look over at Taylor who shrugs, turning the coffee machine on and grabbing some mugs out of the cupboard.

"He wouldn't stop talking about it, so it was the fastest way to get him to shut up about it, really." She laughs.

Leo scowls at her. "Is that why you spoiled me as a child?"

She pats his cheek, smiling widely at him. "You always were a quick study, my dear boy." He continues to scowl while I laugh. My mom takes my hand, leading Greta and me into the living room.

"How was Robert?" I take a seat next to Greta, who's fiddling with her little ball of pink noise. My mom grins evilly. "Oh, my God. You should've seen how fast he ran away from Greta and that Furby."

Leo takes a seat beside me. "Let me guess; he thought it was a sign of the apocalypse?"

My mom laughs, pointing at him. "How'd you guess?" She shakes her head. "Anyway, we'll take them again next month for the weekend before Taylor drags me off to Australia. Most fun I've had in ages. It was even better than watching Taylor dance drunk on a cruise ship with a bunch of men half her age."

I glance at Leo, who blanches at hearing that. Laughing, I

pat his arm. "You're going to Australia?" I ask.

My mom rolls her eyes as if traveling the world is such a chore. "Yes. Taylor wants to see that huge rock and a wombat." Leo scrapes a hand over his stubble, trying to hide his smile.

"But you can see wombats here in the zoo," Charlie informs Taylor who's now bringing coffees into the room and placing them on the coffee table.

"It's not the same." She waves her hand at him. "You'll see. I'll take a video and send it to you."

"You mean you'll make me send it. And what on earth for? They don't do anything. And finding one in the wild might just get your hand bitten off if you approach it."

"Says who?" Taylor frowns. "They're adorable, so cute and fat."

I zone out, looking up at Leo who drapes an arm over my shoulder, melding me into his side. He shakes his head with a quiet laugh, kissing my head. And when I look over at Charlie, whose robot is lying on the couch next to him forgotten, he's got a tiny smile on his face as he looks at us.

Chapter Twenty-Six

"I'LL TRY TO GET HOME A LITTLE EARLIER TONIGHT, BUT I have a lot of work to catch up on that I was supposed to do over the weekend," Leo says, doing up his tie behind me in the mirror.

Turning around, I smooth my hands over his lapels and adjust his tie for him. "Okay. We'll be here." I smile up into his face.

His hands trail up my arms to my neck, wrapping around the back of it and sinking into my hair. "Don't bother making the bed." He leans in to whisper the words to my mouth. I get dizzy, inhaling his cologne and the mint still on his breath from brushing his teeth.

"Why?" I murmur against his lips, my eyes fluttering closed.

His hands roam down my back, pressing me into his chest as his lips softly part mine with the barest hint of a touch. "Because as soon as the kids go to bed, we're going to mess it up even worse than last night," he whispers.

The memory of him fucking my mouth flashes behind my closed lids. The way he spread my legs wide afterward to take me hard and deep while making me hold the headboard as he tortured my breasts mercilessly has a shiver raking over me. Goose bumps cause the hair on my arms to rise. He chuckles, knowing exactly what he's doing to me before finally taking my lips with his and kissing me slowly. His tongue touches but only teases mine before he's pulling away and walking out of the room.

I finally open my eyes when I hear him saying goodbye to the kids downstairs. Snapping out of my daze, I turn back around to the mirror and throw my hair over my head to pull it all up into a messy bun. When I'm done, I grab my phone off the nightstand and head downstairs to finish getting the kids ready for school.

"Can I take my robot in for show and tell?" Charlie asks on the way out to the car.

I shake my head. "It's not your show and tell day yet." I put their bags in the back then hop inside to start the engine.

"I can do special news, though," Charlie says as he opens his door.

"We're going to be late if we don't move it. Ask your teacher if you can bring it in for special news tomorrow."

He sighs but climbs up into the car. Greta finally comes racing out into the garage, slamming the door closed behind her. I wind the window down. "Let's move it, missy."

She laughs, opening her door and getting in. I wait until they've both buckled their seat belts before backing out and closing the garage. Driving down our street, I hear, "Squeeze ma belly," coming from the trunk. "Greta." My head snaps around when I stop at the end of our street. "Did you put that pink furry thing in your bag?"

Charlie snickers at Greta, whose eyes are bugging out of her head. "Um, maybe?"

"Hand him over as soon as we get to school, okay?" I turn around, flicking my turn signal on and heading toward the school.

"It's not a he; it's a she."

Charlie snorts. "It's a weird, noisy ball of fur."

"Is not," Greta says.

"Is too," he says.

"Well, your stupid robot is, is, is … is *hideous*," she stammers out triumphantly.

I'm going to need more coffee. Turning into the school driveway, I park as Charlie says, "It's supposed to be. It's a robot, dummy."

"Hey!" I turn around, frowning at him. "Not cool."

He has the good grace to look a little sheepish.

"All right, let's go." I jump out and grab their bags, making sure to grab the damn Furby out of Greta's before she runs off.

Lola laughs, walking over to me. "Oh, shit. You've been initiated into the, 'help, this thing won't shut up' Furby club, have you?" She takes it from me, tickling its belly and making the damn thing giggle evilly.

"Shush you. Sophie has one too?"

She nods gravely, handing it back over. "Yep, I took the batteries out a month after Christmas. She hasn't noticed yet, thankfully."

That gives me hope. Grinning, I turn around to open the door and place it in Greta's car seat. I close the door and lean against it, watching the kids run into the school as the bell sounds. She leans in next to me. "Have you spoken to Jared?" she asks quietly.

The smile wilts off my face at the thought of him. Remembering that I still need to see him, to talk to him in person. I hope he shows up tomorrow even if I know Leo might lose his shit. I can't leave things how they were on the phone on Friday. He doesn't deserve some bullshit, half-assed explanation over the phone.

"Not yet." I sigh. "I'm going into the shelter tomorrow. I'm planning on talking to Glenda about taking some time away. At least until Jared's finished doing his hours."

She scuffs some rocks below her Converse shoes. "You're going to see him then?"

"I have to," I tell her.

I look over to find her brows furrowing over her sunglasses. "But at what risk? Won't Leo lose his ever-loving mind?" she whispers.

Probably, but I feel stuck about this. "I don't want to upset him; it's the last thing I want to do. Not when things look like they're finally going to work out for us." I chew on my lip for a beat. "But I need to talk to Jared in person. What I've done is pretty shitty on all counts."

"I get it. But you know Leo's probably not going to be happy about it, *at all*," she warns.

That's what I'm afraid of. "I won't lie to him. If he asks, I'll tell him. But otherwise … I'm just worried it'll cause unnecessary drama by letting him know that I want to say goodbye to the guy who was there for me when he wasn't."

She sighs. "Alrighty, then. So." She claps her hands. "Let's go kick some ass." She turns and climbs into my car.

Kick some ass? "Wait, *what?*"

She rolls her eyes. "She who shall not be named. Come on; I have an appointment with my gynecologist at twelve thirty, so we can't take all day." She closes the door.

Um. "What do you mean? Yeah, I'd like to inflict some bodily harm, but I don't know if I can even stomach seeing her yet," I say as I climb behind the wheel.

"I'll stomach it for the both of us. Let's roll."

Feeling worried, I turn the ignition over, and we leave her Mazda behind as we drive away from the school.

On the way, my gut starts to churn as I think of all the times I hung out with Fiona. The times we had coffee, went shopping, had play dates and dinner parties. Then recently, cleaning her house. Trying to help her after her husband found out her dirty secret and left her. Left her because of what she did to my husband and God knows who else.

I start deep breathing as we turn onto her street. I don't know if I can do this. If I can even face her after what she's done—the lives she's almost ruined. Parking in front of her massive house, I turn to Lola, who's been surprisingly quiet.

"Oh, hell." I look out the window to her house. Her perfect fucking house and perfect fucking gardens with her perfect lies hidden behind it all. "What are we even doing here?"

She shrugs. "I don't know, but we need to do something. Let's just go yell at her, maybe punch her in the vagina really good."

I blanch. "Seriously? Let's just go. Looking at those stupid ass lions is even making me sick."

She grabs my hand as I'm about to turn the ignition back over. "If that were my husband, she'd be in unrecognizable pieces and buried in my backyard. And I'd sit there and have tea on my back porch every morning, staring at her final resting place, just hoping she was burning in hell."

My throat bobs. "O-kay … that's a little terrifying," I whisper.

"She's a crazy fucking bitch!" she almost yells. "You were her friend."

"I know," I say quietly.

She points at me. "You were there for her."

"I know," I say a little louder.

Her eyes take on a scary shade of blue as she growls quietly, "You gave her your favorite chocolate just last week, for Christ's sake!"

"I know!" I yell then shake my head. "Okay, wait, Lola. Focus."

She climbs out of the car and slams the door. Shit.

Shit, shit, shit.

"Lola!" I whisper-hiss, jumping out of the car as she beelines up the sidewalk to the front doors.

I scrub my hands down my face. Okay. Looks like we're really doing this then. I slam my car door closed and run after her.

"Lola, Jesus, don't …" I say once my ballet flats slap onto the front porch. But it's too late. She presses the doorbell then grabs the huge knocker and slams it against the wood. The sound reverberates throughout my stiff body. I can't do this. Not yet.

The door flies open and Fiona stands there, her brown hair clean and tucked behind her ears and her gym gear on. Of course. Of course, she looks so put together now. I suddenly want to puke all over her stupidly tight clothes.

"Hey, ladies. Come in. I've been meaning to call you both actually."

Lola doesn't say anything; she just grabs my hand and tugs me inside. My feet drag the whole way, but they don't move past the entryway. I can't. Knowing what she did to Leo here, in this house, has my feet firmly rooted to the floor as Lola glances over at me then sighs, giving up.

"Cut the shit, Fiona. We know what you did." Lola dives right in.

Fiona's pretty face scrunches up in confusion. "What are you talking about?" And that's apparently all it takes for red to blur my vision. My body starts trembling as rage and disbelief battle their way through my bloodstream.

"*You*, raping her fucking husband." Lola points at me, and I step forward, all fear having left my body as Fiona's wide eyes turn to me.

"What the hell do you mean? *Rape* him?" She cackles, legitimately cackles. "*Come on*, as if you can even rape a man." She wipes underneath her eyes, still laughing softly. "That's totally stupid. They all want sex, right?"

I walk right up to her and slap the shit out of her. And when she rights herself, I slap the other cheek with the back of my hand for good measure before Lola pulls me back.

"Are you fucking *kidding me?* So that's why you put something in his drinks, right? *Because he fucking wanted it*?" I screech at her.

She visibly pales even after I've slapped her in the face. She takes a step back, rubbing at her cheek. "I don't know who told you that, but they're lying."

I scoff. "Your husband. He has the tapes, you fucking psycho."

Lola sucks in a breath next to me as Fiona's jaw hangs open. And I've had enough. "Let's go," I say quietly, turning and grabbing Lola's hand.

"You sick fucking bitch," Lola snarls over her shoulder before slamming her front door closed behind us.

"Oh, God. I'm gonna puke." I grab my stomach and stop halfway back to the car, closing my eyes and taking a deep breath.

"Do it," Lola says, "Right here on her precious garden. Tapes? Un-fucking-believable. Leo had better be on top of getting those."

She grabs my hand when I finally manage to get myself together enough to continue walking back to the car. "I don't know what he's doing with them. Dylan apparently has them. Leverage against her or something."

She pulls her seat belt on, and I do the same. "Let's hope he ends up getting the disgusting woman put behind bars then."

I lean forward, dropping my head onto the steering wheel.

"You okay?" Lola rubs my back.

Nodding my head, I sit back up and wipe the tears from underneath my eyes. "Yeah, it's just been so damn hard to wrap my head around."

"And seeing her has made it sink its filthy claws into you, huh?" she asks softly.

"Yeah, I guess." I sniff, turning the car on and checking my mirrors before driving away from that house of nightmares.

Chapter Twenty-Seven

"**D**ID YOU HAVE A GOOD DAY?" LEO ASKS, COMING UP behind me and kissing my neck after dinner. Which he came home in time for, despite being busy.

My lips curl into a smile as I shove the memory of Fiona out of my head. "Yeah, it was … productive." I rinse the pot and put it on the dish rack.

"Oh?" He kisses my jaw and spins me around. "What did you do?"

I know he's probably going to be concerned about my whereabouts for a while, and I know I deserve that. The call at lunchtime and the text message this morning were proof enough that it will take some time for him to get past what I did. But today? He doesn't need to know. I think it was more for me than for him anyway. The pain her actions have caused affects us both. And I think I needed to confront her after all.

Leaning in, I kiss the center of his stubbled chin. "Not

much, just hung out with Lola this morning then came home to catch up on laundry and cleaned the house."

Which isn't really a lie. Cleaning is a great way for me to work out my frustrations. Well, that and chocolate. And sex, but we'll get to that tonight, I'm sure.

He hums and I squish my face into his throat to feel it vibrate against my nose. "I know where you went," he says with a quiet that both terrifies and excites me.

Well, shit. Fucking Lola, I bet she told Trey.

"Do you, now?" I ask his skin.

He folds his arms around me, burying his nose into my neck and squeezing me. "I do. And I love you." He places a soft kiss underneath my ear then releases me and walks out of the kitchen. Feeling cold without his warmth, I rub my arms and smile to myself.

"Shower time, kiddos!" I hear him holler to them from upstairs as he turns the water on.

Okay, I guess he's not mad then.

Driving into the city to the women's shelter the next morning, I can't help but feel a little guilty. Maybe I should've told Leo what my plan was after all. But I know he would've stopped me, and I need to do this. He knows I plan on taking some time away, and he's happy about that, but he doesn't know that I haven't told them yet or that I'm going there today to do that.

And to see a certain green-eyed male with a devious smile.

Parking my car, I jump out and grab my purse. Flicking my sunglasses down onto my nose, I lock it and walk down the street to the front entrance of the shelter. Jared's not out the front and I'm glad that he's not waiting for me. But as I walk inside, I start to worry that he might not show up.

"Dahlia, good morning." Glenda smiles as I approach the staff room.

"Hey, how's everything going?" I take my sunglasses off, sign in, and put my purse away.

She snorts. "Caught someone trying to steal old bread out of the back dumpster on my way in, so I told them we'd make a meal for them for free. They ran off."

I wince, hating when that happens. Unfortunately, some people aren't too proud to ask for help. No, they're simply too scared.

"But good other than that. Lord, it just breaks my heart when all they have to do is ask. I'd thought about putting a sign on the door, just in case they come back."

"Yeah, but we both know it could be some time until they come back this way."

She sighs. "Yep."

"I need to talk to you actually." I take a step back, feeling kind of nervous. "I'm going to have to take some time away. Just for a month or two."

"Oh?" She quirks a brow at me. "This wouldn't have some-thing to do with a tall, dark-haired male with bright green eyes, now would it?"

Shit. My cheeks heat as I struggle to meet her gaze. "Yeah. It does."

She nods, smiling sadly at me. "I figured as much, but don't worry. No one else assumes a thing; the boy is a terrible flirt." She shakes her head. "None of my business. But are you okay?"

I lean against the wall. "I will be. Things have been hard at home with Leo for a while now, but it's looking up. I think we're going to be okay. So it's best to make sure I respect his wishes regarding …"

She pats my arm. "Got it, sweetheart. Don't worry." Sighing, she says, "We'll miss you, though. Don't be gone too long."

"Thank you. Just let me know when he's finished," I find the guts to say.

"Will do. You just take care of you and yours." She pats my arm again and toddles off to the storeroom.

Feeling relieved as well as sad, I head to the kitchen to wash my hands, put my apron and hair net on, and then some gloves. Closing the fridge after grabbing the sausages, I see Jared walking out of the pantry with a pencil tucked behind his ear and his eyes on what I'm guessing is the grocery checklist.

"Hey." I place the sausages down on the counter.

He glances up, his eyes studying my face before his lips curve into a small smile. "Hey, Blondie." He puts the checklist down and walks over to me. "You doing okay?"

"I feel like I should be asking you that." I eye the yellow bruising still evident underneath his eye and along the side of his jaw. My fingers twist together, causing the latex gloves to squeak. "Can we have coffee after?"

He frowns, his beautiful eyes hardening a little.

"Looks worse than it feels and yeah, sure," he finally says. "I'll meet you out front." He grabs his checklist and disappears again.

My shoulders slump. Why does the idea of maybe hurting him get to me so much? I busy myself with preparing lunch with Tilly before finally hanging up my apron then taking my hairnet and gloves off.

Walking out of the bathroom, I fluff my hair and grab my purse. After saying goodbye to Glenda, I walk outside into the bright autumn sunshine. The cool wind has me tugging my gray knit cardigan over my chest as I look around for Jared.

"Boo," he says from behind me, causing me to shriek and a few onlookers to give us wary glances. I spin on my heel, grinning up into his face before taking a step back when I realize how close we are.

"I might be older than you are, but I'm still too young to die, trouble," I grumble jokingly to him as we start walking down the street to the cafe on the corner.

He chuckles, opening the door for me when we reach it. I walk over to an empty booth, watching as he sits on the other side. It almost feels like Deja vu, sitting exactly where we are, a month after that first time I let him take me out for coffee.

"I'm so sorry, leaving the way I did last week." I cringe. "I had no idea that would happen. You know that, right?"

"It's all good." He grins. "Besides, nothing ruins a hard-on quite like an angry husband storming into the room."

I snort, my laughter halted by the waitress who stops by our table to take our order.

"So on with it then." He smiles, but it doesn't reach his eyes.

"On with what?" I ask even though I know exactly what he means.

"You wanted to tell me in person that you're done using me as your plaything, you wicked woman." He winks.

I burst out laughing. "Oh, my God. Shush. You were not my plaything."

He looks down at the menu, skimming a long finger over it then spinning it around on the table. "What was I, then?"

A knot forms in my throat, and I force myself to swallow it down. "You're my friend." I reach over and grab his hand.

He lets me, looking up at me. "Funny, it felt like a little more than that to me." He links his fingers through mine, twiddling my wedding ring around. Tears prick my eyes as I watch him.

"I'm sorry," I whisper.

His shoulders lift. "Can't be helped, Blondie. It was only meant to be a bit of fun, right?"

I frown at him when he finally meets my gaze and lets go of my hand. He laughs. "You can't honestly think I'd want anything serious to happen with a woman who's married and has two kids."

Yeah, that stings. But I get it. "Fair enough," I mutter.

"It was meant to be fun, but I guess you kinda stole something from me along the way."

"Jared …"

"It's okay." He holds up a hand. "My mistake. Next time I'm looking for a distraction or a little fun, I know to be a bit more selective."

We thank the waitress when she places our coffees down. I stir mine, looking over at Jared while he stares out the window at the busy street outside. He takes a sip of his coffee then shifts in his seat, tugging his wallet out and putting a piece of paper down on the table.

"Tell your husband I said thanks, but I won't be needing this." He taps it then picks his mug back up, eyeing me over the rim as I turn the paper around. My lungs seize in my chest as I take in the check for a hundred thousand dollars.

Holy shit.

"He paid you to stay away from me?" I breathe.

He shrugs again. "Can you blame him, really? But yeah. Though it seems a little unnecessary now, doesn't it?" He clears his throat. "Despite his asshole tendencies, I'd say the guy must care about you"—he holds his fingers a few millimeters apart—"just a tiny bit."

I know he's trying to lighten the moment, but I can't laugh when this is anything but funny.

He fucking offered him money to stay away from me.

I get that he doesn't trust me like he once did, but I had no idea it was this bad.

"Things are better then?" Jared asks when I keep staring at the check like it's going to grow teeth and physically bite a chunk out of my heart.

Tearing my eyes away from it, I swallow thickly as I look up at him. "Yeah, they are."

He nods. "What changed?"

He doesn't say it, but I know he knows it's got to do with him. It's not only that, though. "Something happened to him, earlier this year." I blow out a breath. "It, um, well, it messed him up pretty bad. He didn't know how to handle it, and I finally found out what happened."

Nodding again, he picks his mug back up, and I do the same, blowing on my latte and taking a few small sips.

"Bad enough to excuse how bad things got between you two?" He puts his mug down.

Is it? It's hard to judge such a thing really. He should have told me, but I understand his reasons for not doing so. "Everyone deals with things differently, I guess," I settle on saying.

"By making their wife miserable?" His dark brows furrow.

I wrap my hands around my mug. "I don't think that was his intention. He's a good man who was struggling with something terrible. Does it excuse the way he treated me?" I shrug. "No, probably not. But I'm willing to look past it, to forgive him and try again. Especially seeing as he's willing to do the same for me." I eye him pointedly.

He smirks. "Got a good point there, Blondie." Looking down at his coffee, he asks, "So this is a goodbye then, right?"

My heart splinters. But it is, and I'm okay with that, even if it hurts a little. Because I love my husband. Probably more than any sane person should after what I've been through. But I know him. I know the man I married—and I've finally got him back. I'm not giving that up for the world. For anything. "Yeah, it is," I admit quietly.

"Well"—he tips his head back, downing the rest of his coffee—"I'm glad I could help out, babe. Let me know if he ever becomes an ass again. My services will always be available to you." He winks.

Laughing, I shake my head. "That won't be necessary, but thank you." I sigh. "And even if he does, that's not me, Jared. I don't regret knowing you, and I never could, but I won't do something like that to him or myself again."

He bites his lip, staring at me for a heartbeat too long before rising from his seat.

"I guess I'll see you around then, Blondie." He throws a ten-dollar bill onto the table. I give him a watery smile as tears prick the backs of my eyes, making it hard to try to talk. He looks down at me then gently grabs my chin, tipping it up to meet his green eyes one last time. He lowers his head to kiss me softly on the forehead then walks away.

My heart constricts as I watch him through the window, walking into the busy flow of pedestrians before disappearing.

Chapter Twenty-Eight

"I'M GOING TO BE A UNICORN FOR THE BOOK PARADE."

Leo chuckles, cutting into his steak. "How are you going to swing that?" He glances over at me, and I shrug, smiling and trying to hide the bubbling in my gut over today's discovery. *The check.*

"Mommy will make something," Greta says confidently, shoving a mouthful of corn into her mouth and chewing.

He laughs again, keeping his eyes on me. "Right." His blue eyes pierce my skin as they narrow a fraction on my brown ones. I glance over at Charlie. "What are you planning to dress up as?"

He scowls. "I'm not dressing up. That's for babies."

Leo's eyes shift from me to Charlie. "Halloween's coming up at the end of the month. You mean to say you're not dressing up for that either, then?"

Charlie looks as though that's just occurred to him. "Umm."

Greta giggles. "You can't go trick or treating without dressing up. Why don't you go as Mr. Grumpy?"

He scoffs. "No. Why don't you go as Mrs. Annoying."

Greta thinks about it for a second, "There's no such thing—hey!" she squawks when it suddenly registers that he's insulted her.

"Charlie," Leo reprimands even though I can tell he's trying not to smile.

"Think about something you want to go as. Maybe we can make you a robot costume?" I suggest. Charlie's brows rise, his blue eyes alight with sudden interest.

We finish our dinner, and the whole time, I feel as though Leo's eyes are burning holes into my skin. But I try to ignore it. Now's not the time. Because what I'm going to tell him and the argument that it will no doubt cause is best had when the kids are asleep.

"Okay, you two." I stand and take some plates to the kitchen. "Finish up and then it's time for a shower and bed."

"I need some ice cream first!" Greta demands.

"Greta, manners," Leo says firmly as I leave the room. I dig the ice cream out of the freezer and scoop some into two bowls before taking them back into the dining room and grabbing the last of the dirty plates. Leo snags my hand as I'm about to grab his plate and moves his chair back, pulling me down into his lap.

"What's up with you?" he asks quietly, taking the plates from my hands and putting them down before leaning in to kiss my lips.

Greta giggles behind us.

"Nothing. I'll talk with you later." My arms wind around his neck. His hand rubs up my back then glides up into the back of my hair.

"Daddy, you're messing up Mommy's pretty hair," Greta informs him loudly.

"Shut it," Charlie hisses at her.

"Why?" she whispers loudly.

Charlie sighs loudly as Leo and I both shake with silent laughter.

Leaning back, I look down into his eyes for a moment. I lift my hand to trail my finger down the side of his face to his lips as his eyes stay glued to mine. "I love you, Leo Xavier Vandellen."

His brows tug together, but he says it back, "And I love you, Dahlia Jade Vandellen." He then grins at the sound of his last name after it leaves his lips. I shake my head, kissing his nose before climbing off his lap to return to the kitchen and finish cleaning up.

After the kids are bathed and in bed, I hop in the shower too then head back downstairs in my pajama pants and a pink t-shirt. I find Leo in the living room, watching TV and checking emails on his phone, but the sight no longer worries me. Tugging my knitting basket out, I spread the blanket over my lap and get back to work on finishing it while Leo does his thing and the kids are hopefully falling asleep.

"How the hell are you going to make a unicorn costume?" Leo asks distractedly.

Smiling down at the crocheted blanket, I tell him, "I'm sure there's something on Pinterest I can copy. I've got two weeks."

He shifts, sitting up on the couch and stretching his arms over his head. "What's a Pinterest?"

That has me laughing. "In short, it's a website full of

wonderfully crafty ideas."

He grunts, standing up from the couch. "I'm going to take a shower."

"Okay." I look up when he still hasn't moved. "What?" I ask.

He shakes his head. "Never could take a hint, beautiful." Leaning down, he tilts my chin up to meet his mouth. His tongue demands instant entry, and I give it to him, moaning as he skims it over mine. "Upstairs. Now."

Swallowing, I pull back a bit. "I have to talk to you about something first."

He straightens. "Well, come upstairs and do it. Unless you want to do it here." He grins and I feel myself grow heated. I grab the basket, putting my stuff away and rising from the couch. He moves over to the coffee table, grabbing the remote and turning the TV off. "Come on." He takes my hand.

"Leo." I stop in the hallway, and he turns to me. "I saw Jared today."

He drops my hand, rearing back against the wall. "*What?*"

My throat burns as I try to swallow, not wanting to re-peat myself again. He heard me anyway. "I had to go into the shelter to tell them that I wasn't coming back until his hours were done."

He stares at the hardwood floor for a moment then laughs quietly, shaking his head. "And what? You thought you'd kill two birds with one stone?"

"I had to tell him in person. He …" I close my eyes for a second then reopen them. "He sort of became a friend, Leo."

He walks up to me, chest heaving as he crowds me into the wall.

"I know about the check," I blurt, and the stormy

expression falls from his face. "He showed me." I slide passed him to stalk down the hall, turning into the kitchen and snatching it from my handbag. He follows me, leaning against the doorway and tucking his hands into his pockets.

"Here." I walk over and hold it out to him. "He said to say that he wouldn't be needing it." I slap it into his chest when he just stands there.

"Take it!" I demand when he continues to stare at me. It falls to the floor. *"A hundred-fucking grand, Leo?"*

His top lip curls into a sneer. "You're mine, Lia. I'll do whatever it takes to keep it that way."

My heart pounds furiously as I stare up into his angry eyes. "You can trust me, Leo. I don't want anyone but you," I say quietly.

"You sure had a funny way of showing it." His jaw clenches and he glances away. "If you must know, I sent it last week. After ..." He doesn't finish, doesn't need to.

"That doesn't make me feel a whole lot better, but okay."

"I'm sorry. I'm supposed to make you feel better, am I? After I walk into some dump of a hotel room and saw that some asshole was about to *fuck my wife?*" he growls, and I recoil.

There's nothing I can really say to that. Nothing. Even if my throat hadn't closed up thanks to the looming tears that are now gathering in my eyes.

"Tell me, Lia." He takes a step forward, his nostrils flaring. "Why the fuck you'd see him again if I'm the only one you want?" His voice is deceptively soft, putting me on edge. But I tell him the truth anyway. "Because it felt wrong not to at least say goodbye. He wasn't some dirty secret of mine, Leo. Like I told you, he was a friend."

He laughs humorlessly. "Yeah? And what about *me*, Lia? Did you even stop to think about me?" He slams a fist against his chest, growling, *"Did you think about how I'd fucking feel?"*

"Yes." Because I knew he wouldn't like it. "I'm sorry, but I don't regret doing it. He deserved to know what was going on."

He swipes a shaky hand through his hair, exhaling a breath through his nose before turning around and heading for the stairs. "Leo, wait!" I call out.

He doesn't, and he doesn't answer me.

Sitting down at the island, I wipe the tears from my face and wonder what the hell I'm supposed to do now.

I can't let him pull away from me again.

So even though I'm terrified of taking any more blows to my heart, I get up and down a glass of water before going to make sure the house is locked up. But Leo's already done it. I head upstairs, checking that the kids are asleep, and thank God that they are. I walk into our bedroom, but Leo's not here. He's not in the en suite when I walk in there and start brushing my teeth either. After washing my face, I march back down the hall and turn the door handle to the spare room. It's locked.

"Leo." I knock lightly on it. "Let me in."

He ignores me. I lean my head against the door. "Please."

"No," he finally replies.

I lift my head. "I'll sit out here all night, Leo. I'll damn well sleep out here if I have to."

"Go to bed, Lia."

Gritting my teeth together as frustration and fear threaten to take hold, I snap at him, "You're not shutting me out again. I won't fucking let you." I turn on my heel and march back into our room, my heart thumping fast with every step. Grabbing hold of our quilt and a pillow, I tug them out into the hall and drag them to the door of the spare room. Folding it over a few times, I lie down on top of it. If I'm really going to do this, then I'm going to be comfortable, damn it. Well, kind of, I think, as I squirm around and turn onto my side. Shoving the pillow farther under my head, I close my eyes.

I must've just fallen asleep when I hear the door open behind me, and Leo cursing as he bends down to pick me up. I wrap my arms and legs around him, rubbing my nose into his neck. "I'm sorry," I whisper, sleep coating my voice.

He sighs. "You're gonna have to let go of me if you want me to grab the bedding from the floor."

"Don't need it," I mumble, inhaling his scent.

He shifts me farther up his body before turning and heading back down the hall. He passes me my pillow, and I take it as he grabs the quilt and drags it behind him. After kicking the door closed with his foot, he climbs onto our bed. "You're not going," I tell him.

"Don't you think I know that?" he grumbles. "Fuck me, sleeping on the goddamn floor."

I smile into his neck, kissing it as he lays down and pulls the quilt over us.

"Give me that." He takes my pillow from me and puts it on my side of the bed. He rolls to his side and still, I hold him. And he lets me, which I take as a good sign, seeing as if he really didn't want me to, he has the strength to pluck my arms off him.

"It hurts, Lia," he says to the top of my head.

Guilt threatens to swallow me whole but I try to push it away. "How can I make it better?" I whisper.

"Don't talk to him. Don't see him. I thought it was pretty fucking obvious that I wouldn't want you to."

"I know, and I won't anymore. You can trust me. You will trust me again."

His Adam's apple bobs near my nose as he swallows. "I do trust you."

I snort. "You don't have to lie to me, Leo."

"Lia, despite all that's happened, I still do. But not him. I don't think you understand how much seeing that … how much it fucked with me."

"I love you Leo, only ever, always you," I remind him.

His hands wrap around my back, smoothing down my hair. "I love you, too."

We fall asleep like that. And even though I know that he's still not happy with me, I feel like maybe we'll still be okay.

"Greta, you'll eat the yogurt or toast. Pick one," I say when she argues again that she wants Fruit Loops.

"But Grandma Tay lets us eat Fruit Loops when we stay at her place." She crosses her arms.

Leo walks into the kitchen, sneaking up behind her to squish her nose and say, "Well, Grandma Tay doesn't pay for your dental bills. I do."

Greta sucks in a breath. "They're not bad for your teeth! Fruit Loops have fruit in them, duh."

"Ugh, just eat the food already," Charlie groans.

Leo kisses them both, and I tuck their lunch boxes into their bags then turn to say goodbye to him. But all I get is a peck on the head. "Hey ..." I say when he walks toward the entry to the garage.

"Got a meeting at nine. I've gotta go. Bye, guys." He waves over his head.

Frowning, I turn around, finding both kids grinning at me.

"What?" I huff.

"Don't be sad Daddy didn't kiss you, Mommy. When I grow up and get married, my husband will *not* be allowed to kiss me. No way." She pokes her chin out. "Oh, but he can rub my feet. That's totally okay with me."

Charlie and I laugh at her. "What? I'm being serious."

I start the dishwasher then grab their bags. "We know. Come on and grab your toast. We'd better go, too."

We all pile into the car and head over to the school. They run inside just before the skies open and it starts to rain. I wave to Lola on my way out and make the short drive back home. Pulling into the driveway, I stare at the big white and gray painted house that holds so many memories, good and bad, including the argument of last night. While I'm glad I persisted, I can't help but worry if he's still upset with me or if he's trying to push me away again.

Sighing, I put the car into reverse. Well, I guess there's only one way to find out.

Chapter Twenty-Nine

DRIVING OVER THE BRIDGE, I OBSERVE THE WAY THE skyscrapers act like beacons as they light up the gray fog and rain that's shrouding the city of Rayleigh. One of the first towers you see as you come off the overpass into the city is Vandellen Logistics. Handy for trying to get out of traffic every day.

Visiting Leo at work has never been something I enjoyed doing, nor is it something I do very often. The people, while nice enough, are a little stuffy and conversation always seems forced. As if they feel like they need to humor me because I'm Leo's wife. Glancing at the time, I see that it's almost nine thirty and keep driving into the city. Leo will still be in his meeting a while longer, so I park the car outside a French looking bakery and jump out quickly to get underneath the awning before I get soaked. A little bell sounds as I walk inside, smoothing my damp hair back from my face and tucking some behind my ear.

"Hello, what can I get for you?" a woman who looks to be in her fifties asks.

I give her a smile then browse the display of pastries in front of me. "I'll grab two chocolate croissants, a latte, one sugar, and a black coffee. To go please."

She busies herself with making the coffee then grabs the croissants and puts them in a paper bag before handing them over. I give her a twenty, telling her to keep the change. She beams at me, and I grab our drinks and food before running back out to the car. Once inside, I check my phone and decide to just head over there. The morning traffic makes the drive take fifteen minutes anyway. Walking would probably take five. I decide against using the employee parking lot and opt to park on the street when I see a free space instead. Getting out, I quickly shut the door before realizing I forgot our food and drinks. Shit. Opening it back up, I grab them then lock the car, running out of the rain and into the foyer of Vandellen Logistics. I'm a little cold and probably look like I took a dive into the ocean, but I hold my head up high and walk over to the reception desk.

"Dahlia." Sarah looks up from her computer, her red lips pursed as she scrutinizes me over the rims of her black framed glasses. She lifts a hand and delicately pushes them up the bridge of her nose, sniffing then asking, "What can we do for you?"

I hold the snort in, just. She knows I'm here to see my husband. But I smile thinly and tell her anyway. "Just here to see Leo." I hold up the tray with our two mugs and paper bag for emphasis. "Is he done with his meeting?"

She makes a show of checking her computer for a good minute before a frazzled looking young woman rounds the corner. "Oh, you're Leo's wife?" Her eyes bug out as she takes me in. "You're so much prettier in person. Oh, um, instead of the pictures he has in his office," she hurries to say.

My lips curve into a genuine smile as I take in her frizzy red hair, plump figure, and the freckles scattered over her nose. She seems sweet. "You're Leo's new secretary, right?" The one he hired at the start of the year, and I've yet to meet.

She nods frantically. "Yes. Yes, well, not that new now." Rubbing her hands together she turns red in the face. "That's me." She pauses. "Oh, gosh. I'm sorry. My name is Bella." She holds a hand out, and I shove my purse over my shoulder to shake it. "Nice to meet you, Bella. I'm Dahlia."

"Oh, I know." She snorts then startles. "Sorry. You'd like to see him, right? Of course." She shakes her head. "Follow me."

Sarah watches the whole thing with a bored expression on her sixty-year-old, Botox-infused face then returns to clicking away at her computer.

"Thanks," I tell Bella as she leads me to the elevators and presses the button. The doors open, and we walk in as I ask, "How do you like working here?"

She hits the button to the top floor where Leo's office is. The doors close and the elevator glides up. "It's amazing. I love it," She gushes theatrically, causing me to laugh.

"It's okay. I won't tell him. You can be honest." I wink at her.

She chews her lip for a second. "No, seriously. He can be, um, moody sometimes. But he treats us well and puts up with my countless mistakes." Her eyes widen. "Don't remind him of them, please."

Shaking my head, I give her a smile as we step out. "Your secret is safe with me."

She directs me down the hall to the large wooden doors that lead into Leo's office. "He just got out of a meeting five minutes ago, so he should be back by now." She knocks, and his voice sounds on the other side, telling her to come in. Bella opens the door for me, and I walk in to find him leaning back in his chair, a pen in his mouth, and eyes that widen when they fall on me.

"Hey." I smile, walking over to his large desk to put our drinks down.

"I'll just, ah, leave you two to it then." Bella waves awkwardly when I turn to say thank you, almost smacking into the door when she spins around.

Leo chuckles. "Thanks, Bella."

She blushes and closes the door. I turn back to him. "She seems nice."

He smirks. "She is. A bit of a mess at times, but she does well."

I fidget with my hands, glancing out the floor-to-ceiling windows at the sprawling city beyond. And on the other side of his office, windows with a perfect view of the ocean. Which is choppy and gray due to the weather.

"Lia." His chair creaks. "What are you doing here?"

"I wanted to see you," is all I say. Because it's true.

He sighs, tossing his pen to the desk and pulling the tray toward him to grab his to-go cup. Feeling a bit uncomfortable, I chew on my lip as I watch him take a sip and stare out the windows. Oh, fuck it. I came here to see him, so I'm not just going to stand here like an idiot and act as though he's put me in the naughty corner. Moving around the desk, I move some papers out of the way, drop my purse, and take a seat on the desk, swinging my legs over and between his as he watches me with amused eyes.

Then he scowls. "You do realize your dress is soaking wet."

I glance down at it, frowning. Shit, the white cotton is a little see-through, showing my stupidly chosen black lace bra beneath it. Flushing, I look back up at him and give him a small shrug. "I found a parking spot out front and got stuck getting our drinks out of the car."

He leans forward in his chair and places his coffee cup down on the other side of his computer. His hand lifts to my hair, and he toys with a wet blond strand that was resting on my arm, studying it between his fingers. "You don't usually like coming here, Lia. What's up?"

It's my turn to scowl. "It's not that I don't like it ..." His quirked brow halts me. "Oh, fine. But I don't care. I like you, so get used to it, Mr. Vandellen. You'll be seeing a lot more of me."

He gives me that crooked grin. "You like me, huh?" His eyes move to my chest, and my nipples harden behind the confines of my bra. "I more than like you," I reply.

His eyes meet mine, and he leans forward farther, wrapping his arms behind me and bringing my ass to the edge of his desk. "I know," he says with his face close to mine.

Tears prick my eyes as I stare into his. Emotion clogs my throat as I ask hoarsely, "Do you still like me?"

His whole face softens, and he rests his nose on mine. "I fucking love you. Only ever, always you." His voice is rough, and my heart riots as though it's trying to leave my chest to get to him. I dive forward into his lap, wrapping my arms around his neck as he holds me tightly to him.

The phone on his desk rings, and he moves forward to

pick it up. "No," he answers whoever is on the other end of the line. "Hold all my calls until further notice." He slams it back in its cradle.

"Come on. Let's get you out of these wet clothes," he murmurs, kissing my cheek gently.

Pulling my head back, I ask, "How?"

His hands reach up to frame my face as he brings my mouth to his. He kisses me softly, sweetly before responding with, "You'll see. Up." He smacks my ass as he helps me onto my feet. Grabbing our coffees, he passes me mine and my purse then directs me to the door with a hand on my lower back. We step into the elevator, and I'm still wondering where we're going when he checks his phone. "As long as I'm back by one for a conference call that I can't put off, we're good."

"Good? Where are we going?" I ask.

He grabs my hand when the doors open, and I follow as he walks out into the lobby. "Got some shit to do, back in a little while," he tells Sarah and Bella. Sarah frowns at us while Bella waves with both hands, a huge smile on her face. I smile back, already deciding that I like her. Leo stops at my car, taking the keys from me and helping me in before rounding it to the other side. It's then I realize that I forgot our croissants. Damn, I was looking forward to eating mine. Oh well, I guess he'll have a snack for later.

He turns the ignition over after adjusting the seat then looks over his shoulder before pulling out onto the road and driving farther into the city. "Where's Barney's again?" He glances at me.

"Turn left up here then right. It's in the shopping mall on the corner." Hang on. "You're taking me clothes shopping?" I ask with clear disbelief.

He grins, flicking the turn signal on. "Yep. You're not walking around wet, and I'm not quite ready for you to go yet." We turn into the underground parking lot, and I stare out the window, trying to hide the smile on my face.

He waits for someone to back out of a spot before taking it and turning the car off. Grabbing my hand, he helps me out of the car. "Leave your bag here," he says, closing the door and locking it before linking his fingers through mine and walking toward the automatic doors of the shopping mall. I direct us to Barney's, smiling brightly at the pretty brunette who greets us near a display rack. Her eyes rake up and down Leo's body; he fills out a suit like it's his job to model them. I don't care, though, because he's mine. Let her look all she wants. I grab a pair of skinny jeans and check the price, my eyes bugging out while Leo chuckles and takes them from me, draping them over his arm. "Just pick some stuff, Lia."

"You can feed a village in Africa for a month with the amount of money some of these clothes cost," I hiss at him. He only laughs. "Then it's a good thing we already donate a big chunk of money to some of them each year."

He's right, but still. I snatch up a peach sweater dress and a pair of black leggings, taking them with me to the change rooms. The sales lady comes over to unlock it for us before returning to her task at the front of the store. Leo looks up at the ceiling for a beat then shocks me by coming in after me and locking the door behind him.

"Leo," I whisper. "You can't—" He shuts me up with his lips, tugging at my bottom lip with his teeth then pulling away to take my jacket off and lift my damp white dress from my body.

He hums, fiddling with the clasp of my bra. "This should

really go too, but I don't think I like the idea of you going any-where braless," he whispers huskily.

Then his fingers are tugging the cups down and he takes a seat on the bench behind him, pulling me between his legs to take a nipple into his mouth while his hands drift down my back to my ass. "Leo," I pant, grabbing his head to pull him away, but instead, my fingers sink into his hair and I whimper quietly as his hand moves from my ass to skirt over my damp panties.

"Open," he says, dragging his teeth over the skin of my breast before moving to suck the other one into his mouth; his hot, swirling tongue has me swallowing a moan. But when my legs spread, allowing him to move my panties to the side, I let one slip.

"Shhh." His finger pauses in spreading me open as his blue eyes flash mischievously at me. I nod, swallowing hard as he parts me. Removing his mouth from my breast, he watches me while his finger glides through my wetness, dipping into my entrance before dragging it back to my clit and softly cir-cling. He repeats the motion, over and over. "Leo, you need to … You'll make me …"

"Come," he finishes firmly, inserting a finger and thrust-ing in and out while his thumb flicks my clit.

"Yes," I breathe, my head rolling back and my eyes closing as I fall apart on his hand in the changing room of a mall. *Holy shit*. My eyes fly open. He removes his fingers, pulling me into his lap as my thighs continue to quiver. They clench together as I watch him move his finger to his mouth to suck the evi-dence of my orgasm from it. "You're crazy," I whisper, resting my head on his shoulder. He laughs quietly.

"Everything okay in there?" the saleslady asks.

"Fine. We'll be out in a minute," Leo answers, his firm voice not inviting any questions about why he's in here with me.

I giggle into his neck when I hear her heels clipping on the floor as she walks away. Tilting my head, I skim my lips underneath his jaw, feeling his hardness twitch beneath me.

"I guess we'd better get you dressed." He moves me off him, and we both stand. I watch lazily as he tugs my bra cups back up then grabs the sweater dress, ripping the tags off and pulling it down over my head. I push my arms through the sleeves.

"Huh, this is actually really nice." I turn and look into the mirror. "Comfortable, even."

He smirks down at the leggings he's ripping the tags from. "Don't look at the price then, beautiful."

I frown, turning around as he gestures for me to step into the leggings and tugs them up to my hips. Smiling, he adjusts the hem of the sweater dress over my ass.

"Let's have lunch before I have to go back." He turns the lock and goes to walk out.

I pull my hair out of the neckline of the dress. "Oh, the jeans."

Backing up, he grabs them as well as my damp dress and jacket before leading me out to the registers. The brunette raises a brow at us as Leo hands the clothes and tags over, looking like she's about to say something before he hands her his Amex plus a hundred-dollar tip. That has her smiling, putting my damp clothes into a separate bag and even saying that she hopes to see us again. I bite my tongue, linking my arm through Leo's as we walk out of the store and head toward the food court.

He doesn't ask what I want—he never does—but he knows what I don't like to eat. We end up getting wraps and sitting in the back of the food court, trying to avoid the noise. I rub my foot over his leg, raising his pants a little as I unwrap mine from the paper.

"So you're not still mad?" I ask my bottle of water.

"Look at me, Lia."

My eyes lift, and I study the hardness of his beautifully sculpted face, watching the way it softens while he looks at me.

"I'm fucking furious. But just give me time because I can understand why you did it. Doesn't mean I like it or that I think it was fair to me."

I nod. "It wasn't. But a goodbye is just that … a good-bye." I drop my wrap and grab his hand. "It needed to happen. Because I want you. I've only ever wanted you."

He stares at our hands for a heartbeat. "Promise me." He raises his eyes when I don't answer him. "Promise me that you'd never even consider doing something like that again."

"You know I won't," I whisper brokenly.

He nods. "Yeah. But I still want to hear it." Tugging on my hand until my face meets his over the table, he whispers, "Promise me."

"I promise." My eyelids flutter as I stare into his eyes. "You and me, Leo. Just you and me."

His breath leaves him on a ragged exhale, his shoulders slumping as his lips take mine in a sweet, short kiss before we finish our lunch.

The rain finally stops as we're driving back through the city. We pull up just outside his building, and I jump out, wrapping my arms around his shoulders and dragging my nails along his neck. He growls deep in his throat, leaning down to suck my bottom lip into his mouth. My arms move from his neck, skating down his shoulders to dive underneath his suit jacket and smooth over the hard ridges of his abs to his chest. He groans, his tongue tangling with mine while my hands climb back up to his shoulders. Muscles twitch as I tuck my hands underneath the sleeves of his jacket and try to pull him further into my body. "Shit." He pulls his mouth away. "Jesus Christ, you'll make me come in my pants like I'm a damn teenager again." He nuzzles his nose into my cheek.

"Crap, maybe we can—"

He cuts me off, kissing me firmly. "Don't worry about me. Just be ready and waiting when those kids of ours go to bed tonight." He kisses my forehead and steps back onto the sidewalk. I smile, trying to calm my racing heart as he points a finger at the car behind me, telling me without words that he's not leaving until he watches me drive off.

Spinning around, I climb in, readjust my seat, and turn the car on. Looking out the window I find him with his hands in his pant pockets, his hair even messier than usual, and a small grin on his face. And with just that one tiny smile, I know. I know that whatever comes our way, we'll be ready and willing to take it on.

Together.

Chapter Thirty

I WALK TO THE FRONT DOOR, OPENING IT UP FOR LOLA, Trey, and Sophie to come inside. "Hey." Trey kisses my cheek and takes off after Sophie who's run off into the house in search of the kids. I close the door and turn to Lola who hands me a bottle of champagne. "Oh, yum. Thank you," I say as I give her a hug.

"How're things going?" she asks.

It's been a little over a week since I went to see Leo at work and things have only gotten better. "Good." I give her a genuine smile. "I think I need a holiday from all the make-up sex, though." I fan myself, and Lola laughs.

"You've got loads of time to make up for, so saddle up, sweetheart." She nudges me as we walk down the hallway.

Don't I know it. We had a pretty healthy sex life before everything took a turn for the worse. It's Leo, after all. The man used to need a fix at least once a day—which you'd never catch me complaining about. But now, I kind of miss having a full night's sleep as some nights, he wakes me up in the most amazing of ways—which I love—but shit, the lack of sleep is starting to catch up with me. I don't know how it's not affecting him. Not to mention if he lets me sleep through the night then he'll likely wake me up early in the morning for it before he leaves for work.

"Any news on the lady of horror?" Lola asks quietly as I tuck the champagne into the fridge.

I shake my head. "Not really, no. Leo doesn't seem to have anything to share on it either." Though, I think that's on purpose. He seems happy and back to his old self, but he hasn't said much about it since our weekend alone. I still wish he'd agree to go see someone. The way he wants to shove it to the back of his mind like it's something he can lock away and ignore worries me.

"He'll be okay," Lola says, looking out the kitchen window to where the guys are talking on the back deck. "He looks … like that light has come back into his eyes."

"Quit checking out my husband." I snicker, grabbing the tray of fruit from the fridge that I'd prepared earlier.

She laughs. "Shut it. You can't marry a man like that and get mad when other women look."

"You know I'm joking. Look all you want, but you've got your own to ogle." Trey is very easy on the eyes—tall, broad with brown hair and a ruggedly handsome face.

"True," she murmurs, waving at who I'm guessing is Trey out the window and giving him a sultry wink.

She turns around, giggling and coming over to help me carry some of the food outside. "So Charlie's having his birthday here?"

I nod, thanking Trey when he slides the door open for us

and we step outside, placing the trays down on the table. It's his tenth birthday right before Halloween in just a few weeks' time. "He said he wants to go see that new Transformers movie that's coming out with Leo, Sophie, and the twins."

I walk back inside, needing to grab the chips, veggies, and dip from the kitchen. Lola follows, speaking quietly. "He's cool with that? Leo, hanging around her kids?"

"He insists that he is. He knows it's got nothing to do with them. But I'm going to tag along and do some shopping while they're in there anyway." I wink at her.

"So he still talks to Dylan then?" Lola tucks some hair behind her ear, leaning against the counter.

"Yeah, I know they've spoken a few times. He hasn't said anything bad about him. In fact, I've even heard them laughing on the phone together sometimes."

She smiles. "That's so good. Man, what a blow. To find out your wife is some kind of creepy psycho who—"

"Shhh." I glance around. "You don't want any of the kids to hear."

"Crap, my bad." Her eyes widen as she checks that no one is floating around outside the kitchen.

I pull the cling wrap off the dip. "Yeah. When I saw him at the grocery store, before he told me, he seemed to be keeping it together, but who really knows?"

She hums. "Right. Maybe I should ask Trey."

I grin down at the dip. "Great idea then be sure to tell me. I probably won't be seeing him until Charlie's birthday. Not that he'd be honest with me anyway." Shrugging, I say, "He might've been more forthcoming with the guys, though."

Lola nabs a piece of carrot, taking a bite. "Very true. I wonder if she's still in the bay."

Something curdles in my gut at the thought. "I fucking hope not."

"Hello!"

Lola backs out of the kitchen, craning her neck and looking down the hall at the sound of Taylor's voice.

"Quit blocking the doorway and get inside," my mom says.

Smiling, I pour the chips into a bowl and put them on the island with the dip and vegetables before joining Lola in the hall.

"Hello, my lovely." Taylor engulfs me in a hug before getting nudged aside by my mother who picks up my hair, inspecting it before patting my cheeks. "Beautiful. Are you pregnant again? You've got that whole glowing thing going on." She kisses my head and steps back when we hear Leo coughing from behind us.

Turning around, I find a weak smile on his face as he looks from my stomach up to my face. More of a grimace, really. Walking over to him, I whisper into his ear, "Do the math, honey. You're fine." I pat his shoulder and grab the food from the kitchen to take outside. Besides, he knows I'm on the pill. I place the bowls down on the table and look over into the yard where the kids are playing. Or rather Sophie and Greta are playing while Charlie sits on the grass and watches them.

"He's a good egg, sitting out so that Greta can be included for once," Lola says as she stops beside me.

"He's doing much better. Still a bit moody, though."

Lola snorts. "I'm sorry to point out the obvious here, but that kid is exactly like his dad. He's always been *a bit moody*." She uses air quotation marks.

"You're right." I smirk, shaking my head. We move over

to take a seat at the table when everyone else comes outside.

"I'm telling you, they were green, Renee. Green." Taylor scowls at my mom as they walk out onto the deck.

"Oh, for heaven's sake, they were blue. We're taking you to get your eyes tested again."

My head tilts back to look at Leo when he grabs my shoulders from behind and gently rubs them. "What are they talking about?" I mouth.

He shrugs, leaning down to kiss me quickly before walking over to Trey who's at the grill, preparing all the meat.

"What's the point in getting them tested? I'll just wear my glasses." Taylor smirks over at my mom.

Oh, Lord.

"Jesus, you're a nuisance. Why do I still even talk to you?" my mom mutters, picking up a glass and filling it with water.

Taylor lifts a shoulder to her ear. "You love me, and I'm fabulous."

My mom snickers and takes a drink.

Taylor turns to Lola. "How've you been? Still teaching those teenage misfits?"

Lola grins. "Yep. I've recently invested in five cans of air freshener. My English lit class seems to be primarily boys." Her brows rise. "Boys who haven't learned the use of a shower or deodorant yet."

Taylor's eyes widen comically. "Good God. You're kidding me? Do they pay you extra to put up with that?"

Lola shakes her head, lifting her glass of water to her mouth. "Nope, unfortunately not. But I sent home notes about personal hygiene to all the students last week. So maybe two of the fifteen will at least read it." She takes a sip of her water while my mom laughs at Taylor's horrified expression.

"That's unsavory working conditions. I still remember when Leo went through puberty." Leo turns at the sound of his name, frowning at his mom who lowers her voice to a useless whisper, "His waste basket was constantly filled with sticky tissues and dear God, the smell of his gym bag used to have me running for—"

"Mom!" Leo scolds as Lola shoots water out of her mouth back into her glass and onto her lap. Taylors eyes bug out at being caught, but she fixes an innocent look on her face as she turns to him. "Yes?"

"Could we not discuss such things? *Ever?*" he asks, but the firm tone of his voice means he's not really asking.

"Oh, of course, of course." She purses her lips for a moment. "So that means I can't tell them about the time poor Robert found your stash of porno—"

"No." Leo cuts her off, dragging a hand through his hair in exasperation.

My mom laughs. "Leave the poor man alone, you evil woman."

Taylor's shoulders sag as she turns back to us. "It's just so fun, though, you know?" She leans in to whisper to my mom, "Robert looked like he'd seen a ghost. Even put a pair of gloves on and acted as if he were handling a piece of damning evidence for the FBI."

My mom and Taylor fall into fits of laughter as I grab some napkins for Lola to pat the water from her lap. I see Trey nudge Leo's arm and say something to him that has him chuckling, and my chest warms.

The guys finish cooking then bring the steaks, sausages, and shish kebabs to the table as I get up to go and grab some more drinks.

"He looks a lot happier. So do you," Taylor remarks, coming into the kitchen and grabbing some cups from the cupboard.

I stop moving, putting the soft drinks and beer down on the island as I look at her. She laughs lightly. "You thought we didn't know that something had been wrong all that time?" She tsks. "Come on, dear. I may have terrible eyesight, but we both have eyes." She gives me a sad smile, looking out the window at whom I'm guessing is Leo.

"Don't bore me with the details. It's not my business. Just know that I'm glad, and your mother is relieved."

I grip the counter of the island as my shoulders deflate. "I'm sorry. If it's been … weird."

She shakes her head. "Nonsense. But I was married to his father, you know." Her brow quirks at me. "We had our ups and downs, but we also had some really low points. And Leo … well, he's just like his father. Stubborn as all hell. Always taking the weight of the world upon his shoulders as if it's solely his responsibility to fix everything himself." Walking over to me, she pats my arm. "You keep sticking by him, though. Because he *is* just like his father, and that means you won't regret it."

I give her a tear strained smile. "That's the plan."

She pats my cheek. "Come on. Let's go eat then, shall we? Before your mother steals all the good food."

We grab the drinks and glasses, heading back outside to join the others. Leo tugs my chair out for me, and I thank him, sitting down. "What's wrong?" He wraps his arm around my shoulders and whispers into my ear.

Looking into his face when he pulls away to study mine, I lean forward, sealing my lips to his quickly before replying, "Nothing. Everything is perfect."

He continues to stare for a beat then kisses my forehead and goes back to his food.

"Daddy, can I have a robot like Charlie's?" Sophie asks from across the table. Trey, who's seated next to Leo, looks at Leo in horror.

Leo shrugs. "Don't ask me. Mother dearest bought it for him." He gestures to Taylor with his beer bottle then places it down to cut into his steak. Trey's eyes dart to Taylor who simply laughs, lifting a bite of salad to her mouth.

"It speaks three different languages," Sophie informs Trey and Lola.

"That's nice," Trey says, looking back at his food.

Sophie's eyes narrow. Uh-oh. "It's my birthday in November, you know."

"Uh-huh," Trey mumbles around a mouthful of food as Leo snickers next to him.

"So can I have one for my birthday?" Sophie asks, her face pulling tight in frustration.

"Soph ..." Lola cuts in. "We'll discuss it later."

Charlie snickers beside Sophie. She elbows him in the arm, causing him to drop his fork and scowl at her. "What?"

"Don't laugh at me, butthead."

"I was going to let you borrow mine, but I'm not now," Charlie says, picking his fork back up and shoving a huge bite of sausage into his mouth.

Sophie's eyes widen. "Really?"

Charlie shrugs and swallows his food. "Guess we'll never know."

Leo ducks his head to try to hide his laughter. I reach over and rub his back while I take a sip of water.

"What's so good about the silly thing speaking three

different languages when you can't even understand them anyway?" Greta asks from the other side of Sophie.

Sophie and Charlie just stare down at their plates, obviously having no answer for that.

My mom laughs. "*Kids*. Keeping it real since the dawn of time."

Tonight's football game plays on the TV in our bedroom. Leo's fingers weave through my hair as my head rests on his stomach while I read my book. To say I'm tired would be an understatement, but I'm content to stay awake a while longer. After everyone left this afternoon, Leo watched a movie with the kids in the living room while I cleaned up the last of the dishes and put the leftover food away.

Having everyone over today felt good. To have that sense of normalcy back in our lives without that sour cloud of trepidation hanging over my head. Without wondering if Leo would snub me in front of everyone, or say something—or not enough—that would send curious glances my way.

No, it felt like it used to. How it always should have been and I'm forever grateful that those days seem to be behind us.

Turning the page, I start reading the first sentence of a new chapter when Leo says something that rips me from my head.

"Will you come with me?"

"Um, where?" Surely, we're not going anywhere now. A quick glance at the clock on the nightstand says it's almost ten thirty at night.

"If I decide to talk to someone. Will you come with me?" he asks distractedly. As if he's been thinking about it but doesn't want to make a big deal out of it.

Closing my book, I put it on the other side of the bed and look up at him. His eyes move from the TV to me, and I see it again. That carefully veiled vulnerability he keeps hidden from the world. Shifting to move onto my hands and knees, I climb up his body and press my forehead to his. He blinks, still waiting for me to answer.

"You already know the answer to that," I tell him. He exhales, and I inhale it, my lungs constricting as I wonder what I'd ever do without this. Without him. "I'd go with you anywhere," I whisper.

His arm wraps around my waist, flattening my body against his as he holds me to him and uses the other hand to brush my hair out of my face. "Thank you," he says to my mouth before crushing his lips to mine.

Chapter Thirty-One

THE NEXT MORNING, I'M PREPARING A PICNIC LUNCH while Greta entertains us with a wonderful rendition of a Katy Perry song. Okay, I'm totally lying. It's so fucking terrible that I feel as though my ears are about to tear themselves from my head, grow legs, and run away any second now. But I'd never tell her that.

I glance over at Leo who's sitting at the island, trying to check his email while he finishes his coffee. He smiles at Greta, who's standing by the fridge, waving her arms around as she dances. But it's definitely more of a wince. Sticking a finger in his ear, he plucks it out and tries to discreetly inspect it for what I'm guessing is blood. Charlie falls into Leo's side with a loud belly laugh. Then finally, Greta finishes with a dramatic bow. My ears are still ringing as she looks around at us, and as usual, Leo claps. She smiles brightly as Leo gets up and brings his mug over to the sink, whispering into my ear from behind. "I'm still wishing that you didn't pass on your awful singing skills to her."

I spin around, slapping him with the dish towel as he chuckles and grabs it, using it to pull me into his body and place a kiss on my head. He releases the towel, turning back to the kids. "All right, ready?"

It's an unusually warm day for October, but we know it'll probably be one of the last, so we've decided to spend a couple of hours down at the bay and enjoy it.

Leo rounds the kids up, grabbing some towels as I put the last of the snacks into the cooler bag and then follow them out to the garage. He opens the trunk of my car, taking the bag from me and putting it in with the towels before heading to the driver's side. I get in, tugging my seat belt on as Leo reverses out and closes the garage.

"Can we swim?" Charlie asks when we're almost there. We could walk really. It's only a few streets away.

"If the water isn't freezing," I tell him.

They both cheer and stare eagerly out the window as we drive into the gravel parking lot. Leo parks, jumping out and staring down at the water. The kids and I get out, and I move to the trunk to grab our stuff.

"Busy?" I ask Leo when he comes around to grab the bags from me.

"Nope. Doesn't look like many other people are here."

"Won't take them long with a day like this." I close the trunk, and Leo locks the car as the kids run down to the sand.

We sit down, watching the kids toe the water before leaping back with a shriek when they realize how cold it is.

"Come here," Leo says, grabbing my hand and patting between his spread legs. Smiling, I take a seat between them and relish in the warmth of his arms as they wrap around me.

The breeze blows some hair into my face, and I push it back behind my ear. Leo's lips land on the now bare skin of my neck not even a second later as we watch the kids, who start digging and building things in the sand. "I've missed this," he says to my skin.

"Me too."

He's quiet for a moment. "I'm so sorry. I was such an asshole. You guys didn't deserve it."

"Leo—"

He cuts me off. "No, there's no excusing it. No matter what was fucking with my head. There's no excuse."

Watching the kids smile and laugh, I find myself agreeing with him. Even if I can understand his reasons for distancing himself from us like that.

"Well, I love you." I squeeze his forearms that are around my waist.

"And that makes me the luckiest asshole in the world." His hand lifts to my chin, turning my head to meet his lips. Sighing into his mouth, I hold the side of his face, feeling those cracks of my heart slide back into place with every slow glide of his tongue against mine. I feel it happen with every touch, look, and smile he gifts me with. I've come to realize that this soul deep kind of love is an unstoppable force. And while I understand that some things can't be repaired, they can always be remade into something better.

Something stronger and harder to break.

His hand slides into my hair, his teeth sinking into my bottom lip before he sucks it into his mouth. "Look, I'm a mermaid queen!" Greta sings.

Shit. I pull away, flushed and breathing heavily while Leo grins down at me.

Looking over at the kids, we discover that Greta has taken it upon herself to wrap herself in seaweed. Charlie sits back in the sand, squinting up at her. "You know there are probably sea bugs and all kinds of other gross things in there, right?"

Greta screams and starts dancing on the spot. "Get it off, get it off! Daddy!"

Charlie falls back into the sand, laughing and holding his stomach. Chuckling, Leo lets go of me and stands, brushing sand from his perfect ass that's wrapped in denim and jogging down to where they've been playing near the water. He removes the seaweed, and Greta watches as he throws it out into the water.

"Are there any sea bugs on me?" Her bottom lip wobbles as she looks up at him. He makes a big show of checking her, declaring that she's bug free then he joins them in the sand with their shovels.

They play together for a while, and I watch, feeling lighter and so thankful for the three people in front of me. After a little while, I grab the cooler bag and spread a picnic blanket out before setting the sandwiches, chips, and fruit down in the middle of it. Grabbing the water bottles out, I turn around and call them over in time to see Leo bend down to lift Greta into the air. He holds her above his head, spinning her around as she giggles like crazy. My eyes are drawn not only to the corded muscles of his arms, but also to the smile on his face. His strength, that aura surrounding him has always been one of his most attractive qualities. Just for a whole variety of different reasons now.

"Love you more," I say to Greta, turning off her light and leaving the room to go see Charlie. He smiles up at me as I bend over to place a kiss on his forehead. "Love you," I tell him, fixing his blankets over him.

"Love you, too." He yawns.

I go to flick the light off and leave the room when he speaks again, "I'm glad you're happy again, Mom."

Looking back at him, my heart stutters as I search for what to say.

He just smiles. "Good night."

I clear my throat. "Thanks, little man. Good night." I close the door halfway after switching off the light and make my way to our room for a shower before I head back down stairs.

"Hey." Leo pats his lap when I take a seat on the couch beside him. I lift my feet to his lap, and he starts rubbing them while staring at me.

"Greta said that she's not letting her husband kiss her, ever." I smile up at him. "That he'll only be allowed to rub her feet."

Leo huffs, shaking his head with a chuckle. He quickly sobers, though. "I hope she likes this house. She's not moving out until she turns thirty."

Giggling, I nudge his hard stomach with my toe. "She's going to give you hell."

His shoulders straighten, his fingers gripping my feet a little harder. "Bring it on." He says it so seriously that I start laughing again.

He frowns down at me. "I don't know what's so funny about the idea of our girl …" He shakes his head. "Yeah, no. Let's not discuss this ever again."

Smirking, I look over at the news reporter that's talking

on the TV before deciding to change the subject when I remember Charlie's comment.

"Charlie seems to be doing a lot better." I chew on my fingernail, staring down at Leo's strong hands on my feet.

He hums. "I've noticed." He looks back over at me when I remain quiet. "What's up?"

Damn, I don't even know how to say it, but I try to sum it up as best I can. "Is it okay? For a child to be so deeply affected by his parent's relationship?"

His hands pause and my eyes flick up from them to find him frowning at me. "Lia, he's okay. We're all okay."

Nodding, I say, "I know. It's just—"

"Stop." He cuts in. "Stop searching for things that might go wrong. Shit." His head falls back to the couch, and he blows out a breath. "I know I've done this to you. To us. But it's okay to be happy, not to worry. We're allowed to be happy again, Lia."

He's right. He's absolutely right. But when you've lived with only half of your heart for so long—only to have the missing half given back—I guess it's normal to have some moments of fear. It's still fresh. The wounds are still healing. But looking at Leo, I can tell that he gets it, especially when he says with a gentle tone, "Breathe. We have a forever to finish living together. Just breathe."

I stare into his eyes for a heartbeat then shift to move into his side. Resting my head on his chest, I close my eyes.

And just breathe.

Chapter Thirty-Two

"T HAT'S FINE, SARAH. JUST GET HIM TO SEND THE paperwork through and tell him I'll have it figured out by tomorrow." Leo sighs. "No. It'll be fine. Okay … thank you." He ends the call, looking up from his desk in his office to find me leaning against the doorway, watching him. He leans back in his chair, stretching his arms up and over his head. He's still in his running shorts and a baggy sweat-stained t-shirt, having just got home from the gym. "The kids get off to school okay?" he asks.

I nod. "Yep. Got back from dropping them off a while ago." I walk into the room, skimming a finger over the large shelf where a row of photo frames sit. Pictures of the kids. Then the shelf below, Leo and me in college next to our wedding and some family photos. Lifting my finger up, I frown at it. "It appears that your wife isn't doing a very good job of dusting this office of yours," I say, inspecting the fine coating of dust on my finger.

Giving me that signature smirk, he chucks his phone onto the desk and asks, "Really?"

Walking over to him, I take a seat on the edge of his desk and rub my bare foot up his shin. "Really."

"Well, that might be because I've kept her quite busy"—his eyes heat—"doing other ... things."

"Oh?" I raise my brows and climb down into his lap. "What kind of things?" I whisper into his ear, sucking his lobe into my mouth.

He hardens beneath me, his hot breath ghosting across my neck as he says, "Very bad things." His hand climbs underneath my dress then pulls my panties to the side to discover how wet I am.

He groans. "You see, my wife likes to play dirty. She tends to like it rough and hard. A little sweet and a little mean. You get what I'm saying?"

Shivers dance across my heated skin. I hum, but it's more of a moan. "You poor thing. She sounds very ... demanding."

His finger toys with my entrance. "Demanding, indeed. Good thing my cock is always up for the challenge." He thrusts his finger inside, and my head rolls back as I grind myself onto his hand. "She's always so wet, so ready for me." His lips graze a path up my throat. Then his finger is gone, and he's swiping papers and his laptop to the side before lifting me onto the desk. He tugs my panties off, throwing them to the floor before grabbing my thighs and spreading me open as he sits back in his chair and bites his lip, looking at me.

"Leo," I whimper.

"Do you need my cock, wife?" His voice is hoarse, his tone biting.

I lean up on my elbows to meet his gaze as I say, "Now."

He smirks. "Don't even care that I've just spent an hour at the gym, and I'm a sweaty mess, do you?"

I almost growl, feeling so turned on that my arms start shaking as I try to keep myself held up. "Please."

He runs the pads of his fingers over the sides of me, purposely avoiding and teasing. I throw my head back, about to scream with frustration when I feel his mouth on me. He licks up and down my center with hard and slow swipes of his tongue. Humming deep in his throat, his hands move my legs over his shoulders, and he soon loses himself and starts feasting like a starving man.

I fall to my back, my legs wrapped around his head as I rock into each blissful movement of his tongue and lips. Then, with several harder flicks of his tongue over my clit, I come. Hard and loud, moaning his name as pleasure travels through every nerve ending of my body. He gently kisses and licks, drawing it out for me even with my legs probably smothering him to death in their vise-like grip.

With my chest heaving, I gently unwrap them, and he helps me to sit up. Standing, he picks me up, my legs hooking around his waist as he leaves his office and carries me upstairs. He sets me by the sink in our en suite before turning the water on in the shower and stripping out of his gym clothes. My thighs squeeze together as I watch him lower his shorts over the perfect globes of his ass. Throwing me a grin over his shoulder, he stalks into the shower and I just sit here, jaw hanging open before snapping into action. I jump down, tearing my dress over my head then my bra as he starts washing himself, acting as if he's not hard as stone and doesn't need me. Opening the door, I step in and close it, my hands going to his back and gliding over the soapy dips and valleys of his smooth skin. Sliding back down, they skirt around his midsection as I kiss his back, grabbing his engorged cock and moving my hand up and down the velvety length of it.

He curses, his head tilting back underneath the spray of the water. It runs down his face and over his body as I move around him and drop to my knees, taking him in my mouth. His hips start jerking, his hands winding into my wet hair as he starts thrusting as deep as he can go into my mouth. Gagging, I grab his ass with one hand and use the other to knead his balls. He tenses, pulling me off him and turning me around to face the tiled wall.

"Don't want to come in my mouth, husband?" I pant over my shoulder.

He smacks then palms my ass, helping to fuel the fire that's reignited between my legs. "I fucking love coming down your throat. But I know sucking me off gets you hot and bothered and this ..." He trails his fingers over my folds then spreads them open for his cock to nudge at my entrance. "Sweet pussy needs me again."

"Yes," I moan, my back arching as he grabs my hips and slams home in one thrust.

"Fuck, so fucking good," he rasps, hands grabbing my ass cheeks and using them for leverage as he starts thrusting in and out in a punishing rhythm that has me feeling delirious. His thick length drags along that perfect spot, exactly where I need it, every time. A hand leaves my ass and scoops my hair into his fist. "Gonna come again, beautiful?" he asks.

"I ... y-yes, ohhh, fuck. Don't stop," I stutter out in response.

He chuckles darkly, swiveling his hips, and then I'm falling apart, almost slipping as my body trembles. His hand releases my hair, wrapping tightly around my waist as he pumps in and out of me a few more times then stays buried to the hilt. Grinding slowly, he comes with a low, hoarse groan ripping its way out of his throat.

"Shit." He laughs huskily, carefully sliding out of me and turning me around in his arms. "I don't think I'll ever get tired of fucking you, wife." He cups my face, tucking some of my wet hair behind my ear as I look up at him.

"Good." I grin. "Because you did say forever. So you're stuck with my demanding ass."

That amazing mouth tugs into a smirk, and his hands move down to squeeze said ass. "Fine with me." He ducks his head, taking my lips in a gentle kiss and moving us underneath the water. "Only ever, always you," he says against my mouth, kissing it one more time before grabbing the shampoo and washing my hair. I laugh, wiping suds out of my eyes as he attempts to wash it all out. Taking over, I rinse out the shampoo and pass him the conditioner, loving the way he bites his lip as he concentrates on running it through the ends of my hair.

After we're finished washing each other, we climb out and get dried. I'm getting dressed into a pair of jeans, cream blouse, and black jacket when I notice the time.

Shit. "Leo, we're going to be late."

He comes out of the bathroom, rubbing a towel over his hair and glancing at the time. "We'll be fine. I'll grab our stuff and meet you in the car in ten."

He pecks my head then walks into our wardrobe to get dressed as I race into the bathroom, quickly putting some mascara and lip gloss on. Men. Of course, he thinks ten minutes is enough time. I'd roll my eyes, but I'm in too much of a hurry. Snatching my hair dryer from the drawer, I plug it in and tug a brush through my messy, wet blond locks. Five minutes later, it's only half dry, but it'll have to do.

I run back downstairs, finding Leo in the doorway to the garage, my purse dangling from his finger. "Thank you." I grab it, planning on heading straight for his car, but he doesn't let go, causing me to collide with his chest.

"Chill." He smiles down at me. "We'll be there in no time. Besides, I'm the one who should be freaking out."

He's right, damn it. Kissing me on the nose, he lets go of my bag and opens the car door for me to hop in. Rounding the car, he gets in and we back out of the driveway, the garage closing as Leo puts the car into first and speeds off down the street.

Once we're nearing the city, I ask, "You do seem pretty okay about this, or are you secretly freaking out a little?"

He grabs my hand, linking his fingers through mine on his thigh.

"No point in freaking out until I get there." He releases my hand after a minute to flick the turn signal on, exiting the highway and driving into the city. "And I've got you. I don't think you understand—hell, I don't think I understood until recent weeks—how much that helps."

He parks the car outside a new looking brown and black building that's only a few blocks away from his work. I grab his hand again, lifting it to my mouth and kissing the top of it before opening the door and climbing out into the late morning sunshine. The ocean carries a breeze through the tall buildings of the city that has me buttoning my coat closed as Leo waits for me on the curb. Weaving our fingers together again, we walk inside the doors and are greeted by a young man with a kind face and an even kinder smile as he lifts his gaze to us.

"Good afternoon, how can I help you?"

"Leo Vandellen, here to see Dr. Tonks," Leo informs him before we're told to take a seat. The number I found in his car? It was because he'd heard of a therapist, Dr. Tonks, moving here to Rayleigh.

Not even two minutes later, an older male, looking to be in his mid to late forties, comes down the hall and shakes our hands before asking us to follow him into his office. Walking inside, I find myself impressed. Not only by the easygoing manner of Dr. Tonks but also by his room. The building may be new, stylish even, but it's not sterile. The air isn't stagnant or oppressive. The windows are all open, allowing the breeze to filter in and stir the venetian blinds, causing them to slap gently against the glass. The couches are leather and new, but they look comfortable. There are red woven rugs and pictures of Dr. Tonks's family on his desk and on the shelves, next to certificates stating his various degrees.

Leo takes a seat on the couch, lifting a leg and resting his ankle over his knee as he looks over at me. Giving him a small smile, I walk over and take a seat beside him. His hand instantly finds mine, his grip firm as I feel him tense up next to me. We make idle chitchat for a little while, and Dr. Tonks tells us to call him Evan.

"So," Evan finally says, sitting opposite us with his note-pad beside him on the couch. He folds his hands together in his lap as he reclines back a little, looking relaxed as he asks, "What brings you here today?"

He stares straight at Leo, patiently waiting.

Leo clears his throat. "Well, I'm here because earlier this year, my wife and I ..." He looks over at me, his gaze stormy as he swallows. I gently nod, telling him with my eyes that he can do this. That I'm here for him as I squeeze his hand.

He blows out a breath, turning back to Evan. "Earlier this year, we attended a friend's anniversary party …"

Chapter Thirty-Three

"**L**EO!" I HISS, LOOKING AROUND. "NO. GET UP."

The smile on his face as he looks at me has all the frustration leaving my body in a huge sigh.

"Come on." He tugs me down into his lap. "Relax, I've got you."

I throw a startled look at him. "We're going to break the damn thing."

He laughs loudly, causing the kids nearby to look our way.

Even though they're not mine, I give them my best mom glare in hopes that they'll look away. Nothing to see here.

Leo maneuvers me to his side, wrapping an arm around me and hitting the accelerator. We lurch forward, and I cover my mouth as a squeal escapes. "Adults do this too, you know," he says, steering the bumper car away from the kids who just tried to barge into us.

Grabbing his thigh in a death grip, I turn to him. "I know. But aren't you worried someone will see you?"

He narrowly skirts the outside barrier as he snorts. "No. Why should I be?"

My eyes bug out. Well, shit. The changes in my husband haven't been all that huge over the past ten months. He's the same Leo I fell in love with all those years ago at a frat party. But this? His father and his grandfather took so much pride in the business and were so careful about appearances that it was drilled into Leo from a young age to be the same. So the fact that he's acting like a big kid and doesn't seem to give a damn has my heart filling with so much warmth that a dopey smile spreads across my face.

Until some kid slams into our side and their buddy sticks their tongue out at us.

"Oh, it's on now. Move it, mister." I grab the wheel and steer us until we slam into the back of their car as they try to get away. One of the kids flips us off, sneering at us over his shoulder.

"Little punk," I growl. "Where are their parents?"

Leo starts howling with laughter. "Probably watching you, so take it easy." He gently pushes my hands away from the wheel and takes over. Huffing, I spin around and look to see if their parents just saw what their kid did. But the only thing close to an adult that I see is the bored looking teenage girl and her friend, who're supposed to be managing the ride.

We do a few more laps before even Leo starts to get crabby with the kids and decides it's time to wrap it up.

"So long, suckers!" one of them yells as they speed by while Leo's helping me out.

"Jesus Christ." He snickers, tugging me down the steps

and through the small crowds of people milling around the carnival, which comes here every year for various holidays. The latest one being the Fourth of July weekend that was a few weeks ago.

"Unbelievable. I hope our kids don't act like that when we aren't around." The thought has me paling as soon as it leaves my mouth. We skirt around a couple of rowdy teenagers near the drop slide and make our way to the front gates.

"I'm sure they don't." He pauses as we wait at the crossing near the entry to the beach. "Though maybe Charlie …"

I smack his bicep, and he laughs. "I'm joking. He's a grump at times, but he's not that bad."

"Freaking hope not," I mumble. He brings my hand to his mouth, placing a kiss on it before we step off the curb and cross the street, heading to the toy store at the end of the street on the corner. Greta and Charlie had a sleepover at Lola and Trey's last night, and being summer break, I thought it'd be wise to utilize this time to grab some presents for Greta's birthday, which is coming up in a couple of weeks.

The heat from the sun has me appreciating the towering buildings above us as they shade us from its rays for a little while. Leo's quiet but has a content smile on his face as he studies our surroundings. He has committed to seeing Dr. Tonks and never misses his appointment every month. He only has two more sessions to go, but I don't think he minds going because the two of them seem to get along quite well. He addressed what happened with us in his earlier appointments. We even talked about Jared and really got down to the underlying issues of why I did what I did. To sum it up, Jared was my heart's way of crying out for help. Something that I already knew, but I think it helped Leo to dig further and to discuss how he was handling it. Because even though it's been almost a year since I last saw Jared, I can tell it's something he's not likely to ever forget. Not that I can blame him. And it's the same for me.

Those fears, the worry that something will go wrong and our happily ever after will be interrupted once again still lurk in the dark corners of my mind. But every day, they shrink a little more, and I know that one day, I'll be able to look at them and see them for what they are. A way of trying to protect myself because nothing's worse than being blindsided.

Life. It doesn't always follow the rules and plans you lay out for your future. Something always happens to make you realize that while yes, you are in control, some things just can't be predicted. And simply won't fit into the mold of your plans or dreams but rather, will smash them to pieces and force you to rebuild. So finding a way to be happy and live despite that is what matters. It's where you'll find your true strength and find out just how much you have. And mine, well, he's walking alongside me. I'll never take that for granted or sit back and allow us to crumble again.

Fiona was arrested and has been denied bail. Her trial is coming up, and Leo's agreed to testify against her as well as two of the other four males she's assaulted in the past. One of them being Dylan's—who's now her ex-husband—former personal assistant. He came forward when Dylan tried to contact him several months ago. I haven't seen her since that day Lola and I went over to her house, and I'm glad for it. I hope she rots in whatever jail she's been thrown into. But I do feel terrible for her kids. They seem to be doing well, though. Dylan sold the house and downsized. He bought a new one down by the other side of the bay after he was granted full custody of Rupert and Henry when Fiona went to jail several months ago.

They've even come over to our place for playdates a few times, which is another reason I'm glad that Leo stuck it out with Dr. Tonks. But he seems to be able to look past it. He's never treated them any differently, and as far as we know, the twins don't know a thing about what their mother has done. Even though I know they probably wonder, I hope it stays that way for a long time to come.

Walking through the doors, Leo grabs a shopping cart, and we make our way through the aisles as I pull out my list that I've been adding to over the past month. Basically, every time Greta mentioned something, I wrote it down discreetly. Stepping onto my tippy toes, I grab a few of the Barbies that are on my list from the top shelf then keep walking until we get to the stuffed toys. I grab the ones with beady eyes that she wanted and throw them in, too. I keep going, almost getting everything on the list except for a toy baby.

"Does she really need all this shit?" Leo's eyes widen as he stares into the cart.

"Of course, she does. She only turns eight once."

I finally find it on an end display and check the box to make sure it's the right one.

"Right." He moves in behind me, his hands skating over my stomach and his lips going to my ear. "Just like she'll only turn nine once then ten once …"

"Oh, be quiet." I laugh.

He stops chuckling as he eyes the boxed doll I'm inspecting then tugs it from my hands and steps back to look at it. "What the fuck?"

"Leo." I glance around, smiling an apology to an elderly lady who frowns at us.

"It poops, Lia. It fucking poops."

I laugh again. "What do you expect? You can feed it, so it's gotta come out, right?"

He glares at it like it's the most offensive thing he's ever seen. "Christ, it even has diapers …" he mutters disbelievingly to the box.

Rolling my eyes, I tell him, "Yeah, for the poop. Genius."

"And it has a pacifier." His eyes narrow. "Nope. Too damn realistic. You'll put ideas in her head. It's not the same as when she was three years old. It was cute then but scary now," he says resolutely, and he places it back on the shelf.

My hand flies to my forehead as I rub it and beg for some kind of divine intervention. "Leo … it's a doll."

"*For now.* Next thing you know, she'll be coming home from school and saying she's got a boyfriend." He scoffs. "Yeah, no thanks. Let's go; she's got enough shit in here." He moves the cart down the aisle as I stand here, biting my lip to keep from blurting out that little Adam Davies from down the street seems to have already laid his claim on her. He writes her notes and puts scratch-and-sniff stickers on them, telling her she'll marry him when they're old enough to drive. Because you can't get married without a car, he said. I laughed so hard that I almost cried. Then I tucked the note with the others in the keepsake box that I have for each of the kids. Well away from Leo's eyes.

Reaching over, I quickly grab the doll and hold it behind my back, asking a staff member who's walking by if they could please hold it for me until next week while Leo's fiddling with some squishy ball down at the registers. She smiles warily and takes it from me after I warn her to wait until I'm gone. I join Leo just as he hands the lady at the register his Amex after she's finished putting all the items through.

"We're gonna need a bigger house if this keeps up," he mutters while moving the cart back over to the store entrance.

"Our house is plenty big enough. How about we grab some coffee?" I ask in an effort to perk him up a bit. He nods, and we both grab some bags and walk them outside to the car, which is parked halfway down the street.

"Oh. Can we stop by the shelter quickly?" I need to give Glenda the bags of clothes I cleaned out of the kids wardrobes, and I won't be in until later this week. Now, I go in to help on Fridays, and thankfully, no one asked much about why I'd been gone or about the change.

Leo nods, and we both put the bags of toys in the car before making our way over to the other side of the city where the women's shelter is located. Pulling up outside it, I quickly grab the bags of clothes from the trunk while Leo gets out and locks the car.

"Wait up," he says.

Turning around, I furrow my brows as I see him jump up the curb. He grabs the bags from me, holding the door open with his backside and waiting until I walk in ahead of him before following. I think this is the first time he's ever been in here, but I don't say anything. I just smile at Glenda and introduce them both when she comes out the front. Leo hands the bags to her.

"My, my, dear." She smirks at me. "I knew you'd been hiding him from us for a reason." She winks at Leo who chuckles, rubbing the back of his neck.

"Shhh," I whisper and rub his chest. "You'll embarrass him."

We all laugh, and I chat with her briefly before telling her I'll see her on Friday.

She waves. "You're welcome too, Leo. Anytime, honey."

I swear his cheeks go a little red as he responds, "Um, I'll see what I can do."

I widen my eyes at Glenda who just shrugs innocently before Leo and I continue outside. Wrapping my arm around his waist, I smile up at him. "You know you love it."

He guffaws. "What I do know is that I love you." The quick retort has my smile stretching across my face so wide that I probably look a little crazy.

"Blondie," a familiar voice calls just as we're nearing the coffee shop. My heart drops into my stomach as I take in Jared, who's leaning a shoulder against the brick wall outside the cafe and stubbing out his cigarette. He looks the same, but something seems a little different. He's also clearly not afraid of the very tense male who's holding my hip in a bruising grip. The bright smile on his face might have something to do with the raven-haired bombshell in designer clothes who's holding his hand and staring curiously at me.

"Hey." I stop but keep some distance between us as anxiety and happiness war with each other in my brain. Happiness, because I'm glad to see him after so long. Glad that he seems to be doing well. Anxiety over how well, or not so well, these next few minutes might play out.

He takes a step closer, and Leo growls low in his throat. I grip his side in warning.

"Sheath your claws, tiger. I just need a minute of your time." Jared smirks. He freaking smirks while my husband tries to commit murder with his eyes.

"Hi, I'm Dahlia." I wave awkwardly at the woman beside

Jared, trying to defuse the tension. Her blue eyes that were darting back and forth between Leo and me, now stay firmly fixed on me, and she doesn't look so happy to meet me.

O-kay then. I drop my hand as Jared chuckles.

"Don't worry about her. She's a bit of a spitfire." He tugs her into his side, and she turns her withering glare on him, which does nothing. He kisses the side of her head, and I smile as her big blue eyes seem to soften. "Anyway, I'm glad we ran into you …"

"Get to the point," Leo snaps, cutting him off.

Jared looks at Leo. "The number of the PI you used almost a year ago. I need it."

"Why?" I blurt before I can help myself.

Jared shrugs. "Got someone who's proving a little difficult to find."

I look up at Leo, and he drags his hard eyes from Jared to me. I nod, and he knows I'm asking silently if he'll give the number to him.

Leo stares at me for a moment, apprehension and anger swirling in those blue depths before finally nodding back at me. "I'll think about it," he says curtly to Jared, turning us and walking back down the street away from the cafe. I smile over my shoulder, waving at Jared who winks at me before grabbing his girl and walking in the opposite direction.

"Don't. Jesus Christ, Lia."

"What?" I frown up at him.

He stops next to our car. "He called you *Blondie?*" He practically snarls.

"Stop." I lift to my toes to place a kiss on his lips, looking him square in the eyes. "You saw for yourself; he's well and truly moved on."

He continues to scowl, and I know that was probably hard for him. But he knows. He knows he has nothing to worry about anymore.

"Look at me," I say when his eyes look unseeingly over my head. He does. "We'll just send him the number. You can watch me if you want." Though I hope he trusts me a lot more than that.

"Not necessary." He sighs. "Fuck. I'm being an idiot, aren't I?"

"Uh-huh." I nod. "Just a little. But I get it."

"I'm sorry. I trust you."

"Good." My lips curve into a smile.

He hooks his arms around my waist, his hands smoothing up and down my back. "Okay. I'll find it for you tonight."

"Thank you. I'm sure he wouldn't ask unless he didn't have many other options."

He groans. "And that's precisely the only damn reason he's going to get it."

My hands slide up his chest, moving to the back of his head and bringing his lips down to mine. "I love you," I breathe the words into his mouth and watch the last of that hardness fade from his face. "Only ever, always you." I remind him before he seals his lips to mine and makes the chaos of the city turn into white noise as I'm held captive by everything he makes me feel. Even after all this time, his effect on me never lessens. It only seems to grow stronger.

Driving back home, he's quiet. But he gifts me with a smile when I grab his hand and flip it over, trailing my finger over the creases in his palm. He still has quiet moments, times when I've lost him briefly to the shadows that still haunt him, but he knows that when he needs me, I'm here.

Always ready and willing to light up that darkness in any way I can.

And my love for him could light up the whole damn world.

The End

Playlist

Taylor Swift & Ed Sheeran—*Everything Has changed*

City and Colour—*Love Don't Live Here Anymore*

Arctic Monkeys—*Do I Wanna Know*

Brand New—*The Quiet Things That No one Ever Knows*

The All-American Rejects—*Move Along*

Kygo & Selena Gomez—*It Ain't Me*

James Arthur—*Impossible*

Live—*I Alone*

One Republic—*Apologize*

Paramore—*Still Into You*

Acknowledgements

My husband—Even though you'll probably never read my books—thank God—your unwavering support and belief in whatever I set out to do means more than I could ever possibly describe. Thank you, from the deep, dark depths of my heart, thank you. <3

My children—You're the reason I love with a capacity unknown to me before I held you both in my arms. The reason I dare to dream and take risks.

You're also the reason I eat and clean the house, so thank you for always tethering me to real life when I'm drifting away inside of my own head. <3 <3

Mum—Your unshakable faith in me is the best reminder a girl could have. <3

Amanda Burch—A rare gem in a sea of thousands. Your

friendship, advice and feedback has helped in more ways than you could ever know. One day, I'm going to meet you and hug the shit out of you. <3

Paige Velthouse—Thank you for jumping straight on board to beta read for me when I told you I was writing my first solo project. Your excitement and feedback put the biggest smiles on my face and made releasing this book a little less scary. <3

Michelle Clay—Thanks for being one of the first to read this story in its final moments before it was truly the end. Your feedback, kindness, support and enthusiasm means so damn much to me. Thank you for all your help in pushing this book out into the big wide world of readers. <3

Billie—Because you saved my butt at the very last minute. And just because. <3

My editors …

Bex Harper—You're a lady of incredible talent. Seriously, not only can you design with the best of them but your eye for any detail is out of this world amazing and your kindness is truly inspiring. Thank you for not only helping to make my book shine but for your friendship, too. <3

Jenny from editing4indies—Thank you, thank you, thank you. Did I say thank you? THANK YOU!!! This book is what it is because of you. <3

Sofie from Hart & Bailey Design Co.—Thank you so much for the beautiful cover!

Stacey from Champagne Formats—Once again, your ability to transform makes all the difference. Thank you!!

About the Author

Ella Fields lives in Australia with her husband, children and two cats. While her children are in school, you might find her talking about her characters and books to her cats. She's a notorious chocolate and notebook hoarder who enjoys creating hard-won happily ever afters.

Find Ella here:

Facebook:
facebook.com/authorellafields

Website
authorellafields.wixsite.com/ellafields

Instagram:
www.instagram.com/authorellafields

Goodreads:
www.goodreads.com/author/show/16851087.Ella_Fields